SARAH BENNETT has be~~en reading~~ remember. Raised in a family of bookworms, her love affair with books of all genres has culminated in the ultimate Happy Ever After: getting to write her own stories to share with others.

Born and raised in a military family, she is happily married to her own Officer (who is sometimes even A Gentleman). Home is wherever he lays his hat, and life has taught them both that the best family is the one you create from friends as well as relatives.

When not reading or writing, Sarah is a devotee of afternoon naps and sailing the high seas, but only on vessels large enough to accommodate a casino and a choice of restaurants.

You can connect with her via twitter @Sarahlou_writes or on Facebook www.facebook.com/SarahBennettAuthor

Also by Sarah Bennett

The Butterfly Cove Series

Sunrise at Butterfly Cove
Wedding Bells at Butterfly Cove
Christmas at Butterfly Cove

The Lavender Bay Series

Spring at Lavender Bay
Summer at Lavender Bay
Snowflakes at Lavender Bay

The Bluebell Castle Series

Spring Skies Over Bluebell Castle
Sunshine Over Bluebell Castle

Starlight Over Bluebell Castle

SARAH BENNETT

ONE PLACE. MANY STORIES

HQ
An imprint of HarperCollins*Publishers* Ltd
1 London Bridge Street
London SE1 9GF

This edition 2020

2
First published in Great Britain by
HQ, an imprint of HarperCollins*Publishers* Ltd 2019

ISBN: : 978-0-00-833114-6

MIX
Paper from
responsible sources
FSC **FSC™ C007454**
www.fsc.org

This book is produced from independently certified FSC™ paper
to ensure responsible forest management.

For more information visit: www.harpercollins.co.uk/green

Printed and bound in Great Britain by
CPI Group (UK) Ltd, Croydon, CR0 4YY

For M – for everything xx

Prologue

Beaman and Tanner's Christmas Party – Seven Years Ago

Jessica Ridley tilted back her head to watch the illuminated number above the door of the lift as it scrolled past floor after floor on its way to the penthouse level of the luxury hotel overlooking the London Embankment. Beaman and Tanner, the events and PR firm she'd been working for since graduating that May, had hired the entertainment space for their staff Christmas party. With access to the roof terrace above the penthouse included, it promised to be one of the best spots in town to take in a spectacular view of the London Eye all lit up for Christmas later in the evening.

If she could still see at that point. She pressed a fingertip to the corner of her eye, barely resisting the urge to rub, and cursed her decision to wear the contact lenses she'd been talked into trying by her mother. The lift dinged to announce her arrival, and the discomfort of her new lenses was soon forgotten as a hostess in a stunning black dress stepped forward to greet her with a smile. In short order, her name had been checked off on the hostess's list and Jess had been steered towards the ladies' cloakroom to divest herself of her coat and boots.

Hanging up the little backpack she'd used to carry her silver evening bag and black heels, Jess swapped the cosy boots for the strappy, sophisticated shoes and muttered a small prayer of thanks for the gel inserts her mum had reminded her to buy. When her school friends had been cramming their toes into the latest fashionable footwear, Jess had been clumping around in the Clarks wide-fit brogues Mum had insisted upon. She might be blessedly free of corns, hammertoes and other unsightly horrors she'd been warned cheap shoes would cause, but all that growing room meant her size seven adult feet were not the right shape for most high heels within her limited price range.

It took a couple of halting steps before she found her balance on the thick pile carpet. A couple of lengths of the wide area between the cubicles and the sinks later, she was feeling more confident of her footing. Her blasted eye started itching again, sending Jess scurrying over to the sinks to check her make-up in the brightly lit mirrors. Satin-lined wicker baskets rested in the spaces between each white porcelain bowl, stuffed with every imaginable emergency supply a woman could need from tampons to deodorant and perfume. She even spotted a little sewing kit tucked into one corner.

With a damp cotton bud, she managed to remove the small streak of mascara beneath one eye without destroying her eyeliner. Much heavier than her usual neutral shades, the black liner and sparkling silver eye shadow made her olive-green eyes look huge. It was strange seeing the whole of her face without the comforting shield of the dark-framed glasses she was used to seeing perched on the bridge of her button nose. She felt oddly naked without them.

Make-up checked, shoes and bag exchanged, there was really no excuse for Jess to linger in the bathroom any longer. She cast a quick glance towards the cubicles, contemplating the wisdom of a pre-emptive wee, before deciding against it. By the time she'd wrestled down her tights and the enormous Bridget Jones pants beneath them, she'd be all hot and bothered. Before she could change her mind, Jess forced herself to leave the safety of the bathroom and returned to the lobby to find the smiling hostess waiting at a discreet distance. With a sweep of her arm, she ushered Jess towards the entrance to the party then left her with a quiet wish that she enjoy her evening, the siren call of the lift summoning her to greet a new arrival.

Smoothing a nervous hand over one velvet-clad hip Jess took a deep breath, fighting the temptation to tug at the hem of her party dress which suddenly felt at least three inches too short. The midnight-blue sheath had been an impulse purchase when she submitted to her mother's cajoling and joined her in the buffeting, shoving crowds thronging Regent Street a couple of weekends ago. A clever section of ruching stretched from a diamante flower on her left-hand side across to the opposite hip, falling in forgiving waves that disguised any hint of a tummy her support pants had failed to suck in. The wide shoulder straps provided perfect cover for her bra, the front scooped low enough to show off her décolletage without flashing more than she was willing to share with anyone other than a lover – not that she had many of those lined up. Though she'd had had her fair share of boyfriends at university, none had developed into anything long-term.

Only one man had caught her eye since leaving university, and Tristan Ludworth was so far out of her league she could drape herself naked across his desk and he'd probably still not take the hint. Not that Jess did any hinting. Just the sight of Tristan was enough to make her feel giddy and off-balance, like being in a high-speed lift. She could hold her own with him when it came to work stuff, but only by removing her glasses whenever he was in the vicinity. A blurry, out of focus Tristan was a lot easier to cope with.

The only other man she'd had a serious long-term crush on was her older brother's best friend, Steve, back when she was thirteen and first starting to notice boys. He'd always felt like a safe option to practice her new and tender feelings on. Their mothers had been friends for years, and Steve had always been a familiar presence in her life. He'd tolerated her awkward teenage flirting with kindness, and never made her feel foolish.

Nothing about the way Tristan made her feel was safe. Exhilarating, yes, with a hint of something dangerous and outside her comfort zone. Like riding a roller-coaster, when she'd always preferred the steady even pace of the merry-go-round.

For a fleeting moment she wished she'd stuck with the perfectly serviceable black crepe evening dress hanging unused in her wardrobe. It had always been her plan to wear it tonight – sophisticated and understated, her mother had assured her when she'd first bought it as a wardrobe staple, pointing out how the forgiving drape of the material hid the excess weight that seemed to settle around her middle and bottom the moment she even glanced at a slice of cake. *Safe and boring more like*, a mutinous little voice had whispered in the back of her mind – perfect for someone who had never chosen the road less travelled in any of her twenty-two years. Head down, study hard, do the right thing, had been the mantras she'd carried from childhood into uneventful adulthood. Just lately those mantras had started to feel less like sensible rules to live by and more like the restraining reins her parents had made her wear as a clumsy toddler eager to explore.

The arch of her mother's eyebrow when she'd descended the stairs at home earlier might have dented her confidence had her dad not swooped in to twirl her around before planting a kiss on her cheek and declaring she'd be the belle of the ball. Her mum's face had softened then and she too had kissed Jess before bombarding her with such a flurry of questions about what she was taking with her – yes, she had her gloves, no, she hadn't forgotten her personal alarm, yes, she would be careful and take a taxi if she was at any risk of walking on her own for any distance – that she'd not had time to consider whether she should change her dress until she'd been ensconced on an overheated tube train whisking her in from the suburbs, and by then it had been too late. Only now, dithering as she was, she wished she'd stuck to her usual, practical style.

'God, Jess, just open the bloody door,' she muttered, furious with herself.

'Talking to yourself is the first sign of madness, or so they say.' The voice purring just behind her ear sent a shiver down Jess's spine that had nothing to do with nerves. Feeling a blush rising to burn her cheeks, she tilted her head to glance up and back into the face of a fallen angel. And if there was anyone who could tempt her into sin it was Tristan Ludworth. As ever when she met the hint of wicked humour in his chocolate brown eyes, butterflies fluttered in her middle.

He'd joined Beaman and Tanner the same week as her, and from the moment he'd sat down beside her at the company induction day, she'd been drawn to him. She shouldn't like him – they were rivals on the same graduate training programme and, come the summer, they'd be fighting it out for a permanent position on the staff. The trouble was he was so charming and funny it was impossible not to like him.

He was the son of an aristocrat, according to the coffee room gossip mill, and Jess could well believe the lips currently smiling down at her had been born with a silver spoon between them. And there was no way the tuxedo he wore had come off the peg, it fit too well – the jacket hugging his broad shoulders, and the trousers the perfect length to cover the tops of his shiny, patent-leather shoes. His bow tie – classic black, not like those awful novelty ones some men wore – looked hand-tied, and the handkerchief sticking up from the top pocket was a flash of deep maroon silk, not one of those fake white triangles glued to a bit of cardboard. He'd never looked so gorgeous, nor so unattainable.

There was an innate confidence about him, something that could've easily tipped into arrogance had he not been so damn nice to everyone. Where she fretted and worried over saying or

5

doing the wrong thing, he seemed to breeze through the day without a care in the world. Which was why no matter how hard she worked, he would beat her in the final selection, and break her heart in the process.

Shifting position so that he was beside her, Tristan raised a finger to tug gently at one of the tumbling curls she'd left trailing from the complicated up-do it'd taken three hours in front of a YouTube tutorial to arrange earlier. 'I like this,' he said. Lowering his hand, he brushed the shoulder strap of her velvet dress. 'And this.' The deep timbre of his voice sent another shiver down her spine. 'You look fabulous, Jess; like a gorgeous Christmas present just begging to be unwrapped.'

Warmth spread through her. Not because she thought for a moment that Tristan was being serious in his flirting, but because he'd obviously sensed her nervousness and was going out of his way to make her feel good about herself. It was the kind of thing he'd done since that first day they'd met – like the time he'd given her a little pep talk before her first big solo presentation, or the silly congratulations GIF he'd sent via their internal messaging service when she'd been part of the team that had managed to win back a big client who'd briefly left Beaman and Tanner for a rival company.

Feeling brave, she fluttered her lashes at him. 'You'll have to be a good boy and see what Santa leaves you under the tree.' *Oh God. Had she really just said that to him? She hadn't even had a drink yet, and she was already making a fool of herself.*

Mouth kicking up in one corner, Tristan offered her his elbow, covering the hand she rested upon it with his free one. 'I promise to be a very good boy, although this gorgeous dress of yours is going to make that very difficult. Come on, Cinderella, let me be your Prince Charming and escort you into the ball.'

The next couple of hours passed in a whirlwind of laughter, free cocktails and not quite enough of the delicious nibbles on offer to counteract the alcohol. She and Tristan had ended up at a table with a group of co-workers all in their early-to-mid-twenties. So many people had complimented her on her dress, she quite forgot her inhibitions and let the evening carry her away on a wave of fun and frivolity. She barely had time to sit and ease her sore toes before one or other person in their group declared whatever song was blasting across the dance floor as their absolute favourite and away they all went to dance.

As the current song wound up to its climax, Tristan grabbed her hand and spun her out and back in a twirl. Unsteady from too many cocktails and the unfamiliar heels, Jess placed a hand on his chest to steady herself and let out a breathless laugh. Raising his hand to cover hers, Tristan squeezed her fingers lightly. 'Having a good time?'

Jess nodded, regretting the action as it made the spinning in her head worse. 'A bit too much of a good time, I might have to slow down if I want to make it to midnight.'

Whether through fate or serendipity, the music switched from fast-paced to a soft ballad. Around them, people left the floor in laughing groups, though a fair number shifted into pairs and began to sway to the music. Jess made to follow their friends but was stopped short when Tristan refused to release her hand. When she cast him an enquiring glance he tugged gently, drawing her back into him.

'I thought you wanted to slow things down?' he said, with that mischievous smile that did all kinds of stupid things to her insides.

'This isn't what I had in mind.' Her voice came out breathless.

Circling his arm around her shoulders, Tristan held her close, the sway of his body a temptation she was powerless to resist. 'No? It's been all I've thought about since I first saw you in this beautiful dress.'

Not sure how to take his comment, Jess laughed. 'You shouldn't say things like that, or you'll give a girl ideas.'

Expecting him to laugh along with her, she was shocked when the hand resting on her hip tightened. 'Good. I want you to have

7

ideas about us, Jess. In fact, I want you to spend the next couple of hours thinking about the fact that before this evening ends, I'm going to kiss you.' With one last squeeze of her hip, he backed away from her, a knowing grin plastered across his face.

Heart racing, she turned in the opposite direction and fled for the safety of the ladies'. Locking herself in the far end cubicle, Jess pushed the seat lid down and sank onto it, knees wobbling. Though he'd been smiling, there'd been no mistaking the promise in Tristan's eyes as they'd parted on the dance floor. He wanted to *kiss* her! A little giggle escaped her mouth and she clamped her hand over it. What if someone walked in and caught her laughing to herself?

What if they saw Tristan kissing her? This was her first proper job. Getting mixed up in an office romance might ruin her chances of being taken seriously. But, it was Tristan – the man who made her stomach do somersaults, and her heart race a mile a minute. The man who went out of his way to do nice things for her, for reasons other than his general decency perhaps? The man who would be certain to beat her to the permanent position if she did anything to diminish her reputation in the eyes of their superiors.

She might have sat there for another hour mooning over what could never be, had her bladder not decided to remind her quite forcefully just how much she had drunk in the past couple of hours. With a sigh, Jess stood and began the inelegant task of wriggling down her tights and underwear, almost groaning with relief as her stomach was released from the tight confines of her elasticated pants. She was in the process of struggling back into them when the external bathroom door banged open and she caught the tail end of a conversation.

'. . . even more gorgeous than usual in a tux.' Jess recognised the speaker as Michelle, one of the two company receptionists. She froze, not wanting the woman to know she was there. Though she'd never been overtly rude to Jess, there was an undercurrent to the way she treated her, as though she resented being asked to

8

do things by the new girl – even when they were part of her job description and she never seemed to have a problem when anyone else asked her to make a drink for a visitor or to book a courier.

'I know, right? Tristan's so hot, he puts James Bond to shame.' The second voice belonged to Nicola, the other half of the formidable duo who handled everything from dealing with visitors, to answering the phones and sorting the post without so much as a chipped nail or a single hair out of place. Jess had never seen either of them ever looking anything other than perfectly made-up and turned out. 'I'm going to ask him to dance when we go back in,' Nicola continued, her voice distorted in a way that told Jess she was applying lipstick as she talked.

'Good luck with that,' snorted Michelle. 'You'll have a fight on your hands the way Shrek has been hogging his attention all night. God, did you see the way she was hanging off his neck on the dance floor just now? I felt embarrassed for him.'

Jess found herself frozen in place, hunched over, her tights still halfway up her thighs. The bitchy edge to Michelle's voice was harder and meaner than anything she'd heard from her before. And – *God* – had she really just likened Jess to the ugly ogre cartoon character? She clutched at the wall for support as she listened, the pair of them oblivious to her presence.

'Everyone knows Jess has had a crush on him forever.' Nicola said. 'But tonight it's downright embarrassing the way she's traipsing after him like a dog with its tongue hanging out. As if he'd look twice at a fat lump like her.'

'More like a bitch in heat.' Michelle cackled. 'And you're right. How can she possibly think a man like him would fancy someone like *her*? That's the trouble when you're as nice as he is, I suppose – some people get the wrong message. Let's go and find him and let him know we'll run interference for the rest of the night. Give the poor guy a chance to enjoy himself without Shrek stomping on his toes.' The pair's laughter faded as the door closed behind them.

Shocked and humiliated, Jess tried to focus on the task of

pulling up her tights, and not on the burn at the back of her eyes. How was it possible people knew she fancied Tristan when she'd gone out of her way to keep it to herself? Perhaps she wasn't as discreet as she'd believed and the whole office was laughing at her behind her back. Horrified at the thought, Jess yanked at the thin nylon of her tights, manging to rip a big hole in the left thigh which immediately zoomed down to her ankle in a ladder. 'Damn it!'

Vision swimming with tears, Jess kicked off her heels and yanked off the ruined tights. The pale, mottled skin of her legs looked shockingly white in the harsh overhead lighting. *Now what was she going to do?* She couldn't go back out there flashing her dead-fish coloured legs, for God's sake! Despair gave way to hope as she recalled the baskets of supplies on the counter tops. Leaving her heels on the floor of the cubicle, she padded barefoot across the thickly piled carpet and began to rummage. She came up with two pairs of tights, both of them size small. In desperation more than hope, she took one pair back into the cubicle but couldn't get them much more than over her knees before the fibres stretched so thin and tight she knew it was no good.

Feeling wretchedly sorry for herself, Jess tried to push her naked toes into the narrow confines of her heels. Her feet had swollen after so many hours in the unfamiliar shoes, and that combined with the lack of any barrier between her bare skin and the leather made it almost impossible to get them back on. A couple of steps was all it took for her to know she'd rub a blister if she tried to wear them like that. *Why was everything going wrong for her, tonight of all nights?* A hot tear coursed over her cheek, and Jess stumbled over to the mirror to grab at a handful of tissues. No amount of deep breathing, cheek pressing, and dabbing could stem the trickles. She wasn't exactly crying, but her eyes wouldn't stop leaking and the salt of her tears made her contacts start to itch.

Between rapid blinks, she managed to get the right one out, only to drop it. Its slide down the plug hole was the last straw. 'Sod it.' Removing the other one, Jess flicked it into the sink and turned on the tap to flush it after its mate. Her ruined tights were balled up and chucked into the waste basket, the hated heels pried off and shoved into her backpack along with her evening bag. Retrieving her glasses, Jess popped them on and met her gaze in the mirror. A sense of calm descended as she reached up to tug and pull at the myriad pins holding her up-do in place. Curls tumbled around her shoulders only to be gathered up in one of the spare scrunchies she kept in the front pocket of her rucksack.

Securing her hair in a rough ponytail at her nape, Jess then pulled out a knitted bobble hat and tugged it down over her ears. Coat on and zipped to the neck, feet and calves snug in her furry boots, she cast one last glance in the mirror as she slung her backpack over her shoulder. She should've stayed at home tonight. It was clear she didn't fit in here, and the idea of spending another second around people who thought so little of her they made up cruel nicknames behind her back was more than she could stomach. It turned out she wasn't a blue velvet dress kind of girl, after all. And, she thought as she reached for the door handle, that was just fine with her.

Thanks to a points failure, it took Jess ages to get home and by the time she slotted her key into the front door all she wanted was to crawl into her pyjamas and curl up in bed with a mug of hot chocolate. Before she could turn the key, the door was yanked open and she was confronted with the sight of Steve, her brother's best friend, red-eyed, his face an agonised mask. 'Oh, Jess,' he said, dragging her into his arms. 'He's gone. Marcus is gone.'

No. No, no, no, no, no. It couldn't be, he couldn't be, not her darling big brother. After everything they'd been through with him the past couple of years. The endless worry, the thousands of pounds her parents had spent on rehab. A scream echoed down the stairs, inhumane, animalistic, a sound no human throat should be capable of making. As the waves of grief smashed into her, Jess clung to Steve, his strong arms the only thing that kept her from being swept away.

Chapter 1

Present Day – the first week of September

Charlie Tanner, Tristan's boss since he'd left university and the co-founder of a very successful events and PR firm he'd set up with his business – and life – partner Tim Beaman, took a sip of the wine poured by the waiter. Though Tristan had invited him to lunch and was footing the bill, he had left it to the older man to select the wine. Already feeling nervous about the news he was going to deliver, he could only hope the sop of a decent vintage would go some way to ease the news he was pretty sure Charlie wasn't going to want to hear. Charlie raised his glass towards the light spilling in from the window, turned his glass a couple of times as he studied the ruby-red hue of the liquid in his glass before finally giving the waiter a nod. With the ritual of the wine selection over, he turned his hawk-like gaze to Tristan. 'So, when are you coming back to us?'

Okay, so they were cutting straight to the chase. Tristan smiled his thanks at the waiter then reached for his own glass, more to give himself time to word the answer than any real desire for a drink. Both Charlie and Tim had been incredibly understanding when Tristan had taken a twelve-month unpaid sabbatical in order to return home to help his brother, Arthur, and sister, Igraine, manage their ancestral home following their father's death the previous autumn. Though he'd been happy to do everything he could to support Arthur, Tristan was grateful that being the youngest of the triplets meant the family title and all its burdens and responsibilities had not fallen on his shoulders.

During the bleak winter months when it'd seemed to do nothing but either rain, snow or some hideous combination of the two, Tristan had missed his busy life in London. Once the bluebells that had given the family castle its pretty nickname had started blooming and the hard work the three of them had invested started to pay off however, Tristan had found his thoughts straying less and less to the smart apartment he rented in Battersea and his job as a marketing executive in the city. 'Yes, well that's what I wanted to talk to you about,' he said to Charlie with an apologetic wince.

'Oh, balls. Don't tell me we're going to be losing both of you? When you invited me to lunch, I assumed you wanted to get up to speed on our current projects in preparation for your return.' Charlie cast him a gloomy look then took a large swig of the rather fine burgundy. 'Well, you know what they say about assuming things . . .'

It cut Tristan deeper than he'd expected to be letting the man opposite him down. Charlie had been an inspiration to him from the first day he'd started working at the events management and public relations firm. Both Charlie and Tim, chose to encourage rather than control their staff, giving them room to take chances as long as any failures were learning experiences.

Feeling wretched, Tristan braced his forearms on the edge of the table and met the older man's gaze. 'I'm really sorry. I should have given you a warning, I suppose, but I wanted to talk to you face to face and explain. After everything you've done for me, it seemed rude to put it in an email.' Twisting his glass between his fingers, he studied the rich wine as though he could find the answers he owed his boss in its opaque surface. 'If I'd thought for one moment I would find myself in this position then I would have resigned outright rather than requesting a sabbatical.' He glanced up to find Charlie studying him over the steepled tips of his fingers.

'What changed?' There was no censure in this question, only genuine curiosity.

'I fell in love.' When Charlie quirked a brow, he laughed. 'Not like that. As a second son, I always knew there was never any future for me at the castle and somewhere along the way my brain translated that into believing that I didn't want there to be a future for me there. I told myself I was city boy, that life in the country was too slow-paced for me. And then somewhere along the line I found myself standing on the edge of our land looking out over the dales and I couldn't imagine being anywhere else.'

'If that's the case, then you can go with my blessing.' Raising his glass in a silent toast, Charlie took another drink.

Relief flooded Tristan and he returned the gesture in tribute to everything the man opposite had done for him. As his worry over letting Charlie down began to dissipate, something else his boss had said earlier finally filtered through his awareness. 'Hold up. What do you mean losing both of us? Who else is leaving?'

Setting down his glass, Charlie sat back in his seat with a sigh. 'Jessica turned her notice in last month. Did you not know?'

Tristan swallowed. Cocooned in the microcosm of life behind the thick curtain wall of the castle, he'd been a bit lax in keeping in touch with his friends and co-workers. Several unread emails rested in his inbox. Fearing they would be asking him about his planned return, and not sure how to answer them, he'd stuck his head in the sand and ignored them.

'Well, anyway,' Charlie said after giving him a quizzical glance. 'It's her last day today. We're having drinks in The Crown and Sceptre later; you should come along. I'm sure everyone would be delighted to see you.'

Everyone apart from Jessica. They'd been great friends until he'd cocked it all up by coming on too strong at a work's party. So desperate had she been to avoid his crass advances she'd done a runner, then hardly said two words to him on their return to work in the new year. Several years later, it was still a source of embarrassment that he'd managed to read what he'd thought was a mutual attraction so wrong. The fact she'd married some bloke she'd practically grown up with less than twelve months later had told him exactly how mistaken he'd been about the whole scenario.

Even with her own wedding to plan, Jess had still beaten him hands down to the permanent position on the events team they'd both been interning for. Her work ethic had been formidable, even back then. Luckily for Tristan an opening had come up in the corporate affairs side of the business and he'd been able to transfer across. Things had soon settled down between them, and whenever they'd been called upon to work together on a big project it'd been fine. Oh, he still felt a pull towards her whenever she removed her glasses and stared at him, but married women were off limits. No matter how sweet and sexy they were. They'd never quite recovered that close bond forged during their first week as baby interns, both fresh from university and clueless about the real world, though, much to his chagrin.

'Maybe I'll drop in for a quick drink,' he said, having zero intention of doing so. It wouldn't be fair on Jess to appear out of the blue and steal any of her thunder. 'Which of your rivals has been lucky enough to poach her?' Their corporate world was a small one, and staff interchanged across the major firms with some regularity as they zig-zagged their way along career paths all headed in one direction. It was testament to both Charlie and Tim how few of their employees jumped ship for other opportunities. Someone must've made Jess one hell of a sweet offer.

'That's the absolute worst thing about the whole bloody business – she's not moving to a new role, she's quitting.' Charlie shook his head then took another mouthful of wine.

His revelation stunned Tristan. 'But *why*?'

The waiter chose that moment to return to the table, interrupting their conversation as they each selected something from the lighter lunch menu before throwing all their good intentions down the drain by adding a portion of chips to share.

'Carbs will always be my downfall.' As though to underline his point, Charlie reached for a piece of bread from the basket between them and began to slather it with butter. 'What were we saying? Ah, yes, poor Jessica.' As though intent on torturing Tristan, he took a large bite out of the bread and proceeded to chew it slowly.

Poor Jessica. *What the hell did that mean?* Tamping down his need to demand answers, Tristan conjured every possibility. Perhaps her husband was changing his job and they were moving away. She already had a couple of kids, was she pregnant again and had decided to take a career break? Neither of those seemed likely to elicit the sympathy he'd detected in Charlie's tone. Was she ill? Oh God, what if one of the kids was ill? The piece of bread he'd taken was now many crumbs on his side plate, shredded into pieces as he pondered ever more outlandish scenarios.

'Now, normally I wouldn't say anything, but she's been very open about things around the office, so I don't feel I'd be betraying a confidence if I tell you that she and Steve are getting a divorce.' Charlie shook his head, expression sad. 'No one else involved,' he continued, answering Tristan's unspoken assumption. 'Just one of those things, apparently, and they're still very good friends. With him moving out and giving up his job to go back to university, she can't afford the rent on her own so she's moving back in with her parents until she can get things straight. They retired to Surrey, or Sussex, or perhaps it was Somerset. One of the esses.' He dismissed them all with a wave of his hand, the look on his face saying they were all as bad as each other as far as Charlie was concerned. 'But, enough about that, tell me what's been going on with you.'

As they shared their meal, Tristan outlined the goings-on at Bluebell Castle, most significantly the discovery by Arthur's now-wife, Lucie, of a long-lost painting which was going a long way to righting the family's fortunes. 'I saw something about that in the paper,' Charlie said. 'Hidden under the floorboards or something, wasn't it?'

Tristan laughed. 'Walled up in a hidden passageway, actually. There's a heart-breaking story attached to its creation. One of our ancestors commissioned the piece to commemorate his engagement and his fiancée did a moonlight flit with the artist. I've been working with my sister-in-law on the copy for the information boards to support an exhibition in the castle about it. We're hoping to add some of our other ancestors to it as time goes on, bit of a potted history of the Ludworths, you know the kind of thing?'

Charlie nodded. 'You're opening things up to the public then?'

'Yes. My sister, Iggy, did an amazing job with restoring the grounds, and the summer fete was a huge success. We'd like to open a few parts of the castle as well to ensure we've got an all-seasons attraction. That's where I come into the mix – I'm organising some top-end boutique holiday packages. A chance to experience a traditional Christmas in a real castle. I put a teaser up on the castle's blog the other week just to see if there was any interest and I've had dozens of enquiries. I'd also like to do something with the grounds, create a Winter Wonderland experience.'

'Hopefully it won't end up like one of those disasters that seem to crop up on the news every year.' Charlie observed, dryly.

'Tell me about it,' Tristan agreed, fervently. He'd come across some absolute horror stories during his research into it over the summer. 'Thankfully, I've got my own crack team of garden designers on call in my sister and her other half, Will Talbot.'

Charlie raised an eyebrow. 'Not *that* Will Talbot?'

Prior to meeting Iggy, Will had been something of a tabloid celebrity renowned for his wild ways. Happily settled, there was little about him now to hint at that bad boy image, other than a rather arresting scar on his face and a penchant for leather jackets and jeans.

Tristan grinned. It seemed like even someone as urbane and sophisticated as Charlie wasn't immune to a little stardust. 'The very same. They're based here in town now for the most part which is one of the reasons I came to London. They've been working on design ideas, and we're sitting down this afternoon to make a final decision.'

'Cutting it fine, aren't you? It's September already.' Charlie followed his comment with a chuckle. 'But then that always was your style.'

'Hey,' Tristan protested, though he was laughing at the same time. 'I met most of my deadlines.' True, he'd pulled more than a few all-nighters to get the job done, but he'd always delivered when it mattered.

'Well, I hope you've got someone who'll keep you in line.' When Tristan remained silent, Charlie gave him a speaking look. 'I quite fancied the sound of your traditional Christmas in a castle. After the year we've had, Tim and I could do with a bit of luxury pampering, but maybe we'll wait until next year . . .'

'You don't think I can pull it off.' Tristan couldn't keep the disappointment out of his voice.

Leaning forward, Charlie patted the back of his hand in a purely paternal gesture. 'I'm sure you can pull it off, but perhaps it's time for you to do more than that. Christmas is a special time for a lot of people. Last-minute scrambles to get things done shouldn't be a part of that.' Sitting back, he finished the wine in his glass. 'Look, Tristan, you know I adore you – both Tim and I would cut off our right arms if we thought for a moment we could lure you back into the fold – but you've never been one to sweat the small stuff. When you are part of a team, you're unstoppable, and we gave you the structure you needed to succeed. But even you have to admit you're not always on top of all the details.'

Tristan opened his mouth to argue then recalled the unread emails in his inbox. He was very good at focusing on the stuff that interested him, the rest of it . . . 'So, what do you suggest?'

'Get yourself a decent assistant, someone to compliment your enthusiasm with a dash of ruthless practicality.' Charlie offered him a kindly smile. 'Don't look so worried, I'm sure it will be a great success, but this is the first time you've struck out on your own and sometimes it takes a friend to point out our potential weaknesses.'

A friend. Yes, that's what Charlie was, and a mentor too. 'Thank you. And if you're serious about you and Tim coming up for Christmas, I'll be happy to do you a special deal.'

Charlie waved him off, but Tristan could see it had pleased him that Tristan was willing to not only listen to his advice, but take it in the spirit in which it was meant. 'Nonsense. Mates rates are the death of far too many ventures. We'll be happy to pay full price. Do we get a proper four-poster bed?'

'We've still got a couple of old horsehair mattresses if you want that authentic experience. Or I could throw some rushes down in front of the fireplace in the great hall and you can bed down with the dogs for warmth.' The image of Charlie, a walking Savile Row catalogue, being descended upon by the castle's collection of unruly hounds brought a wicked grin to Tristan's face. A mixed bag, most from local shelters or given up by people who had taken on more than they could handle, the castle pack were a sweet, harmless bunch but could be a little overwhelming to someone not used to them. 'I *did* tell you about the dogs?'

'Stop trying to put me off, it won't work. Tim told me the other day I'm getting a bit paunchy.' Charlie touched a hand to the slight roundness of his stomach well disguised by the impeccable cut of his jacket. 'I can already picture myself striding around the Derbyshire countryside with a whippet at my heels.' He frowned, thoughtfully. 'That's what you North-country types have isn't it?'

'Either that or a ferret stuffed down our trousers, yes,' Tristan responded with a wry grin. 'If you want to walk the dogs every day, Arthur will probably love you forever.' He paused to signal to the waiter that they were ready for coffee. 'Seriously though, the castle is set right on the edge of the dales so there's no shortage of walking to be done – weather permitting, of course. And the estate has its own woods and plenty of parkland. There's also stables if you ride . . .'

Charlie pulled a face. 'I can't see myself on the back of a horse, but the idea of getting out of town and away from the endless round of parties is very appealing. We'll have to talk Tim around to the idea, but you can do that later when you join us in the pub for drinks.'

Damn, now how was he going to duck out of it without causing offence? 'I'm not sure if I'll have time, what with seeing Iggy and Will this afternoon.' Probably best not to mention he was staying in their spare room during his visit, or that he wasn't going back home until the day after tomorrow.

'Nonsense. You have to come. Now you're leaving us in the lurch, it's the least you can do.' It was said with a smile, but there was no getting around Charlie's disappointment at his continued attempts to evade the celebration.

'The party is for Jess, I don't want to crash in at the last minute.' Tristan tried one last time to get out of it.

'Rubbish. She won't mind, she'll probably be relieved. You know how she is when there's too much fuss. Hold on a minute.' Before Tristan could say anything, Charlie whipped out his phone and made a call. 'Jessica? Charlie, here. What? Yes, everything is fine with the Centrifuge account, and besides, it's not your problem anymore, is it?'

Tristan listened as Charlie laughed. 'Okay, Little Miss Conscientious, in three and a half hours it won't be your problem anymore. Look, I'm with Tristan, and he's decided to quit on me as well. I told him he should come for drinks tonight, but he's being stubborn. Have a word, will you?' With that he thrust his phone across the table, leaving Tristan no choice but to pick it up.

'Hi, Jess.'

'Hello, stranger.' The phone emphasised the natural huskiness of her voice, and he could instantly picture her, long dark hair wrapped up in one of those practical knots his fingers always itched to undo, a little crease of concentration furrowing her brow as her hands flew across her keyboard. 'Causing trouble, as usual?'

He laughed. 'You know me too well.' *But not half as well as he might wish.* 'I'm staying in Derbyshire for the foreseeable future, and Charlie has decided he's never going to forgive me.'

'I'm not,' Charlie bellowed loud enough to be heard. 'And the same goes for you too, Jessica. Pair of traitors.'

'Here we go again,' Jess muttered, giving Tristan the impression Charlie had put a lot more pressure on her about leaving than he had received. It didn't do much for his ego, but it would be churlish to feel any resentment. Her tone brightened. 'Well at least if you're leaving, too, that takes some of the heat off me.'

'Cheers,' Tristan said, wryly. 'Thanks a bunch. Listen, Charlie wants me to come along to your leaving drinks tonight, but I don't want to crash your party.'

'Oh God, crash it, please crash it!' she begged. 'I told them I didn't want to do anything, but you know what they're like.'

'Any excuse for a party.' It was the company's unofficial motto, and, after all, the way they made most of their business.

'Exactly! Please, say you'll come.' She was quiet for a long moment. 'It'd be nice to see you again.'

Well, hell, how on earth was he going to refuse now? 'It'll be nice to see you too.'

What was he going to wear tonight? He hadn't packed much, having only planned to be away for a couple of days. He'd worn a suit for lunch with Charlie, but that would be a bit over the top for the pub given he wasn't coming from the office. They were only going to the pub, surely a shirt and jeans would suffice? And why was he bothered about it anyway?

'Hello? Earth to Tristan.' Iggy snapped her fingers a bare inch from his nose, making Tristan flinch back in surprise.

'Hey, stop that.' He batted her hand away.

'Well, if you'd stop daydreaming for five minutes, I wouldn't have to.' His sister slouched back in her seat, arms folded across her chest. 'It's not like we've got anything better to do other than give up our time to help you out.'

Tristan didn't know what the hell had got into her, but Iggy had been in a foul mood from the moment he'd returned to the apartment she shared with Will. They'd gathered around the big island in the kitchen that doubled as a table to discuss how to transform the castle grounds into something spectacular, but she'd done nothing but snipe and snap at him since they'd sat down.'

Will leaned over from his seat to press a kiss to the tip of her nose. 'Leave your poor brother alone, he's not going to ruin your garden.'

Iggy scowled at Will, but there was no mistaking the way her body language softened when he tucked his hand under her hair to stroke a light caress. 'He can't even pay attention long enough to listen to what we have to say about it, how can I trust him?'

Now he understood what was at the heart of her mood, Tristan had nothing but sympathy for his sister's position. She loved Bluebell Castle – probably more than he and Arthur did combined – and she'd surprised them all by her decision to move away. It was clear to anyone she adored Will, and he her, and his horticultural business was based in London so the move made sense. They were working to diversify the brand, to leave the refurbishment projects which had been the bread and butter of the business in the hands of their experienced installation team so Will and Iggy could focus on their new passion for bringing gardening to schools and deprived inner city areas, and Tristan understood how important it was for his sister to strive to build a life away from their childhood home. Not because she didn't love it there, but because she'd been the de facto mistress of the castle for several years and she was determined to surrender that role to Lucie. But the gardens were her baby, and Tristan needed her to know that he understood that, that he would honour all the hard work she had put into them and preserve her legacy.

Pulling his chair close on her other side, he slung an affectionate arm around her waist. 'I won't screw this up, Iggle-Piggle, I swear.'

Though his use of her hated nickname earned him a punch in the arm, it was immediately followed by a swift, hard hug. 'I know, it's just . . .'

'I know.' Tristan gave her a squeeze before shuffling his chair back. 'When it comes to the grounds, you're still the boss. Consider me your on-site eyes and ears, but I won't do anything that the three of us haven't agreed in advance.'

'And we'll go up for as many weekends as we can spare. And a whole week at half-term,' Will assured her.

'That's a lot of unnecessary miles,' Iggy protested. 'When I'm just being precious about it.'

'Bollocks to that,' Will retorted, before digging in his pocket with a sigh and dropping a pound coin into a jar on the table. 'I can't believe that meddling assistant of mine talked you into having a swear jar at home as well as in the office. A man should be able to eff and blind in the peace of his own bloody kitchen.'

Giving him an evil grin, Iggy tapped the side of the jar with her finger until he fished out a fifty-pence piece and flipped it in after the pound. 'She showed me a brochure for that luxury spa she visited last month on the back of your dirty mouth,' she said.

Will leaned forward to steal a kiss. 'I thought you liked my dirty mouth.'

'Okay, okay, time out.' Tristan waved his arms to draw their attention away from each other. As happy as he was that his siblings had both found love, it was bad enough watching his brother moon after Lucie every day at home without being subjected to these two and their public displays of affection. 'Can we get back to the matter at hand?'

Chapter 2

The door of the pub swung open and Jess cursed herself not only for her Pavlovian response to it, but the little dip of disappointment she felt when once again it wasn't Tristan who walked through it. She checked her watch surreptitiously, giving a weak smile as a gale of laughter went around the table to some comment she'd missed.

'Here, get this down your neck!' A large glass of rosé was thrust in her face.

'Thanks.' Accepting the drink, she set it down untasted beside the half-full one she'd been nursing for a while. Apart from the odd bottle at the weekend when she was curled up in her pyjamas after the boys were asleep, she was grossly out of practice. From the ever-increasing volume of her friends and colleagues, they were having no such problem sticking with the pace.

'Everything all right, Jess?' Tim was watching her with a frown of concern, making her feel guilty. He and Charlie had put a lot of money behind the bar, she needed to buck up and a least make an effort to have a good time.

'I'm fine, just not used to being away from the boys.' Sitting up straighter, she reached for the fresh glass of wine and took a sip. It wasn't bad at all for a house wine, though not as cold as she preferred it. 'I could do with some ice.' She cast a forlorn look towards the bar. Hemmed in as she was along the back row of a group of tables they'd shoved together, there was no chance of her getting out short of getting on her hands and knees and crawling underneath.

'I'll get you some.' Tim rose at once. 'I'll order some food while I'm at it to soak up some of this booze.'

'That'd be great.' She shot him a grateful smile.

He was back in moments with a large tumbler full of ice which he placed on the table between them. 'I hate warm wine,' he said, fishing out a couple of cubes for himself after Jess had added what she wanted to her glass. Leaning across the table, he lowered his voice with a conspiratorial wink. 'And it won't do any harm to water it down a touch. I can't keep pace these days.'

'We should be at home with our pipes and slippers.' She grinned and finally allowed herself to relax. This would be the last night out she was going to get for a long time, it would be stupid to waste it. Besides, she'd worked with the people gathered around her for the past seven years, and she would miss them. Her eyes flicked to the end of the table to where Michelle, the company receptionist, was holding court with a couple of the guys from accounts hanging on her every word. Well she'd miss *most* of them, she mentally amended.

Even if she could get away with sneaking out early, it wouldn't be fair to Steve or the boys. This was their last weekend together before Steve moved out, and he'd planned a special night in. Knowing how much Elijah and Isaac were going to miss him, she'd told Steve to take the bedroom he'd surrendered to her when they'd finally admitted things were over between them.

They'd been as honest as it was possible to be with a five- and two-year-old, but little Isaac, in particular, had become very clingy and spent more nights curled up with one or the other of them, than he did in the bunk beds they'd put into Elijah's room, to allow Steve to move into the box room, which had previously served as their youngest son's bedroom. She had no doubt the three of them were already sprawled across the king-sized bed, watching cartoons and eating pizza. A pang of sadness struck deep in her middle as she thought about other Friday nights when she'd been a part of those messy, lazy gatherings. So many things their little family would never do together again. She shoved the threatening sadness away. No matter how awful they both felt about it, separating from Steve had been the right decision.

Taking a fortifying sip of her wine, she turned her attention back to Tim, catching a look of sympathy on his face which told her he knew what she'd been thinking about. She couldn't deal with any kindness right now; it would only lead to tears. A distraction was needed. 'Charlie was telling me yesterday that you guys are looking to book a late break, have you got anywhere in mind?'

Tim pulled a face. 'I was hoping for somewhere in the sun, but after his lunch with Tristan earlier Charlie is obsessed with going up to Derbyshire for Christmas. Did you know he lives in a castle? A proper turrets and drawbridge castle.' He reached for the phone resting next to his glass, fiddled with it for a few seconds and then handed it across to her. 'I thought Charlie was joking until I googled it.'

Jess stared at the screen, unable to believe what she was seeing. She'd always known Tristan came from a background of privilege, but she'd assumed he was joking from the dismissive way he'd told her he'd grown up in a castle. A big house – bigger certainly than the standard suburban three-bed semi she and Marcus had been raised in by their parents – but Tim was right. It had *turrets*.

Fascinated, she began to scroll through the website, found a link and clicked on the blog. She recognised Tristan's breezy writing style in the updates. He'd always been a whizz at producing press releases that didn't sound like hard-sell marketing, even if that's exactly what they were. The top story talked about plans for a traditional Christmas and how the family hoped to be able to share it with a few new friends. It sounded so inviting, like an intimate house party rather than a hotel break. She might be tempted herself had common sense not told her it would be way outside her price bracket. Although, once Steve started his course and they were down to one income, a weekend at Butlins would be outside her price bracket. 'It looks glorious,' she said on a wistful sigh.

He shuddered. 'It *snows* up there.'

She couldn't help laughing. 'It snows down here too, sometimes.'

'Not like they get up there. Can you see me wading through the drifts? No, thank you.'

'You can stay in, cosy by the fire. God, look at this!' She passed the phone back to Tim, showing him a picture of a roaring fire in the biggest fireplace she'd ever seen. A gorgeous pair of brindle greyhounds were curled up before it, and a thick swag of greenery decorated the high mantel.

'Mmm, now that is something I could get on board with,' Tim mused. 'A nice glass of port, a Kindle full of books.' He leaned forward to call down the table to Charlie. 'Derbyshire is a go!'

A hand landed on Tim's shoulder and Jess looked up to meet a twinkly pair of brown eyes. Her stomach did that ridiculous little flip thing it did every time she saw Tristan. Even when she and Steve had been happy, had been in love and looking forward to growing old together, she'd always had this visceral reaction to Tristan. 'Now that's music to my ears,' Tristan was saying as he eased himself into a chair someone had vacated for him. 'I thought I was going to have to give you the hard sell.'

'You can thank Jess. She's the one who showed me this.' He held up the fireplace image to Tristan. 'This is the real deal, right? Not creative marketing?'

'Every picture on the website is a genuine image of somewhere on the estate,' he assured Tim as he offered a smile of thanks to a co-worker who'd placed a pint in front of him. Raising it, he toasted the table. 'Well, cheers to you all. I wasn't expecting to have the chance to see everyone on this flying visit so it's a real bonus.'

'Cheers!' Jess joined in with everyone sitting close enough as they clinked glasses. 'I'm really pleased you could make it.'

'Me too.' His expression grew serious for a moment as he spoke in an undertone. 'Everything all right?'

Oh. He knew then. She wondered if it was someone from the office, or if Charlie had mentioned it over lunch. Not that it mattered, she'd decided to be open about it when it was clear things with Steve were beyond repair. She'd never been great at hiding her feelings, and once they understood the reason behind it her colleagues had given her a wide berth on the mornings when she'd turned up red-eyed from lack of sleep and too many tears. 'Getting there.'

He gave her the ghost of a wink before turning away to respond to some banter flying from the other end of the table, giving her the opportunity to study him from behind the shield of her wine glass. He'd rolled the sleeves of his blue and white checked shirt to his elbows, revealing tanned forearms that spoke of many hours spent outdoors. His hair was longer than she'd seen it in a while, the shaggy curls tangling in the back of his collar. A hint of five o'clock shadow dusted his chin the way it always did at this point in the evening. It struck her then that perhaps it wasn't the sort of thing a woman ought to know about a man who wasn't her husband.

Embarrassed, she looked away only to meet a knowing look from Michelle. With the slightest curl of her lip, the receptionist tilted her head to whisper something to the girl next to her, eyes never leaving Jess's. For a horrible moment Jess was back in that toilet stall listening to Michelle bitch about her having a crush on Tristan.

Instinct had always pushed Jess to avoid confrontation and she'd submitted to the subtle bullying of messages not passed on, post misfiled and myriad other little snipes from this woman for years. She'd always told herself she was rising above it, that the lack of respect didn't matter, but it did. It always had, but she'd never done anything about it, too afraid to rock the boat. But this wasn't her boat any longer, was it? Michelle would never again 'forget' to book a meeting room for her because come Monday morning Jess would be trying to comfort her boys as she waited for her parents to arrive and help her pack their belongings.

Part of Jess wanted to wail about the unfairness of life, to curl up in a quiet corner and sob over her situation, but a larger part of her was angry. Angry that she and Steve hadn't been able to find a way to stay together; angry that his plans were having such a drastic knock-on effect on her; angry at the thought of being trapped once more under her mother's loving, but oppressive thumb. Marcus had always been the golden child, and Jess had accepted her role in the background, adoring him as she did. After his death, all that expectation he'd been unable to carry had fallen upon her shoulders. A burden she neither wanted, nor quite knew how to shrug off.

She'd been swallowing this anger for weeks, not wanting to upset the children or descend into pointless rows with Steve that would do nothing other than hurt them both even more than they already were, and now it felt like she would choke. Letting it push to the surface, she locked eyes with Michelle and let all the contempt she felt for the woman rest in that look. It didn't take more than a few moments before Michelle lowered her head.

Reaching for her glass, Jess gave herself a little toast of victory then drained half of what remained in there.

'Can I get you another?'

It was on the tip of her tongue to refuse Tristan's offer, but she gave him a smile of thanks instead. 'Yes, please.'

The food Tim had ordered arrived as Tristan returned with their drinks and everyone tucked into the platters of sandwiches, bowls of chips, onion rings and other calorie-laden treats. Conversation ebbed and flowed, much of it led by Tristan, and she was content to settle into the background and let the evening wash over her.

After the first couple of hours, people started to drift off, home to their families, or in the case of one group on to the bright lights of the West End. They'd done their best to persuade Jess to join them, but she'd never been one for crowded pubs and clubs even in her university days. There were maybe a dozen people left and Jess had finally been able to escape from her position at the back of the table for a well-needed bathroom break. While in there, she loosened her hair from its restrictive bun to scrub her aching scalp before tying it up in a messy ponytail. She freshened the light lip gloss she favoured, although she had to squint one eye shut to focus properly on her reflection to do so. *Time for a soft drink.*

The bar was busy, and she was still waiting for the server who'd given her a nod of acknowledgement to make his way towards her when someone nudged her arm. 'Alone at last.' Tristan's grin looked a little wonky, maybe she wasn't the only one feeling the effects of the free bar.

'Apart from the fifty people standing within about five feet of us.'

'They don't count.' Turning his body to stand sideways onto her, he propped an elbow on the bar effectively shielding them from the rest of their group sitting beyond him. 'I was really sorry to hear about you and Steve.'

'Just one of those things.' She tried for levity but missed by a country mile. 'Seems like we'll both be living back home.'

Tristan gave her a sad smile. 'But I'm the only one of us doing it by choice, right?'

It would be simple to let him believe that, to indulge in her earlier need to bemoan her fate and soak up the sympathy she knew he'd offer in abundance. But that wasn't right. She wasn't a child, nor a passive participant in what was happening in her life. The decision for Steve to quit a job he hated and that was slowly destroying the laughing spirit she'd loved in him since they were little, had been made together. In fact, Steve had been the one to argue against it, knowing how hard it would be for her to move back home – even for a short while.

'It makes the most sense,' she said to Tristan now, echoing the words she said to Steve at their kitchen table months earlier. 'Steve wants to go back to university, and I fully support his decision to do so. I've got a couple of interviews lined up next week, so it won't take me long to find another job.'

'I thought you were taking a break from work?'

The question surprised her. 'No. Why would you think that?'

Tristan shrugged a shoulder. 'When Charlie said you'd turned down his offer to work remotely, I just assumed, I guess.'

God love Charlie, he'd been beyond understanding, and it had been very tempting to accept his offer. But the kind of work she did required too much face-time with their clients and she wouldn't be able to do as good a job as the company deserved, which she wouldn't be able to cope with. Jess liked to do the best she could – *needed* to feel like she was doing a good job. And, no, she didn't need a shrink to tell her where that desire to please came from.

'I wouldn't have been able to give work the attention it deserved. Elijah will be starting school full-time, and both he and Isaac are going to need me around until things settle down. Isaac's too little to really understand what's going on, but poor Elijah is the apple of his daddy's eye. If Mum and Dad lived closer, I might have found a way to juggle everything.' She shrugged. 'It's not a permanent move and I'll take stock at the end of the year. The jobs I'm applying for are both part-time. It'll make things tight, but we've got some savings and not having to pay London rent prices makes a difference.'

The barman finally made his way to her and she ordered a bottle of sparkling water before asking Tristan what he wanted. 'I'll take a bottle of alcohol-free beer, please.'

Drinks in hand they made their way back to the table to find the group had thinned out a bit more. Taking a free seat at one end Jess took a long, cooling drink of her water and started to feel a bit less tipsy. Not wanting to pursue their conversation at the bar, Jess waited until Tristan slipped into the seat beside her and then began to question him about his future plans. 'How many guests do you think you'll have at Christmas?'

Tristan sipped his beer from the bottle. 'Not sure, yet. As many as I think we can cope with and still give them an individual experience. We'll do a few bigger group things, Christmas dinner, of course, and Midnight Mass at the chapel for those who want to participate. But I want each person to feel like they are spending time with family and friends rather than being just guests who I'm trying to screw a load of money out of.' He laughed. 'Not that I won't be trying to do that as well, but it's important they don't feel like that's my aim.' Settling back in his seat, he stretched his legs out in front of him, feet crossed at the ankles. 'Charlie said he liked the idea of walking the dogs, for example.'

'He might be on his own there. Tim wants to sit by the fireplace and read.'

'See, that's another perfect example. The bedrooms in the castle are all different, so it will be important to establish what people want and make sure we give them accommodation that matches those expectations. We've got several different reception rooms available so if one couple is a bit more introverted, we could assign them their own private lounge as well as giving access to a larger one if they choose to mingle some evenings.'

'A proper boutique experience,' Jess mused. 'That sounds brilliant, but it'll be a lot of upfront preparation. You'll also need to provide some kind of concierge service for guests who want to go out and about.'

'You're right. I hadn't considered that, but I'll have to put together an itinerary of available entertainment and ways to access them either by road or rail.' Pulling out his phone, Tristan began tapping notes into it. 'Bloody Charlie was right.'

Not sure if his half-muttered comment was aimed at her,

Jess didn't ask what Charlie had been right about, though she couldn't deny her curiosity was piqued. She didn't have to wait long, because as soon as he'd finished jotting things down, Tristan shoved his phone in his shirt pocket with a sigh. 'I'm just not detail-orientated enough to think of all these things, I'm really going to have to up my game, or do what Charlie suggested and get myself an assistant.' He reached for his beer, then stopped, hand outstretched as he stared at her.

'What?'

Tristan blinked. 'Nothing. Never mind.' Seizing his bottle, he took a long draught. 'Nothing,' he repeated, sounding less certain this time.

'Stop being so bloody mysterious, and tell me,' she demanded, giving his free arm a playful shove.

'I was thinking you and I might be able to offer the perfect solution to each other.' Shifting his chair a bit closer, he slung an arm around the back of hers. 'How do you fancy coming to work for me?'

The wine had not only affected her eyesight apparently, because she must've misheard him. Gulping at her water, she silently admonished herself for that third glass of wine.

'Well, what do you say?'

Incredulous, she shifted in her seat to face him. 'About what? Surely, you were joking.'

He shook his head, sending a lock of his dark hair tumbling into his eyes which he twitched away with an impatient finger. 'I'm deadly serious.'

Maybe he was the one who was drunk. 'I've just told you that my boys need my attention and you expect me to abandon them to come and work for you.' She couldn't hide her outrage.

'Who said anything about abandoning your kids? Bring them with you, of course.' He said it like it was the most reasonable thing in the world.

No, not drunk, mad. 'And do what with them?'

34

'Put Elijah in the village school, and you can keep Isaac with you during the day if you want. We can set up a little play area for him next to your desk, but you can work flexible hours around them. Once he's got used to things a bit there will be plenty of people around to do a bit of babysitting if you need a break. There was never any shortage of willing hands when we were kids, and that's not changed in the past thirty years. We've got acres of land for them to play in, a special children's area of the gardens where they can dig and plant stuff with Constance. Lancelot will give them riding lessons, whatever you want.'

He was talking about people she'd never heard of, volunteering them for roles without the slightest hesitation that they might have better things to do than be saddled – literally in Lancelot's, *Lancelot! Who had a name like that anyway?*, case – with a stranger's children. 'It's ridiculous.'

Tristan opened his mouth as though to argue his point further, then reached for his beer bottle with a shrug. 'You're probably right'

Of course, she was right. As Tristan turned away to say something to Tim, she caught a flash of something on his face, like maybe she'd hurt his feelings by dismissing his outlandish idea so quickly. Annoyed she turned her back to him, her eyes lighting on the phone still on the table. With an exasperated sigh, she scrolled back through the photos on the castle's blog. It was clear that growing up in a fairy tale setting had given Tristan some odd ideas. People like him just didn't understand how things worked in the real world. She couldn't just pack up the boys and make them live with a bunch of strangers.

Her heart clenched at the image of a tyre swing hanging from the boughs of an ancient oak, and she thought about the prim neatness of her parents' back garden. About how her mother had pretended – unsuccessfully – not to mind when Elijah had trampled a row of gladioli when retrieving his football from one of her pristine flower beds. And it wasn't just the perfection of the garden to worry about, there was also the cream carpet in the front room just waiting for a blackcurrant squash disaster. It had really begun to bother her how much her boys would have to compromise to fit into the neat and tidy box her parents called home. They'd have to be small, and quiet, and neat at the very age when they should be able to explore their environment without fear of the constant drip-drip of criticism she and Marcus had been subject to. *A place for everything, and everything in its place.* How many times had she bitten her lip as she watched her mother correct the boys for breaking some rule that only existed in the pristine bubble of Wendy Wilson's perfect world? She imagined Elijah whooping with joy as she pushed him on the tyre swing, of Isaac tumbling around in great piles of autumn leaves; of them just being free. 'I'll have to talk to Steve.'

Sitting up straighter, she nudged Tristan's arm to get his attention. 'I'll have to talk to Steve,' she repeated.

His expression was puzzled for a moment before he gave her that dazzling, tummy-flipping grin. 'Well, okay then.'

Chapter 3

'It's a stupid idea,' Jess said for what must've been the tenth time in as many minutes. When Steve remained silent, she paused in the act of sorting the clothes from the bottom of Elijah's chest of drawers to stare across the bed to where Steve was doing the same task from the blanket box they used for Isaac's things. 'Well?'

Steve held up a tiny pair of dungarees with a dinosaur patch sewn on the front pocket. They evoked a flood of memories of both their boys wearing them. She'd been determined not to put Isaac in too many hand-me-downs, but they were too adorable for her to consign to the charity bag. 'Are you keeping these?'

Downsizing her own wardrobe had been a doddle compared to this. She had no emotional attachment to an array of Dorothy Perkins skirt suits in varying muted shades, and it had been quite liberating to shed the uniform she'd moulded for herself. She'd kept a couple of the newer ones for future interviews, but the two suitcases already stacked against the wall in her room were mostly casual clothes. These dungarees though, the idea of parting with this little scrap of denim was breaking her heart. They couldn't keep everything, though. 'They're too small.'

Steve tugged at a loose thread, 'And this hem is getting frayed.' He gave her a smile. 'Keepsake bag?'

'Keepsake bag,' she agreed, and they shared a laugh. It shouldn't be this easy, to parcel up six years of their lives, but apart from the odd heart pang over a few pieces of old baby clothes she'd found it remarkably straight-forward. Maybe too straight-forward. Crumpling the jumper in her hands, Jess sank down on the edge of the bed. 'Are you sure we're doing the right thing?'

Abandoning his own packing, Steve circled the bed to crouch down before her. 'Aren't you?'

She stared into a pair of blue eyes as familiar as her own and wished she felt more than deep affection. The first storm of passion they'd shared in those dark days after losing Marcus had inevitably blown itself out, leaving the aching realisation they had little in common other than the friendship they'd grown up with, and two beautiful boys who meant the world to them both. 'We're blowing up entire lives.'

Circling her ankle with a hand, Steve gave her a little squeeze. Hugging was too awkward now, but those urges to comfort each other didn't just vanish overnight. 'Because we want something better.'

'Because we deserve something better.' It was the conclusion they'd reached together in those long, painful hours when they'd been coming to terms with the truth about their feelings for each other. 'But what about what we're doing to the boys?'

Releasing her leg, Steve sat back with a sigh. 'They're young enough to adjust. We just need to give it a bit of time. Isn't this better than spending the next twenty or thirty years together when our hearts aren't truly in it and destroying each other with a million tiny acts of bitterness?'

She knew he was thinking about his own parents then. For all she wished her folks would be a bit more honest with each other, she'd never once doubted the love they had for each other unlike the icy war of words that raged constantly under the roof of Steve's childhood home. Though they seemed to have reached something of an *entente cordiale* lately, the Ripleys had rowed constantly when

38

she and Steve had been growing up. Part of the reason Steve and Marcus had become such close friends was Steve's desire to escape from the toxic atmosphere his parents had created.

After Marcus died, she'd been so desperate for something to hold onto as life imploded around her, and Steve had been there, warm and familiar, and just as in need of comfort. They thought they loved each other enough to hold on forever, but they'd been wrong. Or perhaps it was because they still loved each other just enough, that they knew it was time to let go.

Bracing his arms behind him, Steve dropped his head back to stare up at the ceiling. 'Or maybe that's the lie I'm telling myself, so I get to be selfish.'

Now it was her turn to offer comfort. She rubbed her foot against the edge of his. 'We only get one go at this, and archaeology has always been your dream, Indy.'

He laughed at the old nickname he'd given himself at ten years old after the BBC had shown the first three *Indiana Jones* movies over Christmas. Steve had been mesmerised by the wise-cracking, whip-cracking hero and his love of archaeology had been born. 'God, those films have a lot to answer for.'

'Including your love of all things beige,' she teased, poking the leg of his chinos. When Marcus had been experimenting with hair dye and piercings, Steve had stuck rigidly to khaki and beige, as though any moment he might be summoned on an adventure to the deserts of Egypt, or the jungles of South America. Jess had skipped the experimental stage all together – her brother had done more than enough rebelling for the both of them. Even after all this time, the memory of him pricked sharp like a needle. 'No more calling yourself selfish, okay? We made this decision together, in the best interests of *our* family.' They'd both hear enough of that particular accusation when her parents arrived tomorrow.

He nodded. 'United front.' He held out his fist and she bumped hers against it.

'United front.'

They returned to their chores, but the previous easiness between them was lacking as the reality of their choices pressed a little closer. This was the last night the four of them would spend beneath this roof. Her gaze strayed to the freshly painted wall beside the door where they'd drawn marks on the wall to record the boys growing. She closed her eyes. It was just a wall; the memories of those moments were what mattered, and she would carry them in her heart forever.

A couple of hours later, she sealed the final box of toys that were being donated to a local charity and lifted it on top of the half a dozen others also heading for a new home. 'Are we giving away too much?'

'Given the fact the keep pile is about three times the size of that, I'm going to say no.' Steve climbed down from the stepladder he'd been using while he cleaned the top of the wardrobe and folded the dirty cloth into a small square. 'I think that's this room about done.'

There was no helping the lump in her throat as she glanced around them. The little beds looked too bare. She'd wanted to take the bunk beds to her parents, but her mother had refused, saying there wasn't room, that the boys would be fine to top and tail in the second guestroom until Jess got herself back on her feet and had her own place again. A place close enough for Wendy to be able to keep an eye on the boys, and her too, Jess suspected.

'You look done in,' Steve said, dragging her thoughts back to the present once more. 'Why don't you go and have a bath and I'll check on the boys? There's no point in loading anything up until the morning.' Although Steve wasn't taking any more than he could fit in his car – a cheap second-hand runaround he'd purchased after returning his company car – they'd rented a small trailer and attached it to the estate car they'd invested in after Isaac's birth when the logistics of transporting all the paraphernalia of two small boys proved too much for their old hatchback.

'That sounds like a good idea, I might just do that.'

'And I'll order a takeaway.' He checked his watch. 'The Szechuan Palace is open until ten, so there's no rush.'

Jess let him usher her out of the bedroom and towards the bathroom without protest. She was pretty much at the end of a very frayed tether and could feel the tears that always gathered when she was tired, or angry, or hungry, or just about anything on the emotional scale these days. Crying was a default she'd always hated and did her best to fight, but damn it she was exhausted.

Avoiding the bathroom mirror, she began to fill the tub, adding a squeeze of Matey bubble bath because she wanted the comfort of the bubbles but everything of hers bar the absolute essentials was already packed. She was swishing her hand through the water to build them up when a soft knock came at the door. Steve was in the hallway, holding a glass of white wine so cold it was already covered in condensation. 'I decided we both deserve a drink,' he said, showing her the open bottle of beer in his other hand. 'Kids are out like a light.'

'Thanks.' She accepted the wine, feeling awkward because they were now people who knocked on bathroom doors. How many nights had they spent chatting with one or other of them perched on the toilet lid whilst the other soaked away the trials of the day? The tiny threshold strip of metal holding down the carpet separating them felt as wide as the ocean. She turned away, not wanting Steve to see her cry, knowing this was part of the mourning process and not true regret.

'Jess.'

She froze, not daring to turn around in case it allowed any regrets he might be feeling to intrude, then cursed herself for a coward. 'Yes?'

'That stupid idea of yours? I think you should do it.'

This time she did turn. 'You do?'

He shrugged. 'Why not? When else are you going to get the chance to do a job you know you'll love and live in actual castle at the same time?' His enthusiastic grin was infectious. 'Imagine the history in a place like that! And it's like you said, the boys will have all that space to run around and explore.'

'It'll be disruptive. Come the new year I'll be back where I am right now.'

'Maybe, or maybe you'll have had time to work out what it is that *you* want from life. You can say as many times as you like that we're making the decision to split together, but I'm moving on to something positive, and I just wish there was a way for you to be doing the same.'

'If I'm up in Derbyshire, it'll be harder for you to see the boys.' One of the many reasons she'd agreed to move in with her parents was to be close to where Steve was doing his course at Exeter University.

'Stop putting everyone but yourself first, Jess.' There was real exasperation in his tone. 'So what if it's inconvenient for me? So bloody what? This is a brilliant opportunity for you. All you have to do is give yourself permission to take it.' A thin, high wail came from the main bedroom, Isaac disturbed by his father's uncharacteristically loud voice. 'Damn, I'll get him.' Steve took a couple of steps away then glanced back. 'I appreciate that you wanted to consult me about this, but this is one decision you need to make for yourself.'

Chapter 4

'Sit down, Tristan,' His great-aunt Morgana peered at him from over the top of the porcelain teacup which looked as pale and delicate as the hand holding it. 'You're making the place look untidy.'

Though age had shrunken her somewhat from the formidable figure she had cut during his childhood, nothing had dimmed the strength of her character and the old admonishment was enough to still his pacing. With worry gnawing at him, he resorted to staring out of the sitting room window once more. He'd never felt a sense of responsibility towards another person before, well not more than the usual consideration for his family. From the moment Jess had called him that morning to say not only would she be taking the job, but she and the boys were loaded up and ready to hit the road immediately, he'd been weighed down with the knowledge that he'd put himself firmly in the middle of her very delicate domestic situation. The urgency of their impending arrival hadn't given him much time for introspection during the day as it'd been all hands to the pump to get suitable accommodation sorted out, but now there was nothing he could do but wait – and worry.

It wasn't just Jess he would need to look out for. As he and Arthur had cleared out old boxes and rearranged furniture whilst

Maxwell and Mrs W cleaned and Lucie had cut fresh flowers from the orangery and even managed to find a few old toys to brighten up the old nursery, it had struck Tristan that he needed to offer a place of security to two very vulnerable little boys. The doubts niggling at him now were not about his family, they'd taken the news that their new events planner came with some very special baggage with their usual open-hearted acceptance. It was himself he was bothered about. And more especially his motivation for offering Jess the job. Yes, he needed help, and yes, she was the perfect person to do it, but sitting beside her in the pub had reminded him of how much he'd missed being around her and he'd not been ready to say goodbye. Stupid, really, but as long as he kept any foolish yearnings for what might have been firmly to himself, there was no reason they couldn't work successfully side by side as they had these past few years.

His gloomy mood matched the weather beyond the glass. The heavy rain showed no signs of letting up and had now been joined by a thin mist rolling in from the dales. He could barely make out the dark shadow of the protective curtain wall which separated their land from the single road snaking up through the village. A dim light flashed giving rise to his hopes that this might be them at last, but the headlights vanished an instant later, the vehicle passing rather than turning into the heavy iron gates he'd left open. 'They should've been here by now.'

'They'll get here when they get here,' his brother's relaxed voice from somewhere behind the paper he was reading was enough to make Tristan want to punch him in the nose. 'I'm sure Jess is just being sensible and taking her time.'

Their great-aunt harrumphed. 'Phoning out of the blue to say one is setting off without so much as a day's notice to one's hosts doesn't strike me as the actions of a sensible woman.'

'It wasn't out of the blue. I offered Jess the job knowing her circumstances, and that we'd have to move quickly if she accepted it. She was willing to book herself into a hotel for a few days, but what's the point in wasting money unnecessarily?' Hearing the defensiveness in his tone, Tristan attempted to moderate it as he continued. 'I'll try to minimise any disruption, Aunt Morgana, I promise.'

She gave him a look blistering enough to peel the lacquer from the wood panelling at his back but said no more on the subject.

'I'm sure Arthur's right and there's nothing to worry about.' Lucie offered him a reassuring smile. 'Come and have a cup of tea.'

Abandoning his watch with one last glance out the window, Tristan slouched over to drop himself onto the floral sofa next to his sister-in-law. They'd complied with his request to take afternoon tea in this rarely used front parlour rather than their usual cosy family room just off the great hall so they would know the instant Jess and the children arrived. It would be churlish of him to refuse a cup of tea when he could have left them in peace and skulked around here on his own.

'Maybe the weather got too bad and she decided to stop for a while?' Lucie suggested after handing him a plate of sandwiches to go with his tea. 'I wouldn't fancy driving in this on my own, never mind with two little ones on board.'

'Yes, you're probably right.' *But wouldn't she have called?* Tristan slid his phone from his pocket to check the reception. Thankfully, the booster they'd had installed over the summer at considerable expense was holding up even in these dank conditions. It was early in the year for it to be so gloomy, but the forecasters were promising the rain was a temporary blip and high pressure would be moving in to bring one last taste of summer by the weekend.

Half a cup of tea and two sandwich fingers later, he was up by the window once more. Folding his newspaper, Arthur tossed it onto the footstool beside his armchair and rose. 'For goodness sake, if you want something to do why don't you come and take the dogs out with me?'

'You're going out in this?'

'Doggy bladders don't care what the weather's like.' Crossing to his side, Arthur clapped him on the shoulder. 'Besides, if we've worn them out they're less likely to scare our new arrivals.' The last was said to his wife with a wink.

'They can be a bit of a handful if you're not used to them,' she said with a rueful grin. 'Oh, what the heck, I'll come out with you as well.'

Their arrival in the great hall was greeted by a few enquiring woofs from the dogs who were all cosied up before the fire. As the three of them made their way towards the coat cupboard beside the front door, those woofs rose in volume and were soon joined by the skitter of claws on stone as Nimrod and Bella, their pair of matched greyhounds shortly followed by Tristan's wheaten terrier, Pippin, came over to see what was going on. When Arthur appeared from the cupboard clad in a Barbour jacket and flat cap, the excitement level in the hall reached fever pitch and Tristan found himself almost toppled over by the milling pack as he raised one foot to wedge it into his wellington boot. Once dressed similarly to his brother, he pulled open one side of the enormous wooden front door and stepped aside expecting a stream of fur to rush past him. Nimrod stuck his nose outside, gave a sniff and promptly sat down on the stone floor. Tristan couldn't say he blamed the dog, to be honest.

Arthur was having none of it, however, and he marched out the door and down the steps, pausing at the bottom only long enough to toss a couple of tennis balls out across the wide gravel drive. The temptation proved too much and Nimrod shot up and out after the balls, the rest of the dogs following closely on his heels.

Once he was out in it, Tristan decided it wasn't that bad. The earlier wind had dropped, and if he kept his face ducked down, his cap kept the worst of the rain off. Though the rest of the dogs followed his brother and Lucie as they made towards the path leading through the formal gardens and to the broader open spaces of the parkland beyond, little Pippin kept close to Tristan's heels, only circling off now and then when one delicious scent or another proved too tempting to ignore.

Happy to let them range ahead, Tristan found himself breaking away from the path and headed towards the open gates at the end of the drive. As he reached them, he ordered Pippin to wait before poking his head past the heavy stone pillar securing the left-hand gate to stare down the hill. Other than a few static lights shining from the houses and cottages lining the lower half of the hill, all was quiet. The oppressive rain laid a strange stillness over everything like a thick wet blanket. 'What are you doing?' he muttered to himself. 'It's not like staring down the road is going to make them arrive any quicker.' It still took him a few more moments before he could persuade his feet to move.

Not ready to return to the house, Tristan wandered away from the gates towards his latest obsession. Tugging a torch from his pocket, he shone a thin beam of light through the dirt-encrusted window of the old gatehouse. The saggy old sofa he, Arthur and Iggy had persuaded their father to put in the sitting room when they'd claimed it as their private den still stood before the fireplace. It looked more black than the pale green velvet he remembered, possibly a trick of the light, but more likely from mildew. He pulled a face, wondering just what else might be lurking in the depths of its cushions after so many years of neglect. They'd outgrown it after going off to university, and he doubted very much anyone had been inside in the dozen or so years since.

Ever since Uncle Lancelot had taken it upon himself to convert the rooms above the stable blocks from which he ran his successful horse stud, Tristan had been pondering the idea of carving a private space for himself on the castle grounds. It wasn't that the castle didn't have more than enough bedrooms to accommodate them all several times over, but now the long-term future for the castle looked healthy, it was time to start making plans of his own.

A home of his own. He'd have to speak to Maxwell, the family's butler, to see if he knew where the keys were and check the place out before he got too far ahead of himself.

Ignoring the little voice in his head that whispered perhaps now wasn't the best time to take on yet another project when he had so much already on his plate, he circled around to the other side of the gatehouse, shining his torch through each window in turn. The kitchen was small, but how much space did he need? Though Lancelot and Constance lived above the stables, they still joined the rest of the family for most evening meals. The old wood-fed stove was a bit too primitive for Tristan but could easily be replaced with a microwave and an electric hob. He flashed the torch around the rest of the room. The tile floor looked pretty sound and the wooden cupboards were mostly intact apart from one door hanging loose off its hinges.

His progression round to the two rooms which had once served as bedrooms was halted by a sudden splash of light behind him. A car with a mobile trailer box attached had pulled into the drive and come to a standstill. *At last.* Abandoning his plans for the gatehouse for the moment, Tristan hurried across the grass. When he got close he could make out the silhouette of a woman, hands gripping the steering wheel as she stared straight ahead through the windscreen. She seemed lost in a world of her own and gave no sign she was aware of his approach.

Using the butt of the torch he tapped lightly on the glass. With a muffled scream she twisted her head to stare up at him through her window before quickly glancing behind her towards the back seat. Following her gaze, he saw two little figures strapped into car seats, their heads lolling in sleep. The window slid down, and she hissed at him. 'You scared me half to death! What are you doing lurking out here in the bloody dark?'

Adopting the same hushed tones, Tristan bent down. 'I was out taking my dog for a walk and wondering where on earth you'd got to. Is everything all right? Why did you stop here?'

She waved a hand towards the castle. 'Look at it, for goodness sake.'

His eyes followed the direction of her hand. The rain had thinned to a drizzle, casting the illuminated front of the castle in a misty curtain. Looming out of the darkness, he supposed it cut an imposing sight, but for him it was simply his home. 'What am I looking at?'

Her incredulous stare narrowed as she realised he was teasing her. 'Not funny.'

'Well, a bit funny,' he argued, giving her a grin. 'Come on, you must be knackered, let's get you inside in the warm.'

She eyed him for a long moment before nodding. 'It was a tough drive.' As though admitting it brought the reality of what she'd been through rushing forward, her shoulders slumped, and he could make out the lines of strain bracketing her eyes.

'The rain's almost stopped. If you want to leave the car here and walk the rest of the way . . .?' He or Arthur could come back and fetch it in a bit once Jess and the boys were sorted.

'It's so silly, it's only a hundred yards.' When she made no move, Tristan leaned in and turned the engine off before tugging open her door. 'Come on, the fresh air will do you good.'

'Yes, you're probably right.' She still seemed a bit dazed when she climbed out, so Tristan put his arm out to steady her. When she looked a bit more with it, he quickly unzipped his jacket and slung it around her shoulders.

'Mine's in the boot somewhere,' she protested, vaguely.

'And you can get it later.' Tristan moved towards the passenger door and popped it open quietly. 'This is Elijah?' he asked Jess over his shoulder as he crouched down beside the sleeping boy.

'Yes.' Shrugging into his coat, she leaned across Tristan to shake Elijah's shoulder. 'Hey Eli, wake up, sweetheart, we're here.'

A pair of thick sooty lashes blinked open to reveal a set of deep-set green eyes inherited from his mother. 'Mummy?'

She tugged the complicated mechanism strapping him in then

straightened up. 'This is Tristan. Remember I told you about him? He's going to help you out while I get your brother.'

Those big olive-green eyes blinked owlishly as they watched Jess disappear around the back of the car before turning to gaze at Tristan. 'Hello, Elijah.'

''lo.' The little boy made no move to get out, his expression a combination of suspicion and weary confusion.

Glancing behind him, Tristan clicked his fingers towards where Pippin was busy sniffing at the tyres of the trailer behind them. 'Come here, Pippin. I've got a new friend for you to meet.' The little terrier bounced over, his stub of a tail wagging a mile a minute as he put his front paws up on the side of the car and gave Elijah an inquisitive sniff. 'This is Pippin,' Tristan said. 'We've got lots of lovely dogs here at the castle, but he's my special friend. He can be your friend too, if you'd like?'

Still looking uncertain, Elijah held out a tentative hand towards the terrier, giving a little giggle when Pippin licked the tips of his fingers. 'It tickles.'

'Down now, Pip,' Tristan tap his thigh and the obedient dog came to sit at his heel. Turning back to Elijah, Tristan held out his hand. 'Ready now?' The boy nodded and wiggled down from the car. When he left his hand resting in Tristan's he kept hold of it as he rose, making sure to keep his grip loose so Elijah could slip free at any time.

'Well now, who's this?' Jess asked as she returned with a very sleepy Isaac in her arms and Pippin came to sniff at her feet.

'Pip!' Elijah said, then glanced up at Tristan as though checking he'd got that right.

Smiling, Tristan nodded. 'His name is Pippin, but he likes to be called Pip by his friends.' Pippin wagged his tail in agreement.

'Making friends, already? Aren't you a lucky boy, Eli? Now where's your coat?' Jess bent forward, still clutching Isaac to her hip.

Over her shoulder, Tristan surveyed the jumble of toys, pillows, colourful plastic lidded cups and other detritus spilling across the back seat and into the footwells beneath. 'Do you want me to look?'

Jess straightened. 'Thanks. It's a navy puffa-type thing.' At that moment, Isaac straightened in her arms and pulled the kind of face that portended nothing but trouble. As the first wail escaped his lips, Jess jiggled him. 'Shh, it's all right, bubba. We're here now.' Paying no heed to her assurances, the toddler continued to cry.

'Take him in,' Tristan nodded down the drive. 'I'll find Elijah's jacket and we'll be right behind you.'

'Okay, sorry.' Jess gave him an apologetic smile before heading towards the castle, crooning nonsense words to Isaac as she tried to console him.

Crouching once more, Tristan began to turn over everything in the back of the car, but the jacket remained stubbornly elusive. Giving Elijah a quick glance, he asked 'Any idea where your coat is hiding?' Elijah shook his head, his expression falling.

Fearing more tears, Tristan decided to abandon the hunt. The rain was nothing more than the odd spot now, and the boy's sweatshirt looked warm enough for the couple of minutes it would take them to get inside. 'Brave men like us don't need coats, right?'

Clearly liking the sound of being a brave man, Elijah nodded. 'Right!'

After closing the car door, Tristan held out a hand. 'Come on then, let's get inside. Betsy's been working hard all afternoon to make you a very special welcome tea.'

Elijah linked fingers with him, eyes bright with curiosity. 'Who's Betsy?'

'She's our cook,' Tristan said, starting towards the castle. He kept his stride short to make sure the boy could easily keep pace with him. 'Our house is very big, so we need lots of people to help take care of it, and us.' It suddenly occurred to him how overwhelming all this must be and paused to crouch so he was at eye-level with Elijah. 'I'm sure this is all a bit scary for you, but I promise that everyone here at Bluebell Castle is very excited about you and Isaac and Mummy coming to stay with us. If anything upsets or bothers you, tell your mummy straightaway and we will sort it out.' He squeezed Elijah's hand very gently. 'And you can always come and talk to me, okay?'

Elijah gave him a hesitant nod. 'Okay.'

Pippin squeezed in between the two of them, not wanting to miss out on whatever was going on. Tristan scratched behind his ears. 'And Pippin is a very good listener, too. I've told him my troubles lots of times, haven't I, boy?' The dog gave a little bark as though agreeing with him. Meeting Elijah's gaze, Tristan asked. 'Have you ever had a dog?' When Elijah shook his head, Tristan took a moment to show him how to stroke him.

Ahead of them, Isaac's wails had lessened into the odd sniffle. 'Poor Isaac sounds very tired. Let's get him inside and into bed.' Tristan stood and this time Elijah took his hand without him offering it. Feeling like he'd made more progress than he could've hoped for to win the boy's trust, Tristan stretched his legs a little faster so they could catch up with Jess who'd paused at the foot of the steps leading up to the imposing front door.

They made it up the first couple of steps when the clatter of claws on gravel heralded the return of Arthur, Lucie and the rest of the dogs. Acting on instinct, Tristan swept Elijah up onto his hip. 'Brace yourself,' he managed to warn Jess before they were surrounded by a wagging, panting sea of fur.

'You weren't kidding when you said you had a lot of dogs!' Jess didn't sound in the least bit perturbed, thank goodness, and her laughter pealed out as she nudged Murphy, their rambunctious Jack Russell with a gentle foot. 'Yes, yes, I'm very happy to meet you too,' she crooned to the dog as he scrabbled at the leg of her jeans.

'Get off the lady, you flea-bitten mutt.' Arthur scooped the terrier up and held the wriggling bundle of tan and white firmly under his arm as he smiled up at Jess from the step below. 'Hello!

Glad to see you managed to find us in the end. What a filthy day for travelling, you must be exhausted.' He turned all that easy charm to the little boy in her arms. 'And you must be Isaac, hello!' He touched a finger to the toddler's chin.

Any outrage Isaac might have been considering at all the noise around him was negated by the arrival of Lucie. 'Oh, aren't you the most gorgeous thing?' She held out her arms to the bemused toddler who much to Tristan's surprise leaned away from his mother's hold and went straight to Lucie without so much as a peep. 'Hello, Jess,' she continued, brushing a quick kiss on Jess's cheek. 'We're delighted to have you all here. Come in, come in,' she ushered them all up the steps to where Arthur had managed to wedge open one half of the door and still keep his grip on Murphy.

'Is it always like this?' Jess murmured as she walked beside him up the steps.

'Noisy? Chaotic? Slightly bonkers? Oh, absolutely.' Tristan caught Jess's startled expression and gave her a grin. 'Welcome to Bluebell Castle.'

Chapter 5

It was impossible not to feel cheered by the charm offensive laid on by the Ludworths. They seemed genuinely delighted to welcome her and the boys to their home, even at the horrendously short notice she'd given. It hadn't been her intention to foist herself on them so quickly, but the row she'd had with her mother over the late change of plans had been so awful as to have made it impossible for her to go and stay there even for a couple of nights whilst she tried to put some plans in place. Steve had already delayed travelling to university until the very last minute, and though he'd offered to further delay heading off she hated the idea of him missing the start of his course.

When she'd spoken to Tristan that morning, she'd tried to sound casual as she'd asked him about local accommodation she could rent until they'd had time to properly agree terms, but he'd told her not to be so silly, that there was more than enough space at the castle to accommodate her and the boys several times over and just to get in the car and drive. Already beyond the point of feeling capable of making alternative arrangements, she'd done as he'd said. The storm had hit not long after they'd reached the M1, turning a four-hour journey into over seven as they crawled along in the inside lane – the combination of the awful weather and her unfamiliarity with towing the trailer making her too anxious to attempt to overtake.

Isaac burst into another flurry of tears, but before she could attempt to retrieve him from Lucie, he was swept up by Tristan's uncle – the outrageously named Lancelot – and the pair disappeared from the room without so much as a glance in her direction. Before she could worry about where they'd gone to, or the disruption she was bringing to what seemed like a thoroughly nice group of people Lancelot returned with a content-looking Isaac guzzling a bottle of warm milk in his arms. Having successfully dealt with one boy, he then settled down on one of a pair of leather sofas next to where Tristan sat cross-legged on the floor with Elijah and joined in their conversation about all the different dogs and what their names were.

She'd been worried about how Elijah might cope having not been raised with any pets besides a short-lived hamster whose loss had caused such devastation both she and Steve had sworn off any future pets. As she watched Tristan's scruffy little terrier settle himself between Elijah's legs, his head propped on her son's thigh in a distinctly claiming gesture, she realised there was nothing to worry about.

There was no more time to contemplate the wisdom – or otherwise – of their unexpected arrival because Jess found herself taken in hand by Lucie and her mother, who she introduced as Constance. 'Mum lives with Lancelot above the stables,' Lucie offered without preamble as she urged Jess to take a seat on the opposite sofa.

Constance laughed as she sat on her opposite side. 'I only came for a quick visit, but that rogue swept me quite off my feet.' Leaning in, she whispered conspiratorially. 'You have to watch these Ludworth men, they can charm the birds from the trees.' Her face fell almost instantly. 'Oh, but that was crass of me! Tristan told us a little of your circumstances, I shouldn't have been so thoughtless.'

Not sure she was too keen on being the subject of family gossip, but relieved nonetheless that there would be no awkward questions about where the boys' father was, Jess found a tired smile for the woman. 'No harm done. It's been over for a while; it's just taken some time to untangle ourselves domestically.' Not wanting to say any more than that, she turned the conversation back towards Constance. 'So, tell me more about how you and Lucie came to be part of the family.'

As she listened to a story involving an old family diary and a hidden masterpiece, Jess forgot about being tired, or about the million and one things she would have to tackle in the morning and just let the warmth of the room, and the people within it, soak into her bones. It sounded like the Ludworths had a knack of absorbing people into their family. She could see already how easy it would be to get swept along with them and knew she would have to remind herself she was only there on a temporary basis.

'Gosh!' Constance exclaimed a few minutes later. 'Listen to me rattling on and we haven't even offered you so much as drink. What can we get you?'

'Oh, Mum, you're right, where are our manners? Poor Jess, you must be parched.' Lucie said. Her expression all contrition, she stood. 'A cup of tea, perhaps?'

'Pfshh.' The indelicate noise came from the very proper-looking older lady sitting upright in the armchair closest to the fire. 'It's past teatime and I for one am ready for something stronger.' Turning a gimlet gaze to Jess she gave her a thoroughly appraising look which left Jess with the impression this jury of one would be out for a while before passing verdict on her. 'You'll forgive me for saying so, child, but you look in urgent need of something to revive your spirits. I normally take a sweet sherry at this hour, but that's likely not to your taste.'

Definitely not to her taste. 'I wouldn't say no to a glass of white wine,' she ventured.

'Ah, drinks, my specialist subject.' Arthur stood with a laugh and made his way over to a large drinks cabinet, pulling open the bottom doors to reveal a well-stocked fridge.

He was halfway through serving everyone when a very dapper older man dressed in charcoal grey pinstriped trousers with a matching waistcoat over a crisp white shirt swept in through a discreet swing door. Stopping dead with a frown, the man surveyed the room with clear disapproval. 'Really, Sir Arthur, you had only to ring if you required a drink,' he admonished, sweeping the open bottle of wine from Arthur's grasp.

'Sorry, Maxwell.' Arthur's breezy tone said quite clearly he was anything but, though he conceded his spot by the drinks cabinet without protest and resumed his seat.

The man poured a glass of white wine then approached Jess. 'Miss Jessica, you must forgive me for not being there to greet your arrival. My name is Maxwell and I am entirely at your disposal. Should you require anything at all, either myself or Mrs Walters, the housekeeper, will be only too happy to assist. On consultation with Sir Arthur, we've arranged for you and the children to be accommodated in the nursery rooms on the upper level. Once you've had time to refresh yourself, perhaps I can escort you upstairs to ensure you have everything you need.'

Trying to absorb the torrent of helpful information, Jess accepted the glass. 'Umm, that's very kind, thank you.' Apparently that was sufficient for he gave her a brief nod then left her to serve the others. The ice cold wine hit exactly the right spot. Jess closed her eyes for a moment, savouring the taste on the back of her tongue.

'All right?' She flashed open her lashes to find Tristan standing over her, that funny, familiar smile on his lips.

'I think so.' She glanced past him, 'How are the boys?' Isaac had stopped crying, but she was conscious of how long a day it had been for them and it would be prudent to get them fed and tucked in before the novelty of all these new people wore off.

Tristan shrugged, unconcerned. 'Oh, they're fine. Lancelot had years of practice juggling the three of us, so two is a doddle.' He held out his hand. 'If you give me your keys, I'll bring the car up.'

'I can do it.' She would've stood, but he made no move to give her space to do so.

'No, you won't. You'll sit there and enjoy your wine. Give me your keys and tell me what you need tonight. We can sort the rest out in the morning.'

The command in his voice was something new, and she wasn't sure if she liked it or not, but she was too bloody tired to argue. Raising one hip, she fished her keys out from the pocket of her jeans. 'There's a small black case in the boot, that's got our overnight stuff in it. Maxwell said something about us sleeping in the nursery?'

Tristan nodded. 'In keeping with old-fashioned tradition there's a section of the second floor which was set aside as the nursery. We thought you might appreciate a space to call your own as this is going to be home for the three of you for the next few months. It's an ideal set-up with a playroom for the boys, and a sitting room which was originally designed for when the family had a nanny. There's also a little kitchen if you'd rather make use of it although the three of you are more than welcome to dine with us, of course.'

It sounded ideal, though she wondered if beneath the altruism there was a bit of ruthless practicality. From what she could work out, there hadn't been any children in the castle since Tristan and his brother and sister and she couldn't blame a household full of adults for wanting to tuck her and the boys out of the way. 'Did you use it when you were little?'

Tristan shook his head. 'Dad didn't have any truck with using a nanny, even after our mother left him on his own with three small toddlers. He, Lancelot and Morgana looked after us and we attended the village school until we went onto boarding school at eleven. The furniture is a bit dated – but then you could say that about every room in the castle – but Mrs W and Maxwell gave the whole place a thorough clean. It needs a lick of paint and a few things modernising but if you're happy with it then we can sort those out next week.'

Wow, they'd really gone to a lot of effort considering it was less than nine hours since she'd accepted Tristan's off the cuff job offer. 'You've gone to a lot of trouble . . .'

He shrugged it off. 'No trouble. Now drink your wine while I go and move the car.'

'If I'd known you had this bossy side to you, I might have thought twice about taking this job.' She said it with a smile, but just a hint of warning. If he was going to be like this all time, they'd end up clashing.

Tristan held up his hands, rattling her car keys in the process. 'Sorry. The weather stressed me out thinking about you on the roads today. I promise when it comes to work, that once we've agreed the project parameters and boring stuff like the budget with Arthur and the rest of the family, you will have complete autonomy.'

Well, that was a lot more than she'd expected. 'Seriously?'

He nodded. 'It makes sense to divide the workload and if I'm peering over your shoulder every five minutes, it'll drive us both mad. I'm going to have my hands full sorting out all the exterior preparations now I've got a plan agreed with Iggy and Will. I was thinking I'd also manage the online stuff, taking bookings and doing comms with the guests, but the accommodation and entertainment schedule will be down to you.' He frowned. 'Damn, I wasn't going to bother you with any of this stuff tonight, we'll go through it all week after next once you're settled in. Drink your wine!' The last was thrown over his shoulder, together with a cheeky grin as he headed for the door.

Ten minutes later, with Isaac clinging to her neck like a little monkey, Jess found herself climbing up a third – and she hoped, final – flight of stairs. Tristan was ahead of her, helping Elijah who'd wanted to make it on his own, with Maxwell who'd insisted on carrying her case and a kind-faced woman dressed in a neat tweed skirt and stylish, but still sensible shoes bringing up the rear. There was not a wrinkle in her blouse, nor a hair out of place in Mrs W's tidy chignon. She also appeared to have no trouble with the stairs, unlike Jess who was trying not to pant like one of the trains in Isaac's favourite *Thomas the Tank Engine* cartoons. If she achieved nothing else between now and Christmas, climbing these stairs several times a day might shift the last of the baby weight she'd put on carrying Isaac.

Tristan let them in through a white door, the finish on it and the frame dulled to a creamy-yellow which spoke to the age of the paint job. He flipped on the lights to reveal a large rectangular room, the back wall of which was filled with huge lead-lined bare windows. The rain was back with a vengeance, rattling against the glass like bullets and filling the room with noise.

'I sorted out drapes for the bedrooms but didn't have time to find suitable ones for in here,' Mrs W, said, voice apologetic.

'There's no need to apologise,' Jess assured her as she took in the room. 'It's obvious how much effort you've all gone to today.' The smell of beeswax and lemon as much as the shine on the low table and chairs set to one side spoke of hard work. A glow from the overhead lamps bounced back from the sparkling windows, and there was not a speck of dust on the long rail of skirting boards. An open wooden box displayed a collection of wooden building blocks, balls of varying sizes and an antique-looking rocking horse with a white mane spilling over its dappled-grey neck sat in the opposite corner. A thick, fluffy rug had been set down in the centre of the floor an inviting spot for the boys to play, or somewhere the three of them could curl up and read stories together.

The housekeeper gave her a pleased smile as she walked towards a door on the right. 'This is your bedroom.' She pushed open the door to reveal a charming room with a wrought-iron framed bed and a beautiful set of matched furniture. The bed had been made up with pretty pastel-pink sheets and pillows and topped with a quilt smothered in huge cabbage roses. Matching floral curtains covered the windows, and she could see another soft rug had been placed by the side of the bed.

'It's beautiful,' she said, a little overwhelmed.

'Booful,' Isaac agreed, earning a laugh and a chuck under his chin from Mrs W.

'There's a small bathroom off here.' The housekeeper pushed open a door. 'And you've a sitting room here.' She revealed another space, empty this time except for a fireplace. 'We've loads of furniture in storage in the attics, so I thought you might like to choose what you wanted in here for yourself. There's a kitchen, too,' she indicated a door in the opposite wall. 'Though I wouldn't recommend you use anything in there beyond the kettle until we've had a chance to get everything checked over.'

'That's on my list of things to do, tomorrow,' Maxwell interjected. 'I've got the plumber and an electrician coming to give everything a thorough service, but the hot water is working.' He set down her suitcase on the blanket box at the end of the bed. 'Will you be joining the family for dinner this evening, or would you like me to arrange for something to be brought up here?'

The idea of this very kind man lugging a meal for three up all those stairs filled Jess with horror. 'I don't want to put you to any trouble, we can come down.' She glanced at her watch, surprised to find she'd lost an hour somewhere. Oh well, she would worry about proper bedtimes tomorrow.

'As you prefer, Miss Jessica, though it won't be any trouble. I'll be serving dinner at half past the hour. There's soup to start, followed by roast chicken. If you, or the boys have any dietary requirements, I'll be happy to pass them on to Betsy.'

Jess shook her head. 'Nothing specific.' She hesitated, embarrassed about a habit Elijah had recently picked up after having tea at a friend's house, but not wanting to fight that particular

61

battle with him on their first night here. 'Umm, do you happen to have any tomato ketchup?'

'I'll make sure there's a bottle available, Miss.' Maxwell inclined his head as though she'd asked for caviar rather than table sauce. 'Now, if you'll excuse me, I shall go and check on preparations and leave you in the capable hands of Mrs Walters.' With another brief nod, the butler departed.

'You'll get used to his ways,' Mrs W said, after he'd left.

'He's fantastic.' Jess shifted Isaac to her other hip then reached out to touch the housekeeper lightly on the arm. 'I think you're all fantastic, thank you for everything.'

'Oh, it's nothing.' The rosy glow on the housekeeper's cheek said she appreciated the gesture. 'Now, do you want to give the boys a quick bath before dinner? Then they'd be ready straight for bed after.'

It was a great idea, except for one thing. 'I'm not sure about the protocol of appearing at the dining room table with them in their pyjamas.'

'We don't stand on ceremony here. Not for these guys, anyway.' Tristan stood in the doorway, Elijah leaning against his leg in such a trusting way it brought a lump to her throat to see it. 'I've shown Elijah his bedroom and he approves, don't you?' He ruffled Elijah's hair, causing the boy to stare up at him.

'Yes.' It was said with a very emphatic nod. 'It's blue.'

'If only everyone was so easily pleased,' Tristan said with a grin. 'Right, I too shall leave you all in Mrs W's care, unless there's anything else you need?'

'I think we've got everything we need. Thank you again.'

Tristan departed with a wave, and Jess did as both he and Maxwell had recommended and put herself and the boys in the kind, capable care of Mrs W. She showed them into the boys' bedroom which Elijah had already inspected and approved. As well as a matching set of beds set on either side of the room, there was a large high-sided cot sitting against the back wall.

'We weren't sure whether the little one was in his own bed yet,' Mrs W said.

'He's been sleeping in the bottom half of bunk beds for the past few months. It had a low rail along it, which seemed to help with the transition. I'll see how he settles over the next few nights, but the cot is a great back up to have, thank you for thinking of it.'

'Every baby is different.' Mrs W smoothed a hand over the already neat quilt covering one of the beds. 'Even the triplets. Iggy couldn't wait to be in her own bed, but Arthur and Tristan clung to the cot even when the pair of them were almost too big to fit in it together. Silly pair would wake up in a right tangle of arms and legs, but it never bothered them. We had to push two beds together before we could persuade them to try them.'

'You've been with the family a long time.'

Mrs W smiled. 'Yes. I started out as a maid back when their grandfather was still alive, and the castle was a lot busier. I must say, I'm quite excited by Tristan's plans for a Christmas house party. I used to love running between the guests back in the day, helping one with her hair, another with her dress. The castle seemed full of life back then.'

'You won't mind the extra work, then?' It was one of the things she'd been wondering, how the staff were going to take to the idea.

'No, not at all, and we won't struggle to find the extra help we need. We already have a team of people from the village who come up every year to assist with the spring clean. I've already put a few of them on alert and they're delighted at the prospect of a few extra pennies in their purses at Christmas. Once you've worked out the guest programme, perhaps you and I can sit down with Maxwell and work out a staffing rota to support it.'

Well that was one less thing to worry about. 'That would be wonderful. I have a feeling I'm going to be leaning on you quite a bit in the coming weeks as I get up to speed with the place.'

Mrs W beamed. 'Lean away, Mrs Riley, I'll be only too happy to help.'

'Oh, please, you must call me Jess.'

'Jess, it is then. Now shall we get these two bathed and changed?'

Though she could've managed it herself, it was a lot easier to wrangle the boys with an extra pair of hands, especially when Elijah, naked as a jaybird, decided it was time for an impromptu game of hide and seek. Leaving Isaac happily splashing and chatting nonsense to Mrs W, Jess went to hunt down her little escapee. Spotting a suspiciously little boy shaped lump behind the floor-length curtains in her room, Jess made a big deal of searching everywhere else in the room. She pulled open the wardrobe, looked under the bed, inside the blanket box and even underneath the stack of pillows on her bed, all the while pretending she couldn't hear Elijah giggling. Tired as she was, it did her heart good to hear him having fun. When she finally yanked back the curtains to pounce on him, he was almost breathless with laughter.

As she carried him back to the bathroom, she nuzzled him, relishing the sweet familiar weight of him in her arms. He was already heavier than he'd been at the start of the summer, and she'd soon struggle to carry him like this. He was growing up, her sweet little baby. It was enough to make her want to cry.

A little hand patted her cheek. 'Don't be sad, Mummy.'

Glancing down into a pair of worried green eyes, she smiled. So sensitive, she'd have to take extra care not to let things get on top of him over the next few months. 'I'm not sad, darling, I was just thinking about what a big boy you're getting.'

'I'm a brave man,' he told her in a solemn voice. 'Tristan said so.'

'Did he? Well, he's right. You are very brave, and very good, and Isaac is lucky to have such a special big brother. Will you help him feel at home here?'

'Yes.' He paused then, his nose scrunched up in what Steve always called his thinking expression. Oh, hell. She'd forgotten to text him to say they'd got there okay. And her parents, too.

'Come on, brave man, let's get you in that bath.'

She hurried across the playroom towards the bathroom, pausing on the threshold when Elijah said 'Mummy.'

Crouching to set him down, she remained at his level. 'Yes, darling?'

'If I do a bad thing, will you still love me?'

Shocked and stunned that such a thought would even enter his head, Jess gathered him into her lap. 'I'm always going to love you, no matter what. And Isaac too. *Always*.'

'But you don't love Daddy anymore. Did he do a bad thing?' His words came out on a shaky little breath.

Oh hell, and she and Steve thought they'd handled everything with the boys so well. 'Daddy didn't do anything wrong, not one thing, and neither did I. We're still friends, we just don't want to be together in the way mummies and daddies are.' She hugged him close. 'Shall I send him a text and see if you can have a chat later when I put Isaac to bed?'

'Yes, please.'

'All right, then.' She kissed his cheek, then gave him a sniff. 'Cor, I know a smelly boy that needs a bath.' She tickled him as she said it, earning a squirming giggle.

Hoisting him onto her hip, she carried him into the bathroom where he proudly informed Mrs W that he was indeed a smelly boy.

'Well, get yourself in here and get clean, young man!' responded the housekeeper, swirling a hand in the bubbly water. 'Your brother was a bit smelly too, but now he's all clean.'

'Smell!' Isaac declared, proudly, holding his hands up towards Jess.

'Oh dear, what have I started?' Jess tugged down a towel from the rail then bent over the bath to gather Isaac up into it. 'I hope you are going to behave yourself when we go back downstairs.'

'Smell!' he said again.

'Smell!' yelled Elijah from the bath before collapsing into giggles. Oh, dear God, perhaps she should've accepted Maxwell's offer to bring their meal upstairs after all.

Chapter 6

As he'd predicted, the rest of the family had no issue when Jess reappeared in the family room with Isaac dressed in a onesie emblazoned with a picture of Thomas the Tank Engine on the chest, and Elijah in a pair of pyjamas covered in smiling cartoon dinosaurs. Lancelot rose to greet Isaac, and the toddler was soon ensconced on his lap, the pair of them having already formed a mutual appreciation society. So many memories came to Tristan's mind of similar evenings he'd spent as a child safe and content in his uncle's arms. He'd adored their kind, loving father to bits, but Lancelot had always been his hero.

Feeling a bit choked, he turned away from the scene to see Jess frowning over her phone. Edging around the room until he reached her side, he nudged her arm. 'Problem?'

'What? Oh, no, just my mother being her usual self.' She pulled a face. 'In all the fuss of our arrival, I forgot to message them to say we'd got here. I was already in the doghouse, but now I'm in Battersea and up for adoption.' She tilted the screen towards him to show him a message.

Your father's pleased to know you're not all dead in a ditch at least.

'Yikes.' He could sense the frostiness and he'd never met the woman. While he could understand her being worried – God knows he'd been close to panicking when they hadn't arrived on time – given everything Jess was going through, he might have expected a bit more sympathy from the woman. Then again when it came to mothers and their antics, his could probably top anything Jess's tried.

'Indeed,' she agreed in a wry voice. 'Oh well, she'll get over it in another twenty or so years.' She took the phone back. 'Hey, would it be okay to get the code for your Wi-Fi? I've promised Eli he can Skype his dad before bedtime.'

At least that sounded like Steve wasn't giving her a hard time. 'Sure. The router's in Arthur's study and the code's written underneath it. Give me two secs.'

'I didn't mean you had to do it now,' she protested.

'It's no problem.'

He found a scrap of paper in the top of Arthur's desk and scribbled down the code. They had a public Wi-Fi system set up for visitors, but it was an open network and Jess would want the security of the secured family system – even if there weren't currently any visitors to connect to the other one. Returning to her side, he handed her the paper, much to the curiosity of Elijah.

'What's that?' he asked, in that direct way all small children seemed to have.

'It's for the Wi-Fi, so you can talk to your dad later. You'll have lots and lots to tell him about your day, won't you?'

Elijah nodded. 'He's an arkologist. He likes old things.'

'I see.' The last he'd heard, Jess's ex had been doing something in the city.

'He's not an archaeologist yet,' Jess enunciated the word carefully to her son. 'That's why he's gone back to school.' She turned to Tristan. 'He drove down last night, and registration started today.'

'A lot of change for all of you.' He wasn't sure what else to say. Clearly whatever had happened between the two of them,

67

they were still on speaking terms. Part of him wanted to push for information, but again he questioned the motivation behind that. It shouldn't make any difference to him what was behind their split, nor how long it had been in the pipeline. Jess was a friend who needed a break to get her life back on track. He was not going to do anything to try and influence the direction she chose, no matter how much he might want to.

'It sure is.' Jess lifted Elijah onto her lap for a cuddle. 'Your daddy isn't the only one starting school. The first job on my list tomorrow is to go into the village and see what we can do about getting you registered. Won't that be exciting?'

Elijah nodded, but Tristan could tell he wasn't too sure about it. Sitting on the arm of the chair, he slung one arm along the back to support himself as he leaned back far enough to catch Elijah's eye. 'We went to the village school when we were your age. Mrs Winters was our teacher. She's the Head now, so she looks after everyone at the school.'

'Is she nice?'

Tristan smiled. 'Yes. She's very nice. You'll get to do lots of fun things there, and you'll also be able to spend some time with your class up here at the castle. We're just starting a new gardening project with the school, so you'll learn all about how to plant things and where your food comes from.'

'That sounds like fun, doesn't it?' Jess prompted. She glanced up at Tristan. 'It's a new project?'

He nodded. 'Iggy and Will came up with the idea. They created an interactive area of the grounds for children who come to visit and then it grew from there. We've set aside a plot of land for the school to use as a green space. As well as room to plant a vegetable plot, there's enough room for them to do sports activities. There's only a concrete playground area on the grounds of the school itself.'

'It sounds great, and some positive PR for you when you're promoting the castle.'

'I hadn't really thought about it, I don't want it to seem like I'm exploiting them.'

Jess shrugged. 'Well, you'd have to get permission from the parents for any photos you take and publish, but if they're all in agreement then it'd make a nice feature for your blog and you can tie it in with the fact there's a general children's area in the gardens as well. Healthy eating and dietary awareness is all the rage.'

'I'll talk to Mrs Winters about it. Do you want me to come down with you tomorrow? I can do the introductions and then take the boys exploring while you talk to her.'

Before she could answer, Maxwell entered the room to announce dinner and there was the usual hubbub as everyone made their way across the great hall and down the corridor to the dining room. Leaving Jess in Lucie and Arthur's care, Tristan went to offer his arm to Morgana. Trim and fit, she didn't need any assistance, but one of the base standards in the Ludworth household was a lady did not walk unescorted into the evening meal.

'Well, my boy, you've certainly livened things up around here.'

Though her tone was dry, he could see a spark of mischief in his aunt's eye. 'You know me, I like to shake things up now and again.'

'Hmm.'

They entered the dining room to find Maxwell had magicked up a highchair for Isaac from somewhere. Really, there was no end to the man's resourcefulness. As he watched Jess swing the toddler into the chair and strap him into the harness without any sign of hesitation, he realised it must be one she'd brought with her. Pulling out a seat for his aunt in her usual spot at Arthur's right hand he bent forward to whisper in her ear as she settled into it. 'Just you wait and see what she can do. Even you'll be impressed once Jess finds her feet and gets to work.'

'*Even* me?'

Tristan brushed a quick kiss on her cheek, 'Even you.'

Dinner was a noisy, happy affair, and Tristan was impressed once again with how well the two little boys seemed to be adapting to this new, strange environment. The roast chicken went down a storm, especially with Isaac who kept offering his open mouth to Jess like a baby bird every time she wasn't quick with the next forkful of mashed up meat, vegetables and gravy. Elijah managed very well, with a little bit of assistance from Constance cutting things up for him, and a large dollop of ketchup to dip his meat into.

By the time Maxwell returned to clear the table and see if anyone required dessert, Isaac was all but asleep, his head doing that nodding and jerking thing as he kept dropping off and waking himself up again. 'I think that's my cue.' Jess unstrapped the toddler and lifted him out of the chair. 'Come on Eli, bed for you too.'

'But I'm not tired,' Elijah protested moments before he yawned so wide he set the adults laughing.

Faking a yawn, Tristan stretched then stood. 'I don't know about the rest of you, but I'm almost ready for bed.' The murmurs of assent might not have fooled an older child, but it was enough to get Elijah moving once he believed there was nothing he'd be missing out on by going to bed. As he waited for them at the door, Tristan returned Jess's grateful smile with a wink that went over Elijah's head, then followed them out. The climb to the nursery was a slow one, but Tristan kept pace behind Elijah to make sure his tired legs didn't stumble. He waited a couple of steps below the landing to the upper floor, waiting until Jess turned back to him. 'So, did you want me to come down to the village with you tomorrow?'

She hesitated for a moment before nodding. 'If you don't mind. I don't want to keep you from your own work.'

'It's not a problem, besides the sooner we get you all sorted, the sooner you can start work and then I'll be able to sit around with my feet up while you do everything.'

The laugh she gave held more than a hint of her own exhaustion. 'If that's what you think is going to happen, you're going to be very disappointed.'

'I don't think you could ever disappoint me.' The words were out before he knew what he was saying.

Flushing to the dark roots of her hair, Jess glanced away then back. 'Yes, well, I'll see you in the morning.'

He tucked his hands in his pockets in an effort to look casual and not like a bloke who'd just tossed his foolish, unwanted heart at her feet. 'Sure. Shall we aim for about eight o'clock? Arthur will be up and about by then as well and we can get your stuff unloaded while you give the boys their breakfast.' When she opened her mouth, he shook his head. 'No arguments, you can't lug it all up here by yourself now, can you?'

'True, but you don't have to do everything.'

'I'll let you unpack it all, don't worry!' That earned him another tired smile and gave him some hope that he'd managed to steer the conversation away from his embarrassing outburst. 'Well, I shall see you in the morning.' He tugged a hand from his pocket to give the sleepy-looking boy next to her a wave. 'Night, night, Elijah.'

'Night, Tris'an.'

As he trudged back downstairs, he gave himself a stern talking to. Jess was *not* an option, and the sooner he got that idea out of his head the better. Pining around after her was pathetic and it was time he put himself out there and started looking for an eligible girlfriend. Rather than return to the rest of the family who were no doubt settled once more in their usual spots in the family room, he veered left towards his bedroom and settled on the comfy old chair beside the window. Staring out into the stormy night, he considered his options. He'd never *had* to look for a girlfriend before, they'd always just come along in his life through social interactions, or via introductions from mutual friends. Neither of those were a viable option currently, so he'd have to do what everyone else seemed to be doing these days and resort to his phone. After all, they had an app for everything these days . . .

With Arthur only too happy to help, the two of them made short work of the stack of boxes, cases and sundry odds and ends packed into the back of the trailer. Maxwell and Lancelot soon stepped in to assist, and they formed something of a human chain with he and Arthur lugging everything up the main staircase and the two older men ferrying it along the corridor and up the shorter flight to the nursery with the aid of a flat-bed trolley Maxwell kept for moving heavier items. They left a few things downstairs, including a folded down buggy, a bright red scooter and a child-sized pushbike with stabilisers. Neither the scooter nor the bike would be much good on the gravel drive, but there was plenty of hard standing down by the stables where Elijah would be able to practice. But that could wait for another day.

He'd just finished stowing them in the side of the huge porch which framed the door when a yap from Pippin alerted him to the sight of Jess coming down the stairs with the boys, each clad in a padded coat which made them look like squishy little barrels. Jess had belted a bright red raincoat over jeans and a thin sweater, and he was pleased to note they all had sensible trainers on their feet. There was a proper path down to the village, but it would be a steep climb back.

He was just shrugging on his wax jacket when Mrs W entered the great hall, her low heels clicking on the stone floor as she hurried over to him. 'Oh good, I caught you before you left. Betsy needs a few bits from the shop and the main delivery isn't due until tomorrow, do you mind?'

Tristan scanned a quick glance over the list she handed him. 'Shouldn't be a problem.'

'You're a good boy,' she said, patting his cheek just the way she used to do when he'd been no bigger than Elijah was now.

'Despite what everyone else says, right?'

Laughing at his quip, she paused briefly to greet Jess and the boys before heading off to one of the myriad things she did to keep the place running as smooth as clockwork. Some might think they were overfamiliar with the staff, but to Tristan they were a part of his family. He knew Arthur and Iggy both felt the same way.

Grabbing a rucksack from one of the hooks in the boot room he shrugged it onto his back then turned to Jess. 'All set?'

'I think so.' She glanced around, then spotted the folded-up buggy. 'Oh, thank goodness. I thought for an awful moment we'd forgotten to pack it.' Setting Isaac down, she flipped a couple of clips and the buggy unfolded. It was larger than he'd expected, with a single wheel at the front giving it a streamlined shape, and a thick rubber platform stretching between the back wheels.

Tristan held open the door so she could manoeuvre it out and was ready to give her a hand to lift it down the steps but Jess was already walking it backwards. Elijah, he noted, had taken his little brother's hand to keep him from trying to follow her and he was impressed with the way he looked out for Isaac without having to be asked. Pippin came up to them just as Jess returned to collect Isaac and she gave him a quick pet before helping the boys down the steps. 'No, not this time.' Tristan told the terrier, trying to keep him inside as he began to pull the door closed.'

'Can we take Pip for a walk?' Elijah asked, giving the dog the perfect excuse to wriggle through the gap in the door and bound down the steps.

It was on the tip of his tongue to refuse, juggling two children, a buggy and a rucksack full of shopping back up the hill was going to be enough work without Pippin getting in everyone's way, but the look of hope on Elijah's face was too much to resist. 'If we take him outside the grounds, he has to wear his harness.' He fetched it from the boot room, ignoring Pippin's soft growl when he spotted the hated thing. 'Behave,' he admonished, closing a gentle hand around the terrier's muzzle until he quietened and consented to being strapped into the harness.

73

'Would you like to walk with him to the gate?' When Elijah nodded, Tristan showed him how to hold the lead. 'You don't need to yank on it, because he's only little, just keep walking in the direction you want and he'll get the hint. I've given him lots of extra lead for now, but we'll have to tighten it up when we get on the street because we don't want him to get into the road.'

'Make sure you stop before the gate, Eli,' Jess called out as boy and dog began to trot along the gravel driveway.

'Yes, Mummy.'

They watched for a few moments and it was all Tristan could do not to laugh because it was already pretty clear that Elijah was happy to let Pippin lead him all over the place. 'If they do a tour of all Pip's favourite spots, they won't reach the gate before lunchtime.' He watched as Jess gave the buggy a shove to get it going on the stony surface. 'Can you manage that okay?'

'Yes, it's fine now we're moving.' The wide tread on the wheels did seem to be handling the uneven surface just fine so he left her to it as they strolled along, their trainers crunching over the stones.

It was still a bit overcast, but at least the rain had cleared overnight and though there was a hint of autumn crispness in the air, it was still warm enough to be pleasant. As they walked, Tristan showed her the path down towards the formal gardens and chatted a bit about the work Iggy had put in to restore them to their former glory. 'Can you see the tops of those tall trees in the distance?' He pointed to the narrow tips of a long stand of cypress trees just showing over the thick hedges of the formal gardens. 'Just beyond them we've got a fantastic display area, complete with a water garden which is an exclusive Will Talbot, gardener to the rich and famous, design.' They shared a grin at his teasing tone about his sister's boyfriend. We used it for the summer fete, and also pitched a marquee there for Arthur and Lucie's wedding reception. The fountains were the perfect backdrop, and they've got a programmed light display which is stunning in the evening. I want to put on a winter festival with lots of food and drink outlets and the kind of stalls you get in Christmas markets. I've also got details of the guy who helped Will design the lighting for the fountains and I'm going to pick his brains about doing something similar in the woods.' He gestured back behind them towards the thick stretch of trees which bordered one side of the land. 'We installed a couple of easy walks during the summer, including one which is a loop and I thought we could use that.'

'I've been to one of those before, and they're incredibly atmospheric.'

'Yes, I went to a couple around London. And we can set up a catering point at the entrance/exit to the walk so people can warm themselves up with a nice hot chocolate or a glass of mulled wine.'

'Make sure you agree a deal with the caterer that anyone bringing a reusable cup gets a discount. It will cut down on waste and the risk of people dropping their rubbish. Perhaps you could order some with the castle motif on and sell them alongside the drinks – going green is on a lot of peoples' conscience at the moment, and it'll bring it a bit more revenue as well as giving you free advertising.'

Tristan groaned. Not because it wasn't a great idea, but because he really needed to get his arse in gear in sorting out lines for a gift shop. And work out where the hell they were going to put a gift shop. When she looked at him askance, he told her as much, and she laughed. 'You really didn't think everything through before you started, did you?'

He shrugged. 'We did what we could, but the imperative was to get people through the gates and some money – *any* money – coming in. If Lucie hadn't found the painting, I'm not sure we'd still be living here now.'

'Things were that bad? I'm sorry, I had no idea. I mean, I knew you'd come home because your father died, which is terrible, of course, but I didn't . . .' Jess trailed off, her face reddening.

'Hey,' he said, putting a gentle hand on her shoulder. 'Don't worry, I knew what you meant. To be honest, I don't think any of us realised how dire things were until after Dad died – he did his best to shield us from it all, which is I think what killed him in the end. In trying to rescue our finances he got ripped off by a conman.' An old anger stirred in his gut. 'He might be in jail, but ours wasn't the only family who lost more than money because of what he did.'

'Oh, Tristan, I wish I'd known.'

Her sympathy was welcome, but there wasn't anything she could've done. *It might have been nice to know someone was worrying for him, though.* The neediness in that thought made him profoundly uncomfortable. This was a woman in the throes of a divorce and facing a very uncertain future with two children to think about. He should be trying to ease her burdens, not want her to take on his as well. 'I think you had enough on your plate.'

It was her turn to shrug. 'People don't have a finite capacity to care. If you don't ever let your shields down, it's not possible to have more than superficial relationships. When things were going wrong with Steve, my first instinct was to hold it all in, but that would've been a mistake. I knew there were times when I wouldn't be able to cope with everything, and by being honest with Tim and Charlie I got the support I needed before I reached crisis point.'

The logic of her statement was mostly lost on him because his brain had locked onto the word 'superficial' and had gone into a spiral of outrage and embarrassment. Not everyone wore their heart on their sleeves, and if he chose to mask his feelings then what of it? He'd never been one to blubber into his hanky, but that didn't mean he didn't care deeply. If he needed a shoulder to lean on, he had Arthur and Iggy for that. *But Arthur and Iggy were moving on with their lives and had other people, other priorities now.*

As they walked past the old gatehouse that panicky sense he was being left behind clawed at his insides once more. What was he doing with his life? He needed a proper plan, and he needed it quickly. Staring through the dusty windows of an empty building with a headful of dreams and half-ideas wasn't good enough anymore. There was no point in yearning after the kind of happiness and stability his siblings had if he had nothing to offer a potential partner.

It was one of the things he'd stalled out on last night after downloading a couple of the most popular dating apps. They all wanted to know stuff like where he lived and what job he did, and there was no easy way to explain his circumstances. '*I still live at home*', didn't sound great for any thirty-year-old, even if his home was a castle. '*I sort of work for my brother*' sounded even less appealing, and so he'd left the boxes unfilled, his profile incomplete.

Christ, he needed to stop feeling sorry for himself and get a grip. It was time to have those conversations with Arthur he'd been postponing and find out if those dreams could be turned into reality. If they couldn't, if Arthur had a different vision for running things at the castle which didn't directly involve him, at least he'd know and could start making some alternative plans. Iggy had found a rewarding new life for herself away from Bluebell Castle, and Tristan himself had done the same before, too. He'd always been great at selling stuff, at finding the right words for a decent bit of copy. Looked like he was going to have to find a way to market himself.

Chapter 7

Jess watched Tristan usher the children out of the head teacher's office with more than a little trepidation. Though they seemed content enough to go with him, and the prospect of exploring a new place and the promise of sweets from the shop enough to keep them happy, he was still little more than a stranger to them.

'The shop is less than five minutes' walk. If there's any problem, he'll have them back here in a jiffy.' Mrs Winters said, tearing her attention away from the closed door. 'Now why don't you have a seat and let's see what I can do to help you.'

'Those mind-reading skills must come in very useful when you're dealing with the children,' Jess said with a rueful laugh as she took the offered seat on the opposite side of the desk. It was a small room, made cheerful by a wall full of colourful drawings and thank you cards, and an array of potted plants which filled every empty spot on the desk not covered in paper.

'If only! Now, can I get you a drink, only instant I'm afraid, but I've got a nice selection of teas.'

'I'm fine, thank you.' Jess shifted on her seat. 'It was good of you to see me without an appointment.'

'Oh, nonsense.' The silver-haired woman waved a hand. 'We

don't stand on ceremony here like they might have to in a larger school. With the way the economy's going we struggle more each year to hang onto our younger families in the village so there's no problem with fitting your lad into the class.' Folding her hands on the desk in front of her, she leaned forward in a confiding manner. 'If you're here to help boost the fortunes of the castle, then I for one am delighted to welcome you and your family to Camland. The work the baronet is doing is already paying dividends for the village.'

It struck Jess then just how closely the fortunes of the local families must be tied to those of the Ludworths. Though it had been hard to see anything through the driving rain last night, she'd not missed how remote a location it was, and she'd seen no evidence of local industry on her approach. 'I think it's more a case of them helping to boost my fortunes, but I'm happy to be here anyway, even if the circumstances are a little unorthodox.'

'Well, yes, it is a bit unusual, and a shame – Elijah, is it . . .?' Jess nodded and Mrs Winters continued. 'A shame he couldn't have started at the beginning of term with the others, but he's only missed a few days and it won't take long for him to make friends, I'm sure.'

Jess swallowed down a wash of bitter guilt. 'I'd registered him at another school, and they were aware of his later starting date but then everything changed at the very last minute.'

'Because you got the offer of this job?' There was no missing the gentle probing behind the question.

'I wasn't expecting it, that's for sure.' God, that made her sound flighty as a bird. Sitting up straighter in an attempt to not look or feel like a naughty child herself, Jess decided to come clean. 'My husband and I have separated, and I was going to move the boys back home to live with my family in the short term. Tristan offered me an alternative to that, and I think this move is the best for the three of us.'

'Better to move away to a place where you don't know anyone rather than live back home?'

Jess wanted to tell Mrs Winters to stop prying, but she supposed this is what life in a small community was like. 'My parents are very kind, very loving people.' It was true, regardless of how her mother's words hurt sometimes, Jess knew they were never malicious. 'My mum has always been a bit rigid when it comes to rules, and I'm not sure exposing the boys – particularly Elijah – to her uh . . . inflexibility is the best thing for him right now.' It felt horribly disloyal to speak of her mother like this to a stranger, but Elijah needed all the confidence she could give him as they all tried to navigate their way through this turbulent patch in their lives. 'Coming here gives me a bit of breathing space whilst taking a job which suits my career.'

'So, you don't anticipate this being a permanent move?' Mrs Winters steepled her fingers, her expression thoughtful, but there was no judgment in it that Jess could detect.

'I'm here to manage a specific project through to the new year. By then, things will be more settled on the domestic front, and I've got time between now and then to work out what I want to do for the longer term.'

Mrs Winters nodded. 'While it would be advantageous for Elijah to be able to continue his schooling uninterrupted for as long as possible, I recognise that's not always possible. You'll keep me informed?'

'Absolutely.'

'Well, there's paperwork to be done and we'll have to get Elijah registered with the local authority, but I'm content for him to start here on a casual basis until the formalities are concluded. It can only be to his benefit to start as quickly as possible – is tomorrow too early for you? We don't have a branded uniform. Black trousers and shoes, a white polo shirt and a red jumper. They're all easily obtained from one of the big supermarkets, and we've got a donations box because most families are on a tight budget, so they donate anything that's been outgrown that still has a bit of life left in it. I'm sure we can rustle up something for Elijah to tide him over the next few days.'

'He has black trousers and shoes, and I'll get online and order the rest as soon as we get home.'

'Perfect. Let's pop next door and have a look at what we can find, and we can get the paperwork started with the school secretary at the same time.' Mrs Winters led her to the door, then paused without opening it. 'I know I've asked some very personal questions, and I appreciate you've been very honest so far, but can I ask how your relationship is with Elijah's father?'

'We're on speaking terms; better than, really. He's gone back to university as a mature student, so the boys won't see much of him in the coming weeks, but the plan is to Skype most days.' She scrunched her nose. 'It's not ideal, but it's the best we could come up with.'

'The joys of modern technology. We have a girl a year or two older than Elijah whose father is in the military. He's on deployment at the moment, and I know they use it to keep in touch. She's a sensible girl, and very friendly so I might get her to help Elijah settle in a bit as she knows better than most how tough it can be when you're missing a parent.' She patted Jess on the arm. 'Don't worry about Elijah, we will take very good care of him for as long as he is a part of this school.'

The relief swamping Jess was almost overwhelming. Thank heavens there were good people in this world like Mrs Winters. 'Thank you.' It was hard to get the words out around the lump in her throat.

As though sensing her struggle, the head teacher said no more, merely opened her office door and took Jess to meet the school secretary and they were soon too busy sorting through the clothing donations box and making a start on Elijah's registration for Jess to have time to get emotional.

*

The rest of that first week passed by so quickly, Jess barely had time to blink. With the help of Lucie and Constance she managed to get all her boxes unpacked within a couple of days and with their familiar toys and things around them, the boys seemed to have settled into their little attic haven without any major issues. The twice daily walk to and from school with Elijah, as well as multiple trips up and down the stairs were doing wonders for her fitness, and by Friday she could make it to the top floor without feeling even a little out of breath. A trip to the outskirts of the nearest big town had resolved Elijah's uniform issue, and although the Ludworths had offered to redecorate their suite of rooms, Jess had preferred to make a visit to the local DIY store and pick up some colourful posters and wall decals which brightened up the walls without the disruption of moving furniture around, or the smell of fresh paint to irritate sensitive noses.

Between Tristan and Mrs W, she'd had a thorough tour of the place and her mind was already buzzing with dozens of ideas. She'd picked up a new notebook at the supermarket and scribbled notes in it of everything as it came to mind. Her phone was full of photos she'd taken of different rooms – from the guest bedrooms to the breathtaking library with its floor to ceiling shelves and access to the enchanting orangery stuffed full of exotic plants and blooms. By Friday, she was eager to get started, but Tristan was insistent she took the full week to settle in and had arranged a meeting with Arthur for Monday morning when they would try and thrash out the basic details of what they would offer guests so Tristan could update the website.

With Isaac down for a nap and a couple of hours remaining before Elijah needed to be collected from school, Jess had decided to do some solo exploring to help coalesce her mishmash of ideas into something more substantive. Tristan had identified ten rooms in the guest wing he thought would offer suitable accommodation, and while Jess could see the merit in maximising their revenue, she believed limiting the first year to half a dozen couples would not only make things more manageable, it would enhance the idea they were part of the family rather than simply paying guests. Twenty felt like a lot of people, too, when it came to finding public spaces they could comfortably use, unless they spread them out over more rooms which would defeat the intimate feel they were aiming for. Knowing she would have to sell him on the idea, Jess started with a review of the bedrooms, making a list of pros and cons for each of them and ranking them in her order of preference.

She was just shutting the door on the suite which was her personal favourite – a bedroom decorated in shades of cream and gold, with an adjoining small sitting room in muted green shades and a bathroom dominated by an enormous roll top bath – when she spotted a dark velvet curtain at the end of the corridor. Assuming it was a window, she went to tug it back so there would be more light to inspect the corridor and spot any remedial repairs or redecorations. To her surprise, the curtain concealed not a window, but a flight of carpeted stairs. Peering down, she tried to see where they led, but her view was blocked by a half-landing about a dozen steps down. Curiosity piqued, she felt around until she located a light switch then began to make her way down in the gloom of the single bulb still working in the pair of wall sconces. She had better luck with the middle section of the stairs as the lights there were fine, but she needed the torch function on her phone to make it to the very bottom where she found a closed door. More with hope than expectation, she turned the handle and found herself towards the bottom end of the picture gallery being glared down at by a portrait of one of Tristan's very haughty-looking ancestors.

Excited, she turned to check her bearings and gave herself a mental high-five as she spotted the entrance to the orangery. It wouldn't take much to get the staircase refurbished and those dead bulbs replaced giving their guests a private route directly from their bedrooms to the parts of the castle she hoped to utilise as their rest and relaxation areas. Pushing open the door to the orangery, she paused, eyes closing for a second as the warm, perfumed air hit her nostrils. Remembering Tristan's warning about protecting the temperature so as not to risk damaging the plants, she stepped inside and shut the door firmly behind her. She'd seen some glorious spaces around the castle, but this one might just be her favourite. Each plant had a neatly penned label at its base, which would likely fascinate those with a passion for horticulture, but Jess couldn't care less about the names or genus listed below the English in Latin. It was more about the atmosphere for her, the colours and vibrancy of the leaves, the scents of the various blooms and the oxygen-rich environment.

Weaving her way through the plants, she noted there were already two or three groupings of seats which would serve perfectly as reading or contemplation spots for guests. She wouldn't have to do much more than add a few comforting touches like soft throws, not that anyone would get cold per se, but just for the snuggle factor. It wasn't just the view inside either. The orangery backed onto a rolling lawn and beyond that was the rear of the stables, the stone walls thick with ivy. Towards the far end, she could see the edge of the woods, the leaves on the cusp of turning were still more green than brown but hinting at a glorious autumnal display to come. In the heart of winter, with perhaps even a dash of snow on the ground, the contrast between the inside and outside would be even more stunning.

Having made her way back to the centre of the room, Jess used a set of double glass doors to let herself into the library. The variance between the warm, slightly heavy air of the orangery and the dry, leather-filled scent of the books lining the shelves was another sensory delight. As she trailed a finger lightly over the spines to her left, she pictured the kind of furniture she wanted to install in the large, empty centre of the room. A couple of sofas facing each other over a coffee table, perhaps a chair or two off set in quieter corners for anyone seeking solitude with a book. A thump from somewhere overhead startled her. 'Hello?'

'Oh!' She recognised Lucie's startled voice before the redhead came to peer down over the railing of the upper mezzanine floor. 'I didn't hear you come in. How's it all going?'

Jess couldn't help but return the other woman's warm smile. She didn't know her very well yet, but what she'd seen so far had given her a glimpse into a kind and generous heart. A sweet foil for Arthur's more outgoing nature, she liked the way they complemented each other, how Lucie shone in his obvious affection, how he softened in her quieter presence. 'It's good. Great, actually. I've been scouting around some possible locations for our guests to use over Christmas.'

'And you were thinking of the library as one of them?'

The slight hesitancy in Lucie's voice brought Jess up short. 'Is that going to be a problem? I didn't realise it got much use.'

'Only by me. This is my office.' Lucie spread her arms to encompass the mezzanine. 'I'm building the family record archive up here.' Perhaps Jess's expression gave away some of the disappointment she was feeling, because Lucie began to hurry down the stairs towards her. 'Don't worry, though! It's not like I'm planning to do much work, if any, over the holidays, and I can always sort out what I think I'll need beforehand and transfer it to Arthur's office.'

'I don't want to put you to any trouble. The idea is to try and make this work with as little disruption to you and the rest of the family as possible.'

Lucie laughed. 'Arthur and I have already resigned ourselves to hosting duties. Oh, don't look so worried, we're quite looking forward to it. It will be our first proper outing as Sir Arthur and Lady Lucinda Ludworth.' She rolled her eyes. 'Lord, what a mouthful that is!'

Jess couldn't help giggling. 'It does make you sound terribly posh.'

'And I'm anything but. Morgana has been trying to teach me all the proper etiquette for things like afternoon tea, but I'm rubbish at it compared to her.' A suspicious gleam entered her eye. 'I'll have to get her to invite you to tea. It's an experience not to be missed.'

'I'm not sure that sounds an entirely good thing . . .'

'Lucie grinned. 'Oh, no, it's wonderful, I promise. We might even be able to persuade her to host one for the ladies over Christmas. She really is a marvellous hostess, and I'm sure the guests would love to hear stories of how life in the castle has changed over her lifetime.'

'Well, if you think she'd do it, it sounds like a brilliant idea.' Tim and Charlie sprang to mind. If they did indeed book to come, then Tim with his sweet tooth would die at the chance for proper afternoon tea. 'It might appeal to some of our gentlemen guests, too. Do you think she'd object to a unisex event? We can balance it with another more rigorous outdoor activity to keep the numbers manageable.'

'I don't see why not. Let's see if we can have a chat with her when we gather before dinner. We could give her the option then to pick and choose whether she attends any of the other group meals. I know she's keen to play her part, but I don't want her to feel obligated.'

'That's a really good idea. I certainly don't want anyone in the family to feel obligated to participate, which is one of the reasons I want to establish a clear division of spaces where both the guests and you guys can relax in private.' Jess glanced around them at the rows of shelves. 'This is such an atmospheric room which is why I wanted to use it. And the orangery as well. I also want to use one of the bigger drawing rooms, hopefully one quite close to where we are now so they're all interlinked.'

'Have you seen the west drawing room? It's just along the

corridor.' Lucie pointed to the door opposite the one where Jess had entered.

'I've seen quite a few of them, I can't remember all their names to be honest.'

'Here, I'll show you.' Lucie led the way, turning left just after they left the dining room and pushed open a door not more than fifty feet away. 'I thought it was a bit spooky when I first inspected it when I was updating the castle inventory.'

As soon as she saw inside, Jess remembered the rather gloomy room and her excitement waned a bit. It would take a lot of work to create an inviting space here.

After flipping on the lights, Lucie hurried across the room to draw back the thick, heavy drapes. 'Once you let the light in, it totally transforms it.' Moving at right angles, she drew another set of curtains. 'See?'

Jess blinked at the transformation. With light flooding in through the huge picture windows, it was already a million times more welcoming. Feeling better, she began to inspect it more closely. 'This fireplace is lovely, and the mantel is nice and wide, perfect for decorating.'

'Yes,' Lucie agreed, coming to stand beside her. 'A roaring blaze in there would make such a difference.'

Her little sigh made Jess turn to face her. 'What is it?'

'I have a theory that this was once used by Thomas and Eudora, and that's why it always makes me feel a little bit sad when I come in here.'

'Who are they?'

Pushing aside the protective covering on a nearby sofa, Lucie sat then patted the seat beside her, inviting Jess to join her. 'Thomas was Arthur's several times great-grandfather. It's because of him that all his ancestors have those mad names. He was absolutely obsessed with King Arthur and the Knights of the Round Table, to the point he developed a theory that Camland was once the ancient seat of Camelot.'

'I thought that was in Somerset? My parents live about forty minutes from Glastonbury and everything down that way is linked to the legends.'

Lucie shrugged. 'I know, but I did a little bit of digging and there are some alternative suggestions that the original Arthur was a northern warlord. Anyway, Thomas latched onto the idea and when he got married, he and his wife named their four children after various characters from the legend, and it was a tradition passed down through the first-born line ever since.' She pulled a face. 'I know Arthur's going to want to do the same. He's going to have to give me a very big bribe, that's all I can say.'

'Make sure it's a *very* big bribe. Eudora must've been a very understanding woman.' More understanding than Jess thought she might be in the circumstances.

'Oh, Thomas never married Eudora! Silly me, of course, you won't know the story. Thomas ran around with a very arty set in his youth and fell for Eudora, who was an artist's model in a grand passion. He commissioned a painting of her to commemorate his love for her only she upped and ran off with the artist, leaving poor Thomas devastated. He walled up the painting and tried to banish her from his mind, and eventually moved on and married. I don't think he ever forgot her though – I found a sketch of Eudora in one of the drawers of that desk over there.' She pointed to a shrouded piece in the corner. 'That's how I got on the trail of the painting, you see.'

The painting Tristan had told her had been instrumental in saving the family fortunes. As the pieces tumbled into place in her mind, Jess looked around the room. If she could tie the theme of the room into this fantastic family legend, the guests would love it. 'Do you still have the sketch?'

Lucie laughed. 'Oh, yes. It's locked in the safe in Arthur's room. It's unsigned, but it's been authenticated as a preparatory sketch JJ Viggliorento did before he painted Eudora's portrait.'

Jess whistled through her teeth, recognising at once the name of one the most famous British artists of the past couple of hundred years. No wonder they'd been able to save the family with one painting if it was an original Viggliorento. 'Well, that puts my plan of hanging it on the wall in here out of the question!'

'Yeah.' Lucie scrunched her nose in thought. 'I could try and get a copy made, and there's a portrait of Thomas in the long gallery we could relocate here while the guests are staying. And I'd be happy to give them a private tour upstairs to show them the secret passage where we found the painting. Though I'd have to check with Arthur first because it runs from our private suite to the castle's tower, but I'm sure he wouldn't mind it as a one-off.'

Jess shook her head. 'No. We can't be invading your personal space like that.'

'Well, there is an external door into the tower, so we could do it that way. Take them inside and show them that end of the tunnel and keep the door at the other end into our rooms locked. JJ used the tower as his studio, you see, so we can give them all the lurid titbits of the illicit romance by showing them how Eudora crept in to see him.'

'Okay, you've sold me! We're definitely going to use this room. I think the guests will love a bit of family history, especially when it's such a juicy story.'

A cough and a grumble came through the speaker on her phone, and she pulled it out of her back pocket. Tilting the screen to show Lucie the image of Isaac stirring on her baby monitoring app, she couldn't help but smile. He looked like an angel, those dark curls he'd inherited from her tumbling over his forehead. He was in dire need of a haircut, but she couldn't quite bring herself to snip away the last of his baby locks just yet. 'Looks like someone is about to wake up.'

'Such an angel,' Lucie said, echoing her thoughts. As though he'd heard them talking, even though Jess had muted her end of the app, Isaac scrunched up his face and gave an outraged bellow at waking up alone.

'That's my cue. I'll see you at dinner, if not before!'

'Okay, don't forget we're going to have that conversation with Morgana, too.'

'Thanks, I appreciate your help, Lucie,' Jess called over her shoulder, her pace already quickening as another yell of displeasure echoed from the screen in her hand. Turning on her mic, she began to reassure Isaac she was on the way.

Unfortunately, Isaac's bad mood lasted for the entire walk down to fetch Elijah from school and back, and well into the early evening. She'd thought at first his cheek was red from where he'd been laying on it, but a feel around his mouth when they'd returned revealed the rough edge of a tooth just breaking through his gum. Of course, when she checked in the bathroom, there was no sign of the tube of soothing gel she was sure she'd packed, and she hadn't got around to putting any of his teething rings in the ice box. An emergency run to the kitchen had secured some ice wrapped in a clean flannel and resulted in Isaac being 'kidnapped' by both Betsy, the cook, and Mrs W which had at least given Jess a chance to spend an hour one-on-one with Elijah going through his day at school. With him settled happily on the cosy rug in the playroom in front of his favourite cartoon, she headed back downstairs to retrieve Isaac so the ladies could finish preparations for dinner in peace.

Halfway along the first-floor corridor, a bedroom door swung open and Tristan stepped out in a cloud of warm, amber after-shave, his shaggy hair still damp at the back from a shower. The navy linen jacket he'd teamed with dark denim and a red and white checked shirt looked a little formal for dinner with the family. He looked smart enough to be on a date. A set of keys jangled in his hand as he closed the door behind him. *Oh.* It looked like he was going out, after all, and given it was Friday night and he was very handsome and very single, then why wouldn't he be going on a date? She wasn't quite sure why, but the idea of it bothered her. The boys were just getting used to everyone in the castle, if Tristan was going to introduce somebody new to the equation, it could throw the balance. Yes, that was the only possible concern she might have over Tristan's personal life. 'Off out somewhere nice?'

'What?' His startled greeting proved he hadn't noticed her until she spoke. 'Oh, hi, Jess. Umm, yeah, I'm popping into town to meet, umm . . . a mate of mine.'

The sudden rush of relief she felt threw her totally off balance, and it took her a few moments to register his awkwardness through her own. In all the years she'd known him, she'd never seen him flustered, never mind as outright uncomfortable as he looked now. 'Is everything all right?'

'Yes, yes, everything's fine. No problems here, how about you?' With a stain of red on his high cheekbones and the way his eyes met hers for a second before skating away, he looked like a man with a guilty secret.

Nonplussed, Jess replied. 'Isaac's been having a bit of trouble with a new tooth today, but other than that I'm good.'

'Good. That's good, well I'd better get going. See you later!'

Staring at his retreating back, Jess didn't know what to do other than shake her head. It had been like talking with a stranger, not the warm, affable, caring man who'd met her at the gates on Monday night. She couldn't believe he'd brushed off her comment about Isaac without even bothering to ask how he was. Not when he'd shown nothing but kindness and concern for both her boys from the moment they'd arrived. *Who are you, and what have you done with Tristan?*

Now, she thought about it, he'd been distracted over breakfast which was the last time she'd seen him, and he and Arthur had left the breakfast table together and disappeared into Arthur's study. Had something happened, something that might affect her job? They hadn't officially agreed any terms, she didn't even have anything in writing from him stating his intention to hire her. If they'd changed their mind, decided the budget didn't include enough money to pay Jess, she wouldn't have a leg to stand on. Gripped by panic, she ran after him but by the time she reached the balustrade overlooking the great hall the only sign he'd passed through there was the forlorn-looking terrier staring up at the closed front door.

As she reached the bottom of the stairs, Pippin came over to greet her. Sitting down, she scratched him behind the ears. 'What's got into your master, eh, Pip?' The terrier whined and licked her hand. 'I'm sure it's nothing to worry about,' she said, lifting the dog into her lap for a cuddle and wishing like hell she could believe it.

Chapter 8

It was late by the time Tristan let himself back into the castle. Closing the door behind him, he shushed the sleepy dogs who'd padded over to greet him, walking them back to the tumble of cushions in front of the fireplace and crouching down to stroke one or two until they settled back down to their slumbers. Only Pippin refused to sit, the little terrier circling his ankles like he'd been gone for a month rather than a couple of hours.

Though he should probably head straight upstairs to his own bed, there were too many thoughts chasing around inside his mind for him to be able to get any sleep. Hoping a brandy might help him unwind, he wandered instead towards the family room, Pippin at his heels.

On entering, he was surprised to find a lamp still lit, casting a small circle of light over a supine figure curled up on one of the sofas. Though a tangle of dark curls obscured her face, he knew instantly who it was, and his heart skipped a beat. 'Jess?'

There was no response to his quiet question, and he realised she was out like a light. The fire had burnt down to little more than a few glowing ashes in the grate, leaving a slight chill in the air. Pulling a throw off the back of the sofa, he placed it gently over the lower half of her body. Though she shifted a little at the touch of the soft material, she didn't wake. Leaving her to sleep, he poured a good slug of brandy into a glass and settled into the armchair across from her to turn over the events of the past few hours in his mind.

Already regretting his decision to arrange a date with Nicky, a woman he'd been chatting to on one of the dating apps, almost bumping into Jess whilst trying to slip out unnoticed had thrown him completely off guard. He'd told himself it was stupid to feel guilty, that he owed Jess no loyalty other than that of a friend and colleague, but it hadn't stopped him feeling like he was making the biggest mistake of his life. It was a feeling that had only grown over the course of the evening. Not that there had been anything wrong with Nicky. In fact, she'd been as charming and funny as she'd come across in her messages. They'd met in a popular bar, but it had still been early enough for them to find a quiet table in the corner where they could talk, away from the speakers pumping out music over the bar.

A junior solicitor, with hopes of making partner in the next year or two, Nicky had been frank about her previous relationship ending because her other half had resented the amount of time she'd been spending at work. Tristan had admired her ambition, and under any other circumstances would have found that drive to succeed sexy as hell. The same went for the black dress she'd worn, fitted in all the right places with a soft floaty skirt that skimmed the top of her knees. Classy. Pretty. Smart as a whip. She ticked every box on his list, except for one. She wasn't the woman he wanted. He'd told her as much over their second drink, and to his relief she'd laughed, but told him he still owed her dinner.

They'd moved onto the Italian restaurant she'd suggested, and the rest of the evening had passed in pleasant conversation. Though she'd asked, he'd refused to be drawn much on Jess, feeling it really was too low to talk about another woman even if they weren't officially on a date anymore. Nicky had shared a few anecdotes about some of the other men she'd met on the app, leaving him with no doubt he'd be the subject of one her stories soon enough. By the time they parted on the pavement, they were well on the way to being friends and he'd promised to give her and her parents a guided tour one weekend if she brought them over to the castle for a day out.

So what was he going to do now? Two-thirds of the way down his brandy and he still had no idea. Nothing had changed. With a sigh, he reached out to set his glass down on the table, but he misjudged his aim in the dim light and sent the slate coaster rattling off the edge and onto the floor, the noise startling Pippin who'd been slumbering at his feet. The calming hand he set on the terrier's head came a moment too late to stop the high yip of surprise. *Damn.*

'Huh?' Jess sat up, spilling the throw he'd placed over her onto the carpet. 'Oh, did I fall asleep?' She reached for the phone beside her, checking something on the screen. 'Goodness, it's late. Why didn't you wake me?'

'You looked too peaceful to disturb. I was just finishing my brandy and then I was going to wake you before I went up. What were you doing down here?'

Jess rubbed her eyes, then swept her hands back over her hair to settle it in a neat fall down her back. 'I was waiting for you.'

His stupid heart faltered, but he managed to keep a firm grip on his hopes. 'What was so important it couldn't wait until morning?'

Uncurling her legs, she set her feet on the floor and leaned towards him, elbows resting on her knees. 'I don't know, Tristan, you tell me. You were so odd when I saw you this afternoon that I've been worrying all evening about it. Look, if you've changed your mind about us being here, just tell me straight. God knows I'll have to live with weeks of "I told you so" from my mother, and wrenching Elijah out of school when he's getting settled is the last thing I want, but I'd rather you told me the truth so at least I have the weekend to try and sort things out.'

Whatever he'd been expecting her to say, even hoping she might say, it certainly wasn't this. 'What on earth put that idea inside your head? Do you think me so untrustworthy that I'd offer you a job knowing your circumstances and then pull the rug out from under you?' He couldn't help the hurt creeping into his voice.

Throwing her hands up, Jess scowled at him. 'What was I supposed to think when you treated me like a stranger, earlier? You couldn't wait to get away from me, so what else was I supposed to think.'

'Jesus Christ, not *that*. You must think me a first-class shit if you think me capable of doing that to you, or the boys for that matter.' Grabbing for his brandy, Tristan downed the last of it then crossed to the cabinet to splash more in his glass.

'Then what is the problem?' Jess twisted round in her seat to face him.

'It was nothing.' He sipped at the brandy, wishing like hell he'd gone straight up to bed as soon as he'd got in.

'Fine. If you're going to be like that I might as well go to bed. Isaac's feeling better, by the way,' she snapped as she stood and headed to the door.

'Wait, what? Hold on, what do you mean he's feeling better. What was wrong with him?'

'You really didn't hear a thing I said to you this afternoon, did you?'

Embarrassed, he stared down at his glass of brandy. 'I was a bit distracted.' He raised his head. 'Isaac is okay, though?'

She nodded, wearily. 'Teething, so he had a pretty miserable afternoon and evening. He enjoyed being fussed over by Betsy and Mrs W, though and once I managed to chill his teething ring, he calmed down a bit. He had a spoonful of Calpol as he was a bit feverish before bed and thankfully dropped off during story time and hasn't made a peep since.'

'I'm sorry I left you to deal with all that.'

'Not your problem, is it? I didn't expect you to drop everything and sit by his bedside, but I didn't expect you to brush me off like that, this afternoon.' Jess folded her arms around her middle, in a way that made her look small and vulnerable. 'God, Tristan, I'm sorry. I should be the one apologising. I've been using you all week as a substitute for Steve, and that's not fair on you. Getting used to handling the boys on my own has been a bit of a shock to the system, that's all.'

The smile she gave him was so sad he wanted to vault over the sofa and drag her into his arms. He clenched his hand around his glass, forcing his feet to remain on the spot. 'You don't have to be sorry, I've been really enjoying spending time with them. No one expects you to do this on your own, I told you when I offered you the job that we'd all be happy to pitch in and help, and I meant it.'

'Thank you.' She rubbed her hands up and down her arms, seemed to catch what she was doing and dropped them to her sides. 'Anyway. we've got our routine sorted, so I'll make sure I remember the boundaries from now on. And, I'm sorry again for overreacting. I had a bit of a panic over not having a contract in place for my work here.'

Tristan felt a bit sick over the fact it hadn't even occurred to him. He knew his word was solid as a rock, but he didn't have anyone else to worry about other than himself. 'I'll make sure there's something drawn up for us to discuss on Monday along with everything else. Arthur had the solicitor draft an agreement for Lucie when she started working here, I'll get a copy and we can make any amendments necessary.'

'That would be good. I'm sorry, I know you're not going to just turf us out, I don't know how such a foolish notion got into my head.'

'We still should've put it in writing for you.' Shoving his glass onto the sideboard, Tristan rounded the sofa to stand in front of her. 'I'm sorry I made you feel vulnerable about your position here, it was the last thing I wanted to do.' *Don't do it. Leave it at that and let her go to bed.* Ignoring the sensible voice in his head, Tristan reached for her hand. 'I went out on a date tonight.

That's where I was going when I bumped into you, and I didn't want to say anything.'

Cheeks reddening, Jess ducked her head until her hair spilled forward to shield her eyes from him. 'Oh. I wondered as much, but then you said you were meeting a mate . . .' She glanced up at him through a spill of curls. 'Your private life is your own, you don't have to explain yourself to me.' She would've pulled her hand free if he'd been willing to let it go.

'But I want to.' Turning her hand over, he smoothed his thumb over the plump softness of her palm. 'The woman I met tonight should've been perfect for me, but she wasn't.'

'*Tristan.*'

'Shh. Don't say anything, just listen to me for a minute. I know it's too soon, but I'm going to lay my cards on the table. I'm not saying you're the perfect woman for me, Jess, but damn it, I think you might be and I'm tired of pretending otherwise. I'm happy to wait for as long as you want me to. *If* you want me to.'

Her fingers closed around his thumb. 'But how am I supposed to know? And say I was attracted to you, it's going to take Steve and I at least a couple of years to resolve everything legally. I can't ask you to wait that long.'

Tristan edged a little closer, brushing a curl from her forehead with his free hand. 'You can if that's what you need.'

Her head dropped to rest on her chest. 'I don't know what I need,' she whispered.

Knowing he'd already pushed too far, Tristan bent to press a kiss to the top of her hair then released her hand and stepped back. 'You don't need to do anything other than take care of your boys and do the job I'm hiring you to do.'

When her incredulous eyes met his, he nodded to show he was serious. 'I've laid down my cards because it didn't feel like I was being honest with you if I didn't. But there's no obligation for you to pick them up. Not tonight; not ever. I'll not even speak of it again, unless you bring it up.'

'I don't know what to say . . .'

Just don't say no, not without thinking about it first. Instead of saying that, he took her shoulders in a gentle grip, and turned her towards the door. 'Say good night.' Releasing her, he returned to the sideboard to retrieve his brandy, keeping his back to the room.

The silence stretched so long between them until every nerve and fibre of his body braced for the rejection he felt sure she was working up to.

'Good night.' It was barely a whisper, followed almost immediately by the snick of the door closing behind her.

Raising his brandy in a mocking toast to his reflection in the glass window of the drink's cabinet, he drained it and set it down with a click. 'Tristan Ludworth, you're a bloody idiot,' he told himself, with a sigh. She hadn't said no, at least, and that gave him hope. It was only as he reached the top of the stairs and turned towards his bedroom that the old adage came unwelcome to his mind. *It's the hope that kills you.*

The next morning he managed to catch his brother and Lucie before they entered the dining room for breakfast. 'Hey, Luce, I need to borrow Arthur for a bit. Any chance you can take Jess and the kids out to explore some of the grounds this morning?'

'Of course, it's such a lovely day we should try and make the most of it. I'll see if Mum and Lancelot want to come with us. I can take them to see the stone circle.' One of Tristan's forebears had created the folly in the heart of the woods, a scaled-down replica of the huge ancient monolith which rose on an escarpment overlooking the dales a few miles from their boundary line.

'Thanks, you're a star.' He pecked Lucie on the cheek, then ushered them towards the dining room.

'Nothing wrong, is there?' Arthur asked, resisting when Tristan tried to push him forward. Though he'd not been on the rugby pitch for some years, Arthur retained the solid bulk of a prop, and nothing would move him until he was ready to move.

'Just need to pick your brains, that's all,' Tristan assured him.

'Well that'll be a bloody short conversation!' Arthur tapped the side of his skull.

Jess was already in the dining room with Isaac strapped into his highchair and Elijah perched on her knee eating a slice of toast. Though she greeted Lucie's suggestion with enthusiasm, the silent look she cast in Tristan's direction said plain enough she knew where the idea had originated.

Having seen the exploration party off with a wave and a kiss for his wife, Arthur closed the front door and leaned back against it, arms folded. 'Are you going to tell me how you got on last night?'

They'd always told each other everything, so of course he'd sought his brother's help before finally posting a profile on the dating apps. 'She was very nice.'

Arthur snorted. 'I sense a but, coming.'

'But, she's not the one for me.'

'And who is the one for you?' Rolling his eyes, Arthur uncrossed his arms and pushed away from the door. 'Oh, bloody hell, Tristan, no.'

Tristan shrugged. 'What can I say?'

'You can say that you're not in love with a married woman with two little kids,' Arthur retorted, voice full of exasperation. When Tristan remained silent his brother raised his hands to his head and pretended to yank out handfuls of his hair. 'You're an idiot.'

'Probably.' Tristan agreed. 'I think it's genetic.'

They laughed before Arthur's expression grew serious again. 'So, what are you going to do about it?'

'Nothing. The ball's in her half of the pitch. She'll either pick it up when she's ready to play, or kick me into touch.'

'Okay then.' Moving in, Arthur gave him a quick hug then a

slap on the shoulder. 'You'll let me know if I can do anything?'

'Sure. But Jess isn't what I wanted to talk to you about. Grab your coat, I've got something I want to show you.'

Arthur circled the old gatehouse, peering through each of the windows in turn much as Tristan had done a few nights before. 'It's a bit of a tip.'

'Nothing that can't be put right, though.' Stepping up beside him, Tristan cupped his hands to the glass and studied the main living room. 'I can't see any sign of damp, so I think the roof is sound. All it needs is gutting, redecorating and some modern fixtures and fittings. Apart from the plumbing, I reckon I can do pretty much everything else. I've got plenty of savings put away so I'm not asking you to fund any of it.'

Arthur straightened up to face him. 'You just want my permission to do it?'

'Yes. Unless you have plans for it, yourself, of course.'

That drew a laugh from his brother. 'I can't say I've given it a single thought for years, even though I drive past it every day.' Tucking his hands in the pockets of his Barbour jacket, he began to wander around to the rear of the gatehouse once more. 'And the plan is to set up your own events management business?'

Tristan nodded. 'I'll still do as much as you want me to as far as the castle is concerned, but I figured that will gradually tail off as things get established and you need me less.'

Arthur raised an eyebrow. 'What gives you the idea I'm going to need you any less than I do now?'

'I don't know, I just figured the more settled into your role you become, the less there'll be for me to do.'

'At least you're not abandoning me like Iggy did.' Arthur said with a scowl. 'When you told me you wanted to talk, I assumed you were going to tell me you wanted to go back to London in the new year, and that's what this business with bringing Jess to work here was all about.'

'What on earth are you talking about? I told you I'd handed my notice in.'

'I know you did, but then in the next breath you said you'd recruited some old friend of yours to organise the house party as she was perfect for the job, so I figured you were hedging your bets.' A sly look came into his brother's eyes. 'That's before I realised you'd lured her up here in the hopes she'd fall madly in love with you.'

'Balls! That's not why I offered her the job.' At Arthur's raised eyebrow, he relented. 'Well, not consciously anyway. She's really good, Arthur. I wouldn't jeopardise the castle's future like that.'

'I know, I'm only pulling your leg. Big brother's prerogative.'

It was Tristan's turn to roll his eyes. 'Five minutes doesn't give you that much clout.' Only it had. Those five minutes had decided the future for all of them, making Arthur the first-born son and heir instead of him. 'You know why Iggy had to go, don't you?'

Their sister was the eldest of the three of them, but ancient inheritance rules entailed the title and estates to the first eligible male heir. Since leaving university, it had been Iggy who'd managed the bulk of their estate on behalf of their father, including running the household as their aunt Morgana had taken a step back. When Arthur married, she'd worried Lucie wouldn't feel comfortable in her role as the lady of the castle with her looking over her shoulder, so Iggy had taken the tough decision to move away.

'No. I don't know why she had to bloody go!' Arthur kicked a loose stone which had fallen from one of the external windowsills. 'Oh, I heard all that stuff about not wanting to usurp Lucie's place, and it's rubbish. My darling wife couldn't give two figs about running the castle, she's got her own career and one she's very happy with. Now she's stuck pretending she cares about menu planning, and which of the tenant farmer's wives has had a new baby, and all the other stuff Iggy used to handle with her eyes shut.'

Tristan groaned. 'And have you told her this?'

Arthur kicked the stone again. 'How could I? She wanted to go off with Will and I wasn't going to stand in her way now, was I?'

'What a pair of idiots you both are! She didn't want to leave, and you wanted her to stay and yet neither of you said so.'

Arthur leaned back against the wall of the gatehouse then slid down to sit on the scruffy grass with a sigh. 'It's genetic.'

Laughing, Tristan slumped down next to him. 'Arthur,' he said, clapping a hand on his brother's thigh. 'I don't want to leave Bluebell Castle.'

Slapping his hand down on top of Tristan's Arthur gave it a squeeze. 'Good, because I don't want you to bloody well leave.'

Chapter 9

It was like Tristan had turned the clock back to those awkward, painful weeks after the Christmas party kiss that never was, and Jess was furious with him for it. They'd been getting back to that lovely easy friendship they'd first enjoyed, and he'd thrown not just a spanner, but an entire bloody toolbox into the works. She rubbed her fingers over her palm feeling the ghost of his thumb stroking it, a reflex action she caught herself making numerous times a day. Several times over the weekend following his outrageous promise she'd contemplated packing the boys up and making a run for it, certain she'd not be able to face Tristan without blushing and generally acting like such a fool the entire household would soon be aware there was something going on between them. Which would make the whole situation ten times worse because there wasn't anything going on between them – there couldn't be.

But how could she do it to Elijah? Drag him away from somewhere he clearly adored being. Over the weeks when she and Steve had been unpicking their life together, she'd watched, helpless as her darling boy crept ever deeper into a protective shell. During their exploration of the woods, Lancelot had hoisted him into the air and spun him around and around eliciting giggles of delight which had bubbled through her bloodstream like the finest champagne. Hearing the pure joy and excitement in that sound had driven home how rare it had become, how much her sunny, funny little man had withdrawn into himself.

Isaac too was thriving on all the attention, and for all she'd told Tristan she could and would manage her family without help, her baby boy spent more time in the company of the older residents of the castle than he did in the playpen she'd set up for him in the corner of her sitting room when she was working during the day. If it wasn't Betsy popping up with a flask of tea and some treat or other she'd baked and casually offering to take Isaac out for a stroll around, it was Constance or Lucie seeking her out for a quick chat that somehow led to them bearing him off to 'give her a bit of peace and quiet', like the two of them didn't have their own work to do. In fact, if it hadn't been for the ever-simmering tension between her and Tristan, Jess might have ventured to think her life at that moment was pretty much close to perfect.

Not that Tristan showed any sign of feeling that tension, of course. When she'd met with him and Arthur to thrash out her contract, he'd acted as though nothing had changed between them. Affable and polite, he'd excused himself while she and Arthur talked numbers and tweaked a couple of the clauses in the draft contract offer, returning afterwards to argue robustly with her about her suggestion they limit the number of guests to a dozen. They'd compromised on fifteen in the end, giving him the flexibility to offer some single spaces for people who might be spending Christmas alone, but who didn't want to be by themselves.

Agreeing the programme of activities had proven much simpler. Arthur had offered to host a welcome cocktail party in the great hall on the first night, and Morgana was on board with the afternoon tea suggestion for a quiet day between Christmas and New Year. Though they would be arriving too late for the winter fete, the illuminated walk would still be in situ, so they'd pencilled in an evening for that, including a bonfire at the stone circle to toast marshmallows and drink brandy-laced hot chocolate. Christmas Eve dinner would be an extravagant buffet to be followed by Midnight Mass in the village church for those who wanted to attend. A traditional turkey roast dinner with all the family was the main feature for Christmas Day, with stockings full of little luxuries to be placed at the foot of each guest bed the night before and the option for a group present opening under the tree Jess was planning for the great hall. They'd agreed to leave some days unorganised so people could relax and enjoy the castle and its estate at their leisure, with an option to pre-book events happening in the local area.

The only awkward moment had been when Jess had suggested a black-tie masquerade ball followed by a private firework display to usher in the new year. As she'd watched Arthur and Tristan exchange a look she knew she'd put her foot in it somehow, but wasn't sure how. 'I know a company who can design a display which doesn't require an on-site technician. They're very reliable, and we used them several times at Beaman and Tanner events and always got great feedback. And it doesn't have to be a masquerade ball, but I thought it might be fun to get a big box of craft supplies and let people have a go at making their own over the preceding week.'

'It's not that . . .' Tristan paused to scrub a hand over his face. 'Arthur, Iggy and I did a private send off for Dad last New Year's Eve.'

'Oh. And you think it will be too upsetting? I can understand if you want to keep the evening free to do something private. I wasn't suggesting the family had to attend the ball, and I can manage the fireworks, myself, I've done it before.'

'It's the fireworks that are the issue.' Arthur gave her a sad smile. 'We had Dad's ashes incorporated into some rockets by a specialist company and sent him off with a bang so to speak.'

Jess didn't know what to say to that. She hadn't realised such a thing was even possible. 'I see,' was about all she could manage.

Tristan glanced at his brother. 'The guests will be expecting something on New Year's Eve.' When Arthur did respond, he turned to Jess. 'Leave it with us, okay?'

'Sure.' The ball would be fine on its own, and if she got some of those indoor sparklers and really went to town on decorations, no one would miss the fireworks. *Hopefully*.

The events list went up on the castle's website without mentioning fireworks, and Jess had to admit Tristan had created a stunning landing page for the house party. The teaser photos they'd chosen included a montage of the most spectacular plants in the orangery, a leather armchair they'd dragged into the library and placed strategically against a backdrop of book-lined shelves, and the dining room table looking resplendent with a full china dinner service laid out. They'd also added a couple of staged images of one of the bedrooms, including the roll top bath full of steaming water with a scattering of rose petals floating on the surface, and a tuxedo and a breathtaking sequined gown in shades of bronze and gold laid out on a bed made up with crisp cotton linens. The gown had been provided by Morgana after overhearing her discussing ideas for the website with Tristan over dinner, and Jess was simply dying for a glimpse into the older woman's wardrobe to see what other delights might be lurking in its cedarwood scented depths.

All in all, Jess thought as she stared out of the window of her sitting room-cum-study and reflected on her first month at Bluebell Castle, things were going better than she could've hoped for. Now, if she could only ignore the Tristan-shaped elephant in the room. The heat in his eyes when he'd declared his feelings that night, the depth of sincerity in his words had made that impossible. She'd always been aware of him on a visceral level from the very first day when he'd sat beside her

107

at the office induction and her fingers had tingled for ages after they'd shaken hands. The intervening years and the first happy years of her marriage had quashed that awareness, but now it had come roaring back to life. Whenever she saw him, nerves and anticipation fizzed in her belly. The scent of that amber aftershave he favoured seemed to linger in the air in unexpected places, waiting to catch her unawares and drive whatever thoughts she had right out of her head for a moment. But it was his voice that really undid her, the deep, even timbre bringing the hairs on her arms to tingling attention. And, *God*, the way he laughed, an unguarded roll of humour which never failed to make her want to join in, even as it sent her wobbly around the knees. Though her head said 'no', and not just no, but '*hell* no', her body and perhaps even a traitorous little piece of her heart said, 'hmm', and 'what if', and '*maybe* . . .' It was driving her to distraction.

Realising she'd been daydreaming about him for a good ten minutes, Jess gave herself a shake and turned her attention back to the nine sheets of paper she'd stuck to the wall above her desk, with a polaroid image of each of the rooms pinned to their top corners. Four of the doubles had a red asterisk inked in the opposite corner to indicate a confirmed booking.

A pile of clippings she'd cut from various catalogues and magazines littered her desk. She'd discovered over the years that she worked better with physical images she could mix and shuffle around until she found the perfect design combination. Picking up a picture of a set of bedding covered in delicate cherry blossoms, she stuck it on one of the suites she had in mind for a single guest. She was just adding a masculine alternative of deep navy and pale blue stripes when a knock at the door was followed immediately by a buoyant looking Tristan.

Ignoring her, he made a beeline for the large playpen in the corner where Isaac was sprawled on his belly watching episodes of *In the Night Garden* on a loop and swooped down to pick him up. 'Guess how many bookings we've taken overnight, sunshine,' Tristan said to Isaac as he lifted him high over his head. 'Go on, guess how many.'

'Tris, Tris, Tris!' Isaac crowed, stretching out his chubby little hands towards Tristan who drew him in for a cuddle.

'That's right, you clever little sausage, it's three!'

Forgetting all the angst he'd been causing her, Jess spun around in her seat to face him. 'Three! Seriously? That's brilliant.'

Perching on the corner of her desk, heedless of the mess he was making of her pile of cut outs, Tristan jogged Isaac up and down on one knee. 'Only two more to go and we've got ourselves a full house.'

'Singles or doubles?' She asked, reaching for her red marker.

'Two singles and a double. I've sent confirmation emails, including your preferences questionnaire.' In order to try and offer a truly tailored experience, Jess had drawn up a list of questions to send out with each booking, including dietary requirements, favourite drinks and foods, reading and other entertainment. 'And,' Tristan continued, 'I've already received deposits in the bank from two of them and a promise the third will pay this evening when they're home. The singles are both female, and the couple are empty nesters looking for a distraction as it's going to be the first Christmas when none of their children are coming home. They sent a lovely, chatty reply and I'm sure we'll get lots more useful info from them when they return your questionnaire.'

'Great,' she muttered as she inked three more red asterisks on her working wall.

'Well, you could sound a bit more enthusiastic about it. I thought that was the kind of stuff you wanted to know about the guests.'

Sinking back into her chair with a sigh, she held out her arms to Isaac and tucked him onto her lap for a comforting cuddle. Not that *he* was the one in need of any comfort, but Tristan's comment about empty nesters had reminded her of something she'd been avoiding. Namely what she was going to do about Christmas with her own family. Though she'd told her parents exactly what her temporary role at the castle entailed, she hadn't made it explicitly clear that she would be busy over the whole of the holiday period. There was also the tricky situation of Steve to tackle. Naturally, he would want to see the boys, but quite how they were going to manage that when he lived in student digs two hundred and fifty miles away she had no idea. 'Sorry, I was thinking about Steve,' she said without thinking.

'Right, okay. Well, I leave you to it.' Posture as stiff as his words, Tristan rose and marched from the room before she had chance to call him back and explain her offhand comment.

As the door clicked shut behind him, regret sparked into anger. Why should she feel the need to apologise to Tristan for the mere mention of her ex's name? How on earth did he think they might have any kind of future together if he bristled anytime she spoke about Steve. Did he expect her to pretend the past six years hadn't happened? That her children were some fatherless miracle visited upon her from up on high? Besides, he had no right to behave like this; it wasn't as if she'd made any promises in return.

The unfairness of that popped the little bubble of anger. She'd made no promises, sure, but she also hadn't set him straight. Every day that passed without her being honest with him and telling him there was no chance of a future between them, she was stoking his hopes. She would have to set him straight – and the sooner the better. Whatever lingering crush she might have on him were the foolish dreams of a naïve girl. Life wasn't fairy tales and happy ever afters, and for her to even contemplate starting a new relationship when she was still hurting from the failure of her marriage was beyond stupid. 'Out of the frying pan, into the fire', or so the saying went. No thanks. 'Once bitten, twice shy' needed to be her motto for the foreseeable future. And Tristan wasn't the only one she needed to be straight with. She needed to sort out with Steve when and how he was going to see the boys, and also make sure her parents were aware she wouldn't be around for Christmas.

Standing to place Isaac back in his playpen, she winced at the thought of her mother's reaction. If Jess thought things were frosty between the two of them now, she needed to brace for the arctic conditions to come.

The matter of access came to a head a lot sooner than she'd anticipated when she wandered into the boys' bedroom later that evening as their scheduled Skype chat with their father was winding up. 'Say good night to Daddy, Eli. It's almost your bedtime.' She busied herself with folding and putting away the clean laundry in the washing basket Mrs W had brought up earlier as Elijah and Steve exchanged silly kissing noises and said good night to each other. Isaac had already crashed out and she paused to slide his sleep-heavy body under the quilt and settle his head on the pillow.

As she reached for the tablet to turn it off, Steve surprised her by saying. 'Hey, Jess? Can we have a quick chat?'

Other than a hello and goodbye when he spoke to the children, most of their current communication was via quick emails, confirming convenient times for him to Skype, sorting out the last of the bills which had come through from the old house, that kind of thing. They kept it short and brisk, polite but careful to avoid slipping into the old patterns of conversation which had been second nature during their marriage. 'Okay,' she said, after a moment. 'Can I call you back once I've got them down?'

'Of course, speak soon.'

It didn't take long to get Elijah into bed, and she gave a little prayer of thanks to the technology gods as she found a story for him to listen to quietly on the tablet and turned off all the lights apart from the little night light that cast stars onto the ceiling. She took a few more minutes to make herself a cup of tea, then curled up in the armchair in her sitting room and clicked the Skype app on her phone.

'Everything all right?' She asked by way of greeting as Steve's image filled the screen. He looked tired from what she could see of his face in the dim light cast by the lamp on his desk.

'Busy. And my brain hurts. I don't remember university being this tough the first time around.'

'That's because you spent most of it getting pissed in the student bar,' she said, with a smile.

'Yeah.' He scrubbed a hand over his already messy hair. 'God, how did we cope burning the candle at both ends like that and still make it to lectures?'

'Not all of us were party animals.' Jess had spent her first year too worried about failing to go to more than the odd party and found herself hiding in the corner of the few she did attend. Everyone had seemed so much more confident than her, so full of certainty about everything from their career ambitions to their politics while she'd still felt like an unmoulded lump of clay.

She'd finally begun to get into the swing of uni life in her second year when, Marcus had been admitted to hospital for the first time, so out of his head on drugs and drink he'd been close to a fatal overdose. As she'd raced down the motorway in her little second-hand Fiesta, she hadn't realised it would be the first of many such desperate dashes home. Any taste for a party lifestyle had been shocked out of her at the sight of him strapped to a gurney, her white-faced parents perched on a pair of uncomfortable plastic chairs beside his bed.

'By the time I make it through the required reading, all I'm fit for is a cup of tea and my bed.' Steve's rueful grin chased away the ghosts of the past and she managed a little chuckle.

'Poor old man. Now what did you want to talk to me about?'

Slumping back in his chair, Steve reached for a can of Diet Coke and took a long mouthful. 'My mum's been on at me about when she can see the kids.'

'Ah.'

'Yeah. She's been talking to your mum and they've clearly been winding each other up. You know what they get like.'

She did, indeed. Friends since they'd been at primary school, the two women saw each other almost every day, and spoke on the phone on the rare days they didn't. The move by both sets of parents to the same small village in Somerset had been their idea, and they'd often said they felt more like sisters than best friends. Jess and Steve had grown up enduring endless comments about how it was ideal they'd had a boy and a girl so their children could get married one day. When that prediction had come to pass, their mothers had been ecstatic, neither woman capable of comprehending that Jess and Steve had been running away from them rather than towards each other. They thought it was some kind of master plan, a love story written in the stars, and other such nonsense. Jess got the impression from Steve that his mother wasn't any nearer to accepting the finality of their split any more than her mum was. Both were in for a serious disappointment.

Filled with trepidation about where the conversation was leading, she took a careful sip of her tea. 'Dare I ask?'

'They've got it into their heads that the eight of us should spend half-term together at Centre Parcs.'

'*What?*' Jess bolted up in her chair, spilling tea on her lap and almost knocking her phone off the arm rest. Yanking a tissue from a box on the table, she blotted the tea stain on her leggings. 'Please tell me you're kidding, that's the week after next.'

'Hey now, don't shoot the messenger,' Steve said, holding up his hands, palms facing the screen. 'I'm not exactly thrilled about the idea. I've got a massive project due in the first week of the new term, but they seem dead set on it. Mum sent me a load of links about the one at Sherwood Forest which looks to be about an hour and half from you.' He paused, then pulled a face. 'They've already booked and paid for a four-bedroom luxury lodge.'

'Without speaking to either of us first? Christ, they are

113

unbelievable!' Even as she said it, she knew it was all too believable. Once they got something into their heads, Wendy Wilson and Isla Ripley were an unstoppable force. The fact neither of their husbands ever showed much inclination to thwart their plans only added fuel to their fire. 'How come this is the first I'm hearing about it?'

'I guess I'm the advance party, and Wendy will be on the phone to you in the morning.' Steve raised his eyes to the ceiling. 'Parents, who'd bloody have them?'

Hold on a minute. 'Advance party? Don't tell me you're going along with this madcap scheme of theirs.'

'Well, it would be nice to spend some time with the boys, even if the timing isn't brilliant' Steve admitted. 'I really miss them.'

Jess closed her eyes. They really missed him too, for all they got to chat to him, it didn't make up for physical contact. Oh, bloody hell, she was going to have to go along with it too, wasn't she? 'I've got so much work to do, I can't come for a whole week.' She hugged her knees close to her chest and propped her chin on them, feeling suddenly chilly. 'And we can't play happy families and pretend nothing's changed, no matter how much either one of them might wish us to.'

'I know,' Steve agreed. 'I was thinking we could find a way to divide the week between us. If you could spare a day at the beginning and the end of the week to bring the boys down and back again, then I'll do the rest. I'll fit in my study around their bedtime, and I'm sure the olds won't mind if I shut myself away for a few hours during the afternoons. If you want to stay over either night, I'll sleep on the sofa.'

'You know they're going to get on our backs about giving things another go.' She buried her face in her knees, already picturing her mum and Isla on the wrong side of a bottle of wine and holding forth on the difficulties of marriage, telling her she needed to try a bit harder.

'Jess.' Steve rapped a knuckle on the screen to capture her

attention. 'Jess, look at me.' When she lifted her eyes, he was sitting forward, his face filling almost the entire screen. 'No matter how much I miss the boys, and God knows, I do, I haven't had any second thoughts about this.'

'Me either.' A guilty flush stole up her throat, and she was glad of the shield her knees provided to conceal it. She hadn't given getting back with Steve any thought, because she'd been too preoccupied with the possibility of being with Tristan at some point in the future. 'I'm happy here, and so are the kids.'

'I'm glad. You look better than you have in ages.'

'Thanks. I was just thinking how tired you looked!' They laughed, and she realised she'd missed this part of them. The thing they had always been and should've remained – friends. 'Send me through the dates and I'll square away a couple of days off. At least it will give the boys something to look forward to. And while you are at it, have a think about what you want to do over Christmas. I'll be flat out here, so you need to decide if you want the boys for part of the holidays, and how you're going to manage it. I'd like to present a united front when we see our parents before they get any more ideas.'

Finding a good time to broach the topic of having time off was taken out of her hands at breakfast the next morning when an over-excited Elijah announced to everyone he was going swimming in the park with Mummy and Daddy. Wishing she'd waited until she'd spoken to Arthur and Tristan first, Jess hastily explained the whole family was getting together for half-term. She kept it succinct, the breakfast table not being an appropriate place to discuss awkward sleeping arrangements and interfering parents. 'It will be a couple of days, not the whole week.'

Arthur smiled at her over Elijah's head. 'Not a problem with me. We deliberately made your hours flexible to cover stuff like this. Besides, you're entitled to time off, isn't that right, Tristan?'

'Of course.' For all their similarity in looks, his smile was a bland mask compared to Arthur's open countenance. 'Jess has autonomy to manage her workload.' He cast a cursory glance at the watch on his wrist then folded the napkin from his lap and placed it on the table. 'Speaking of which, the lighting guy will be here soon, and I need to do a few bits of final prep. If you'll excuse me?' From the glances exchanged around the table, Jess wasn't the only one who'd noticed the stiffness in his posture. Cheeks flaming, she made a fuss of wiping Isaac's messy hands and face and knew she'd have to bite the bullet and talk to him soon. Only, how on earth was she going to find a way to let him down without making her position at the castle impossible?

Chapter 10

Tristan had been in a shit mood for ten days. The fact it was a situation entirely of his own making didn't make it any easier to shake off. It was his own damn fault, for speaking up in the first place. If he could turn back the clock and take back that embarrassing declaration, he'd do it in a heartbeat. He'd jumped the gun and shot himself in the foot in the process. If only he'd been patient, the way he'd intended to be then there might have been a possibility of something developing naturally between him and Jess, the way they had in his siblings' relationships. Only Tristan couldn't keep his big mouth shut, and now Jess was running scared. Perhaps even running back into the arms of her ex. They must be reconsidering things if they were holidaying together so soon after splitting up. He swished the stick he'd picked up off the ground at a pile of leaves one of the gardening staff had painstakingly raked up, sending them scattering into the wind like the tatters of his hopes and dreams.

'I knew you couldn't be trusted to look after my gardens.' Turning at the sound of his sister's familiar voice, Tristan found his temper easing at the sight of Iggy and Will striding hand in hand towards him.

'Hey, what are you doing here?' He opened his arms to a hug from Iggy, then exchanged a warm handshake with Will.

'Spot inspection,' Iggy said. 'And none too soon by the looks of it. I hope you haven't made a complete hash of everything in my absence.'

If only she knew. 'Your plans have been followed to the letter, your majesty, don't worry. I've also signed off on the design for the lighting plan for the woods, it's in my office if you want to check it out?'

'Maybe later, after hours being cooped up in the truck, I need some fresh air.' Come to think of it, she did look a bit pale.

'Everything all right?' He glanced from Iggy's white face to a frowning Will. 'What's going on?'

'Everything's perfect thanks to Will Talbot and his super sperm,' Iggy grumbled, rubbing a hand over her belly.

'You were the one who said you wanted to try for a baby,' Will said in the exasperated tones of a man who'd made the same point on more than one occasion.

'*Try*, I said.' Iggy snuggled into Will's side, her arms curling around his waist. 'Trust you to be an overachiever and manage to knock me up at the first attempt.'

Hugging her close, Will pressed a kiss to the top of head. 'What can I tell you? I'm that good.'

'Arrogant pig.'

'Grumpy mare.'

Tristan watched the interaction play out between them with some bemusement. 'Is this the point where I'm allowed to say congratulations?'

Loosening her hold on Will, Iggy stepped once more into Tristan's arms for a hug. 'I'm scared,' she whispered. 'Happy, but absolutely terrified, and if you tell anyone I said that, I'll pull the heads off all your action men.'

'Your secret's safe with me, sis,' Tristan promised, smiling in amusement at the memory of when Iggy had done just that. It hadn't been funny at the time, especially as she'd swapped them all with heads off her own collection of Barbies and refused to tell him what she'd done with the originals. 'What did you do with those heads, by the way?'

'I buried them out in the woods,' she confessed with an unrepentant grin.

'You always did have an evil streak.' Slinging a free arm around Will's shoulders, he turned them back towards the house. 'Come on, lets break the news to the rest of the family, and wet the baby's head.'

'I don't think you're supposed to do that until it's actually born, which won't be until next summer,' Will pointed out. 'Besides which, your sister has made me promise to go dry until then.'

'I just want you to share in as many of the delights of this pregnancy as possible, my love.' Iggy cackled.

Tristan laughed, then gave Will a sympathetic pat on the shoulder. 'Evil streak, what did I tell you?'

The unexpected arrival of his sister, and the good news she and Will brought with them did wonders to lift Tristan's bad mood. Sulking about his own romantic misfortunes seemed churlish in the face of their radiant happiness. And for all of Iggy's grumpiness, he could tell she was delighted with the prospect of expanding the family she and Will were building together. The only awkward moment was when their great aunt queried over when they'd be getting married.

'We're not,' Iggy said, taking Will's hand as they sat together on one of the sofas in the family room. 'Don't give me that look, either, Morgana. What if we get married and our first child is a girl? I know there's a lot of what-ifs between here and there, but if neither Arthur nor Tristan have an heir, then I won't put my children in the same position I faced because of some stupid, archaic law.'

'You'd let the title die out, then? After four hundred years of an unbroken line? Preposterous!' Morgana sniffed.

'Umm, I think everyone is getting ahead of themselves, here. I can't speak for Tristan's plans for the future, but when the time is right, Lucie and I intend to start a family.' Arthur intervened. 'Whether Iggy and Will choose to marry or not, is a matter for them and no one else.'

'Hear, hear.' Tristan well remembered the hurt and confusion it had caused all three of them when their father had tried to explain why Arthur would be his heir and not Iggy when she'd been the first one of them born. It made no odds to Tristan either way as he'd been the runt of their little litter, but it had affected Iggy deeply – more deeply than even he'd realised until now.

Leaving her place beside Will, Iggy knelt beside their great-aunt's chair. 'Please, Morgana, I don't want to fall out with you.'

'Oh, child.' Leaning forward, Morgana cupped her cheek. 'You always did like to forge your own path. I've only ever wanted what's best for this family, and I suppose I'm just old and set in my ways. Whatever misgivings I might have about your choice, you'll hear no more about them, and I look forward to meeting my first great-great niece or nephew.'

'Thank you.' Iggy wasn't the only one feeling a little teary, and Tristan couldn't even blame it on his hormones. God, he was blessed to have such an amazing family. Heart full, he glanced across the room to where Jess had been sitting a moment ago, but her seat was empty.

Making his way out into the great hall, he saw her heading up the stairs. 'Jess?'

She stopped, and turned, but remained where she was about halfway up. 'I was just going to check on Isaac. If I'd known your sister had such personal news to share, I would've made myself scarce earlier. I didn't mean to intrude.'

'No one thought you were intruding, not for one minute.' He walked to the foot of the staircase, wanting to go to her, to apologise for his bad mood and to find a way of bridging the gap he'd created between them.

She shrugged. 'Well, anyway, I need to start sorting things out ready for Monday. The forecast for next week looks so changeable, I'm going to have to pack for all four seasons.'

The reminder of where she was going next week, and who'd she be spending time with stung, but Tristan refused to give in to another bout of the sulks over it. It was past time he pulled himself together. 'I'm sure you'll have a great time, and the boys must be excited about seeing their dad.'

'They are. As for having a great time, I'm not holding out much hope.'

'But I thought . . .' Tristan cut himself off, what he thought was neither here nor there. It was Jess's personal business.

She wasn't going to let him off that easily, though. Climbing down until she was just a few steps above him, Jess stared down at him. 'You thought what?' Her voice was soft.

'That you and Steve might be thinking about reconciling,' he admitted. 'That perhaps that was the reason you haven't said anything to me about . . . you know.'

'Oh, Tristan.' She took one more step down until they stood eye to eye. 'Steve and I aren't getting back together, no matter how much our families might try and throw us together. Next week is a stupid ploy by our mothers to do exactly that, but it isn't what either of us want.'

Guilt sliced him like a razor. He'd been pouting around the place feeling sorry for himself while she'd been dealing with all this on her own. 'I'm sorry they're giving you a hard time.' He took a deep breath, then ploughed on. 'And I'm sorry that I put you on the spot the way I did. It was stupid and selfish of me, and I wish you would just forget all about it.' Jess tugged at her lower lip with her teeth, eyes looking anywhere else other than at his and he cursed himself for embarrassing her once more. 'I'll leave you to it. Go and get your packing sorted out. If I can do anything for you – walk down and collect Elijah, or whatever, you only have to ask.'

He turned to walk away, knowing he had to do what he'd asked of her and forget about it, too.

'Tristan.' She sounded further away, and when he glanced over his shoulder it was to see she was almost at the top of the stairs. She took another step away from him, as though she regretted calling out, before reaching out to grip the bannister. Time stretched to an almost unbearable tension as they stared at each other, neither one seeming able to move. 'There is one thing you can do for me,' she said, at last.

He returned to his spot at the foot of the stairs. 'Name it.'

'Wait for me.'

Before his stunned brain could form a response, she spun on her heel and fled up the rest of the stairs to disappear around the corner. He took three steps after her, before pulling himself up short. He'd almost blown it once – twice if you included the way he'd handled things all those years ago. *Wait*. That's what he'd promised her, and that's what she'd asked.

Fair enough, he could do that.

Chapter 11

Jess checked her watch. They'd been at Centre Parcs for six hours and thirty-seven minutes, and it was as awful as she'd anticipated it would be – and more so. From the moment she'd pulled up outside the lodge and her door had been yanked from her grasp by her mother, it had been an endless litany of comments such as, 'Isn't this lovely, all of us together again?' and 'Steve was just saying how much he'd missed you all.' Wendy Wilson had all the subtly of a brick, and Isla wasn't much better.

She'd tried appealing to her dad when he'd taken her keys and said he'd move the car out to one of the perimeter car parks as soon as it was unpacked. 'Please,' she'd begged, following along the little path. 'Tell her she needs to stop this.'

'I'm sorry, flower,' her dad, said, giving her a hug. 'You know how she is. She's never been very good at facing reality if it doesn't suit her.'

They'd both fallen silent, then, remembering how she'd failed to recognise the seriousness of Marcus's addiction, choosing to believe him when he told her he was fine, turning a blind eye to the money that went missing from her purse, until it had been too late. 'She's going to have to get used to it,' Jess said, when they finally broke their embrace. 'And fast.'

Her father touched her cheek. 'All right, love. I'll speak to her.'

By the time she went back inside, Wendy and Isla had been through the case she'd brought with the boys' things in it and were stripping the boys down to change them into their swimming things, and Jess hadn't had much choice other than to go along with their plan to take the boys to the huge glass dome housing an array of swimming pools, and water slides for the bigger children. The dome amplified the noise of dozens of other family groups chatting, laughing and in some cases, arguing. Everywhere children shrieked and splashed and screamed until Jess's head pounded and she felt a bit like screaming herself.

When they'd finally worn the boys out, they'd trooped back to the lodge for the next enforced bit of family jollity – a barbeque. Steve had managed to escape to his room to study, and Jess had taken her time over unpacking the boys' things as they napped for an hour, the pair of them exhausted from too much excitement. Finally, running out of excuses, Jess had returned to the main living area to find hers and Steve's dads out on the patio having a beer while Wendy and Isla prepped the meat and salads in the kitchen. 'Anything I can do to help?'

'You can tell that husband of yours to get his nose out a book, for a start,' Isla said, pointing the bread knife she'd been using to cut up a crusty loaf.

God, give her strength. 'If you want *your* son to do something, I suggest *you* go and speak to him yourself.' When Wendy and Isla exchanged a look, Jess finally lost it. 'Enough!' she snapped in a tone she'd never used with her mother in all her twenty-nine years. 'Unless you want me to wake the boys and pack them straight off back home with me, you'll both stop this ridiculous pretence that everything is fine.'

'What's going on?' Steve poked his head out of the nearby bedroom. 'Jess?'

Frustrated to the point of tears, she swiped her arm across her face, getting angrier by the moment that she'd let them push

124

her buttons like this. 'I told you this was a bad idea, I told you what they'd be like.'

Coming to stand beside her, Steve folded his arms and faced the women across the kitchen. 'Jess and I have made a decision in the best interest of our family.' When Isla opened her mouth, he held up his hand. 'It's not up for debate. Now, you can either accept it and choose to have an enjoyable week with your grand-children, or I'll be helping Jess to pack her car.'

'Every couple has their ups and downs.' Jess might have known better than to believe her mum would let it go. 'You just need to give it time.'

'No, Mum.'

'No, we don't.' Steve agreed. 'Come on, I'll help you with the boys.' He walked away towards the bedroom where she'd left them napping.

'Are you really going to do this?' Jess stared from her mother, to Isla, and back again. 'Are you really going to make us deprive Elijah and Isaac of the chance to spend time with you, because you're not getting your own way?'

The glass patio door slid open behind them. 'What's going on?' It was her dad, a couple of empty beer bottles laced between his fingers. 'Wendy? I thought we talked about this . . .'

Jess didn't respond, keeping her attention glued to her mother. Her stomach churned, and she could feel herself shaking a little from the adrenaline surging in her veins. She'd never stood up to her mum before, and even knowing she was in the right, the little girl inside who'd only ever wanted to please hated it. As she watched the tears forming in her mother's eyes it was all she could do to stand her ground and not rush over to comfort her. If she gave in to those tears now, she'd never have proper control of her life. 'What's it going to be, Mum?'

'All right.' Taking a tissue from her pocket, Wendy Wilson dabbed at her eyes, though there weren't enough tears to spill over, never mind spoil her make-up. Putting on a bright smile, she turned to her husband. 'The meat's all prepped, so if you and Greg want to fire up the barbeque, I'll bring it out in a moment.' Jess watched incredulous for a moment as her mum went back to chopping a head of lettuce.

'Here you go, Alan.' Isla handed Jess's dad three bottles of beer. 'Take one for Steve, he's just gone to wake the boys.'

He accepted the bottles, glanced at Jess who couldn't do more than shrug at the question in his eyes. It was like someone had pressed a reset button and the past few hours hadn't occurred. 'If everything's all right here, I'll give Steve a hand with the boys.'

'Lovely,' her mum said. 'When you've done that, we just need to put the salads back in the fridge and we can open a bottle of wine. She glanced at her husband. 'If you light that patio heater, we can probably all sit outside.'

It wasn't the most comfortable evening she'd ever spent, Jess thought, but at least her mum and Isla seemed to have got the message. They didn't say anything when she and Steve chose seats at opposite ends of the outdoor table, choosing to focus instead on the big binder full of activities available within the park and debating which ones would be suitable for Elijah. Jess mostly kept quiet, leaving it to Steve to decide what they should do as he would be the one looking after the boys once she left in the morning. When it came to bedtime, she stayed in the kitchen to do the washing up, listening to the familiar murmur of Steve's voice as he read a story to Elijah. She was just putting the last glass away in the cupboard when he came and joined her. Opening the fridge, he pulled out a bottle of beer. 'There's a bit more wine left if you want some?'

She shook her head, moving to switch on the kettle. 'I have to drive in the morning, I'll have a cup of tea. Do you want to see if the olds are ready for a hot drink?'

'In a minute. There's something I need to tell you.'

Pausing in the act of getting a mug, she glanced over her shoulder. 'What's up?'

126

'I think I might have met someone.'

Oh. Jess paused for a moment to check how she felt, and was relieved to find it didn't bother her in the slightest. It would've been hypocritical of her if she had, considering what she'd blurted out to Tristan the other afternoon. But this was the first time she'd had to think about the possibility of Steve being with someone else. Setting down the mug, she turned her back to the kettle and rested against the counter. 'Only *think* you might have?'

He shrugged, cheeks colouring a little. 'Jesus, this is seriously awkward.'

She giggled. 'It really is, but I'm here if you want to talk to me about it. About her.'

Steve swigged at his bottle. 'She's a geologist, a research assistant. Her department's in the same building as mine. We've had coffee a couple of times, that's all.'

'But you think that might not be all?'

'Maybe? Is that all right with you? Even though its over between us, I didn't want you to think I went rushing out to meet the first woman I could.' He scrubbed at his hair the way he always did when he was feeling tired or uncomfortable. 'We got talking one morning, and . . .' he shrugged. 'She's nice.'

She wondered how long it would take his geologist to learn all his little tells, those secret things only couples knew about each other. How long it might take her to learn all those things about another man, the one she'd told to wait for her even as uncertainty racked her over whether she should've done. 'Thank you for telling me.'

He cast a quick glance at her from under his lashes. 'You don't mind.'

'I don't want to go on a double-date with the pair of you,' she said with a laugh. 'But, yes, of course, it's all right.' She sighed. 'I just wish the government would get on and pass that legislation they promised.' There'd been an announcement earlier in the year that the government planned to introduce a form of no-fault divorce to make it easier for couples like them who didn't fit into any of the archaic strictures of the current law.

'It would make it clear to everyone we're serious about this,' Steve agreed. He took another mouthful of beer, his expression telling her he had something else on his mind. 'What about you, Jess? Do you think you might have met someone? Elijah's got a serious case of hero worship for this Tristan guy. You've known each other for a long time now . . .'

'I don't . . . we're not . . . it's not that easy.' She couldn't give him a straight answer, because she didn't know herself. Yes, she told Tristan to wait for her, but she still wasn't sure when she'd be ready to explore things with him – or if she ever would. It had been a long time since she'd been with Steve, not since before Isaac was born, and she'd got used to going without those intimacies. Her body wasn't what it had been, not that she was embarrassed by the scars and stretch marks carrying and birthing two healthy babies had left behind, but it was one thing to be comfortable with them herself, and an entirely different one letting someone else see them. It seemed crazy at twenty-nine to be able to write herself off the market when it came to sex, but she felt like the past couple of years had settled over her like ancient tree sap oozing and trapping a fly. She hadn't quite ossified into amber, but there was a temptation to allow it. To ignore herself and focus on giving the boys a healthy, happy life.

'That's the thing about living your best life, Jess. I don't think it's meant to be easy.' Putting down his beer, Steve closed the space between them, brushed a kiss on her cheek then walked off in the direction of the boys' bedroom. It wasn't a romantic kiss in any way, more an acknowledgement of their past.

And though they'd said it a hundred times before, it felt like their final goodbye.

Chapter 12

Jess hadn't said much when she'd returned from dropping the children off for half-term, and even less when she went to pick them up. Though it had killed Tristan to give her space, he'd thrown himself into his work, the word 'wait' echoing around his head until he was sure he was muttering it to himself in his sleep. They'd had several questionnaires back from the guests who'd booked for the house party, so he'd forwarded them to Jess to deal with and focused on the final preparations for the winter festival. With Iggy feeling a bit delicate in the early stages of her pregnancy, and things slowing down with Will's gardening business for the year, they'd decided to extend their visit home, and Tristan was taking full advantage of them.

Will had happily taken over supervision of the installation of the lights display in the woods, happy to get out from under Iggy's feet, Tristan suspected, because she wasn't one of those women who embraced being pregnant like a glowing, beatific Madonna. Always a bit spiky, she'd morphed into a hormonal timebomb and there was no accounting for what might light her fuse. Deciding to sacrifice himself for the well-being of the rest of the family, Tristan roped her into helping him with the festival. Many of the vendors they'd attracted for the summer fete were already booked to come back, and as Iggy knew them already, they were delighted to have her as a point of contact. When she got too irritated at being cooped up, or started to look a bit green, Tristan took her out to the showground area and they walked the plot endlessly, planning and re-planning the layout of the various stalls as people dropped out, and latecomers came on board.

'Are you sure about not having a Santa's grotto?' She asked, as he scribbled a couple of notes on the latest version of their plan. 'Won't people be expecting it?'

'That's why I'm marketing it as a winter festival, rather than calling it anything connected to Christmas. I looked into it, but it would cost a fortune to build a really decent one, and then there's all the health and safety hassles around what you can and can't give as presents.'

'Have you spoken to the wildlife park over at Skelton? I'm sure they've got some reindeer there. They might be willing to bring a couple over and do an educational thing for the kids in return for a free advertising display.'

It was certainly an option to investigate. 'I'll give them a call.'

'See, you're useless without your big sister around to help you out.' Iggy stretched her arms over her head, jaw cracking in a huge yawn. 'God, I'm so tired all the time. If I'm like this now, what will I be like when I'm the size of a whale and waddling about the place?'

Tristan laughed at the ridiculous image. His sister had always been fit and active, and he couldn't imagine that changing much even when she inevitably gained the extra weight that came with having a baby. 'Why don't you go and have a nap? It does the world of good for Isaac when he's feeling grumpy.'

'I'm not grumpy.' She swatted at him, a blow he easily ducked.

'Of course, you're not. It's lucky for all of us that God gifted you with such a sunny personality.'

Iggy stuck out her tongue. 'I'm the best sister in the world, and you love me.'

'I love you even more when you're asleep.' Tristan hooked his arm through hers. 'Come on, enough work for one day.'

'Okay.' She rested her head against his shoulder for a moment. 'I know I'm being unbearable, thank you for trying to distract me. Poor Will, it'll be a miracle if he doesn't leave me.'

'He tried that once before, remember? Face it, Iggle-Piggle, the bloke's madly in love with you, and the bean.'

She grinned up at him. 'He is, isn't he?'

Dinner that evening was a quiet affair. Iggy hadn't felt like coming down so she and Will had stayed in their room with a tray. Mrs W popped into the family room just before they were due to go into the dining room to say Elijah had a temperature and a sore throat, so Jess would keep him up in the nursery in case he was contagious. As soon as he'd finished eating, Tristan excused himself to head back to his office and finish updating the changes he and Iggy had made that day to the layout for the festival. He'd made that call to the wildlife park, and they'd promised to get back to him in a few days to confirm one way or the other whether the reindeer idea was a goer. He marked off a corner of the showground for it just in case. There was plenty of parkland beyond, so if the animals became restless, or unsettled they could set up a temporary pen out of the way where the reindeer could be transferred if necessary. If it didn't come off, it would be easy enough to spread out a couple of stands to cover the gap.

With the plan completed, he would be ready in the morning to begin allocating the plots to specific vendors. He had a list of requests from those who'd been at the summer fete so would do his best to accommodate those where possible. Checking his watch, he was surprised to find it was almost ten-thirty. Definitely time to call it a day. He entered the great hall to see Jess coming down the stairs with a bundle of sheets under her arm. 'I heard about Elijah, how is he?'

Jess wrinkled her nose. 'A bit better. He was sick earlier, poor

131

thing, but he managed to fall asleep and he's been down for the past hour. I'm just going to put these in the wash.' She scrunched the sheets into a tighter ball.

'I'll walk with you. I'm heading to the kitchen to rustle up a hot drink.' They cut through the empty family room and entered the backstairs area via the servant's door. As he held the door to let her through, Tristan found himself yawning. 'Sorry. I got caught up in work after dinner and didn't realise how late it was until just now. I should've probably headed straight for bed, but I can never seem to settle without a cup of tea.'

'A cup of tea sounds like my idea of heaven,' Jess said with a tired sigh as they drew level with the laundry room.

He held that door open for her, too. 'I'll make a pot. Come and find me in the kitchen when you're ready.'

The kitchen blind had been left up, and Tristan found himself staring out at the blanket of stairs across the velvet night sky. Nights like this were what made him want to stay in Derbyshire. Crisp and clear, without the ever-present orange glow from light pollution. On a whim, he dug around in the cupboards until he uncovered a thermal flask. The tea was steeping in the pot when Jess came to stand beside him so she could wash her hands at the sink. 'I'll pop down in the morning and run the sheets through the dryer. They won't do any harm being left in the machine overnight.' Having dried her hands, she pressed them into the small of her back and stretched. 'I'm more than ready for that tea.'

'It's ready. I'll pour you a mug, or . . .' He held up the flask to show her. 'I can put enough in here for two and you can join me for a walk. I could do with a bit of fresh air before bed.'

'I can't really leave the boys . . .' He could tell from the way she nibbled at her bottom lip she was sorely tempted, though.

'We can stick to the immediate area around the castle. You've got that monitoring system hooked up to your phone, haven't you?'

She nodded. 'That's true.' She pulled her phone out of her

pocket and checked the screen. 'It all seems pretty quiet, so go on then.'

A couple of minutes later, they were wrapped up in coats and a couple of scarves they'd appropriated from the tangle of accessories in the boot room. The heavy front door creaked as Tristan swung it open, tempting a couple of the dogs away from the fireplace to investigate. And so they found themselves at the head of a small furry contingent as they crunched across the gravel of the driveway. The moon hung low and full just above the treeline, its light enough to guide their feet to the edge of the grass. Tristan had stuck a torch in his pocket which he flicked on to show Jess the path he wanted to take. 'Mind the step here.' He held out his hand to guide her over the low rise.

When he would've let go, she kept hold of his hand, her fingers threading though his until they rested palm to palm. He tried not to let his delight show, choosing instead to raise the beam of the torch to show her a wide expanse of hedge up ahead. 'If we stand behind that, it should block most of the light coming from the castle and give you the best view of the stars.'

Jess tilted her head back to stare overhead. 'It's already incredible. I can't believe how clear it is here.'

'Big skies. That's what my dad always used to say.' He wasn't interested in the view overhead because he was enjoying watching Jess as she craned her neck further back. The messy bun she'd secured her hair in caught in her collar, and he used his free hand to lift it out of the way. The scrunchy came loose sending a waterfall of hair spilling almost halfway down her back. 'Sorry.' Tristan untangled his hand to sheepishly offer her the fabric-covered ring of elastic.

Laughing she held up her hands, one still enmeshed with his, the other carrying the tea flask. 'Don't worry about it. It feels good to have it down when it's been up all day.'

Shoving the scrunchy in his coat pocket, he led Jess along the path until he could show her the gap in the hedge which

133

wouldn't have been visible until they were almost on top of it, even in broad daylight. 'I thought it was solid all the way along.' Jess sounded surprised when he waved the torch in a slow arc to reveal the hidden section of the garden.

'Whoever originally designed the formal gardens had a sense of fun, I think, because there are lots of little quirks like this.' He tugged her over to where a pair of benches bracketed a miniature spring. Though it looked as though the water bubbled from a natural fissure in the moss-covered rocks, he knew from the extensive repair works Iggy had overseen that it was an entirely man-made structure. A tiny folly created to delight the senses. Leaning down, he tested the wooden planks on one of the seats with the back of his hand. 'A bit chilly, perhaps, but I don't think it's damp if you want to sit for a bit.'

Sitting involved surrendering his hold on her hand, but she sat close enough for their bodies to touch from hip to thigh so he found he didn't mind the loss of her warm fingers too much. The dark enveloped them, the air still and silent apart from the gentle burble of the spring and the odd sniffle or whine from the dogs who'd wandered off to explore.

'Gosh, it really is dark away from the castle lights,' she murmured, as though not wanting to break the night's spell. 'Have you got the torch handy?'

While he held the torch so she could see, Jess removed the cup which acted as a lid, unscrewed the seal of the flask and poured a steaming mug of tea. Tristan propped the torch between their thighs, casting enough light for them to share the tea without ruining their night vision. When they'd finished, he shook out the dregs on the grass, resealed the flask and set it on the floor at his feet. He clicked off the torch once more, and the darkness swallowed them in its midnight embrace.

He felt Jess shifting against him in the dark, the brush of her shoulder, a whisper of her soft hair against his cheek as she twisted and turned her head to study the stars. 'It's beautiful,' she whispered. 'I just wish it didn't make my neck ache looking back all the time.'

'Hold on.' Tristan shuffled to his left until he was seated in the far corner of the bench then patted his lap. 'Why don't you lie down, so you've got a better view.'

She was silent for a long moment. 'Perhaps we should go back in.'

Realising he'd spooked her, Tristan fumbled for the torch and switched it back on. 'Jess. You've asked me to wait for you, and that's exactly what I'm going to do. Any steps we may or may not take forwards in our relationship lie entirely in your hands. I just thought you'd be more comfortable.'

'Sorry. I'm overreacting, aren't I? It's just . . .' she trailed off into silence.

Just what? Tristan bit his lip, keeping the frustrated question to himself. This waiting business was damn hard. With a soft sigh, Jess shifted around on the bench until her head rested on one of his thighs. She lifted it almost immediately and a soft warmth covered his other thigh where she'd pulled her hair out from under her and draped it over his leg. She settled once more. 'Oh, that's much better'

She'd get no arguments from him on that score. Having flicked off the torch once more, Tristan hooked his arms along the top of the bench, rested his head back and stared up at the incredible display overhead. He'd known the names of the constellations once upon a time, but now, though he recognised a few of the clusters beyond the universally known Ursa Major and Minor – the saucepans as Iggy had called them when they were little – and Orion and his famous belt, the names of the others escaped him for the moment. They'd had a book when they were kids, perhaps he could dig it out and see if Jess wanted it for Elijah.

He was about to mention it when Jess spoke. 'Do you remember New Year's Eve?'

Was she kidding? The image of her laughing up at him as he

135

twirled her on the dance floor had been permanently imprinted into his mind. 'Hard to forget when you ran out on me, Cinderella.'

'I did not!' Her outraged little huff made him grin into the dark.

'Hard for a chap to take it any other way when he declares his affections to a woman he's adored for months and she vanishes into thin air.'

'Adored,' she scoffed, softly. 'You do exaggerate.'

'Adored,' he countered, firmly. 'From the moment you peered over the rims of those glasses of yours, I was hooked. And it wasn't just that you were the prettiest thing I'd seen in a long time, you were hellishly smart to boot.' A thought suddenly occurred to him. 'What happened to your glasses, by the way, I never see you wearing them.' More's the pity. Sexy and smart was a deadly combination, and he'd always found her both.

'My parents gifted me with laser corrective surgery for my birthday a couple of years ago.' Her head shifted in his lap, and though he couldn't see a thing in the pitch black, he got the impression she was staring up at him. 'I didn't leave the party just because of you, but you were part of the reason.'

The guilt over ruining her evening stung even after all this time. 'I didn't mean to overstep. I didn't realise at the time you had a boyfriend.'

'What? Oh, you mean, Steve? I wasn't seeing him; we were just friends. I just didn't know how to deal with you, or the likely consequences.'

Deal with him? He hadn't pushed his luck. He'd declared his intention to kiss her, sure, but he hadn't behaved in anyway inappropriately. 'What on earth are you talking about?'

'Come on, Tristan, you know what you were like back then. You had enough confidence for half a dozen men, and more than enough charm for twice that many. I was still living at home with my parents and could count the number of boyfriends I'd had on the fingers of one hand. Less than half the fingers on one hand to be exact. I had a crush on you, *oh boy*, did I have a crush on you, but I never had any expectation it would come to anything, so it was safe to fancy you, like having a book boyfriend.'

Now he was completely lost. 'What's a book boyfriend?'

'Oh, you know, when you read a book and fall a little bit in love with the hero,' she said, impatiently.'

'Can't say that's ever happened to me. Though I will admit to having a thing for Emma Watson back in the day. I suppose you could count her turn as Hermione Granger as a book girlfriend, or a film girlfriend rather, as I never got around to reading the books.'

'You fancied *Hermione Granger*?' Her incredulous laughter filled the air.

'Smart and sexy, it's my Kryptonite.' Reaching down, he stroked a hand through her long curls. 'And don't laugh at me; I bet you had a crush on Harry Potter.'

'Never. It was Ron Weasley all the way for me.' Her laughter faded. 'Anyway, you have to admit it would never have worked between us back then. I was too young, too uncertain of myself as person. I'd have let you overtake me, bent to whatever you wanted because I didn't know what I wanted for myself. You'd have soon grown bored of me.'

He liked to think better of himself than that, but he had to admit he'd been a cocky little bastard. 'And what about now?'

'Now . . . Well that's the million-dollar question. Not whether or not I can handle you, but whether or not I want to.'

'Christ.' He barked a harsh laugh. 'Am I that unappetising a prospect?'

'No! Not at all, if anything you're too damn tempting for your own good. I've hardly been able to concentrate on anything these past few weeks. None of my hesitancy now has anything to do with you, it's about me.' He felt her fingers touch his chest. 'Things between Steve and I weren't right for a long time, and I kind of switched off the parts of me that weren't either focused on the kids or on work.'

Oh.

'You're very quiet.'

'Sorry.' He ran his fingers over her hair as he tried to figure out the right response. He didn't want to be glib, to tell her it was fine, and it didn't matter because it did. He wanted everything from Jess, including an intimate physical relationship. 'I think you're beautiful, Jess. I always have.'

'But I'm not the same girl you fancied back then. My body's different for one thing; having children does that.'

'Is that what you're worried about? That I won't find you physically attractive because of a few imperfections? I'd hope you'd believe me worth more than that.'

'I'm not talking about your reaction to my body, I'm talking about my own. I want to be able to come to you confident in myself, and I'm not there yet.'

Tristan wanted to reassure her, to tell her she had nothing to worry about as far as he was concerned and then he stopped himself. This wasn't about him, she'd said, so what he thought wasn't the point. 'I appreciate you being so honest with me. And if you get to the point where you're ready to take that step with me, I will treat you with all the care and respect you deserve. For now, I'm content with this.'

'Oh, Tristan.' Her fingers brushed his and he curled his own around them. Holding her hand, feeling the weight of her head on his thigh, the softness of her hair beneath his other hand, he truly was content. There were many levels of intimacy, a hundred little steps they could take until they took the ultimate one, and each one would be special.

Because it was her. 'I still wish I'd kissed you that night,' he confessed to the dark.

'Part of me wishes you had, too, but then my life would've been too different. I wouldn't have had the boys, and . . .'

'And what?' he murmured softly, fingers stroking her hair.

'There's so much you don't know about that night, some silly, inconsequential stuff that contributed to me leaving, but also . . .' she sighed. 'My brother, Marcus, died that night.'

Jesus. He'd been pining over some missed opportunity to kiss her whilst her world had fallen apart. 'Oh, Jess, I'm so sorry, I had no idea.'

'I know.' She curled on her side on the bench, head still resting on his thigh. He lowered his hand to rub her back, trying to comfort her, and knowing it could never be enough to fill the terrible void she must carry inside. 'I didn't tell anyone at work because I was ashamed. Not about what he'd done, but because I hadn't been able to help him. He'd had an addiction problem for a while, and it wasn't the first time he OD'd . . .', her voice hitched on a breathy sob. 'But it was the last.'

'I don't know what to say.' Sorry seemed pathetic, but what else could he offer her?

'Marcus and Steve were best friends, and it broke him almost as much as it did me. If it hadn't been for him, I'm not sure how I would've got through it, and it was the same for him.'

The pieces started slotting into place. The change in personality he'd put down to her wanting to avoid him after his clumsy pass had in fact been nothing to do with him. The sudden appearance of a new boyfriend on the scene no one had heard of before and her subsequent marriage. 'That's how you ended up together.'

'Yes.' It was barely a whisper. When she spoke again, her voice was stronger; steadier. 'We needed each other, to survive, and eventually to heal. Grief drove us together, but that's no foundation for a healthy relationship, and as time passed we realised we didn't need each other anymore. I loved him, and he loved me, and I'll never regret bringing our two wonderful boys into this world, but Steve's not my happy ending.'

As he stroked her back and listened to her soft breathing, Tristan swore in his heart that when the time was right he wouldn't let her get away again. Prince Charming and Cinderella he'd called them that long-ago Christmas. And, damn it, he wasn't too old to believe in fairy tales.

139

Chapter 13

That stolen hour beneath the stars with Tristan marked a turning point in their relationship. Though the big questions remained unresolved, there was a tacit understanding of the connection between them. When they'd parted at the bottom of the stairs leading to the nursery, he'd lifted his fingers to stroke her cheek before bidding her good night. A ghost of a touch which had left things inside her shivering more than even a kiss might have done, and she went to sleep with a smile on her face and the possibility of them wrapped around her like a blanket.

She didn't have long to dwell on it when she was startled awake, what felt like five minutes after closing her eyes, by a screaming cry through the monitor on her phone. She was staggering across the playroom when Elijah came running to tell her Isaac was poorly. Dispatching Elijah with a quick hug to snuggle down in the warm patch she'd left in her bed, she spent the rest of the night trying to soothe her youngest who'd come down with the same bug which had laid Elijah low. His little body seemed to take a worse dose, and the next twenty-four hours were attritional. Eventually, Jess reached the point of wondering if she should just leave Isaac in the bath as she seemed to spend most of her time washing off the results of his latest mishap. One of the washing machines was in constant use thanks to her multiple trips downstairs with sheets, towels and pyjamas.

How could such a tiny body produce so much vomit, she wondered as she yanked off her T-shirt and chucked it into the sink alongside Isaac's latest pair of soiled pjs. 'Oh, I know, I know, my poor baby,' she crooned as she rocked the poor little mite against her shoulder.

'Mummy, Tristan's here.'

The bathroom door swung open to reveal her half-naked state not only to Elijah, who'd had to stay home from school for forty-eight hours as per their rules, but Tristan a few feet behind him at the threshold to the playroom.

'Oh! Oh, blimey I'm sorry,' he said, turning his back to her offering her a view of his shaggy hair tumbling over the collar of a perfectly crisp, clean cotton shirt.

She glanced down at the bright red lace bra she'd put on that morning because her two favourite everyday bras were lurking in the bottom of her washing basket, her own laundry needs neglected in the face of the mini disaster area in her arms. If that wasn't bad enough, she hadn't had the time – or the energy – to wash her hair and it was currently scraped back off her face in a greasy knot. Ah, well, if he was serious about wanting to be with her, best he learnt sooner rather than later the reality of life with two small boys. Especially, she thought, as she turned her gaze to Elijah who was grinning up at her, when one of them was hellbent on mischief. 'Why don't you make yourself useful, Eli, and fetch Mummy a clean T-shirt?'

'I can do that for you,' Tristan said, sounding desperate for an excuse to get away. 'I only popped up to see how Isaac was.'

'Thank you. There should be one in the second drawer of the dresser in my bedroom.' As soon as she said it, she remembered the state she'd left her room in. She hadn't even had time to make the bed, and there were a least two dirty mugs on her bedside cabinet waiting for her to have a minute to catch up on the washing up. Perhaps there was such a thing as too much reality, but it was too late now to call him back.

Ignoring what couldn't be helped, she tugged a towel from the warmth of the radiator and wrapped a shivering Isaac up in its soft heat. 'Who's Mummy's brave boy?' she asked him as she sat him on the closed lid of the toilet and ran a flannel under the hot tap. Crouching down she wiped his sweaty face with the wet cloth, then brushed his straggling fringe from his forehead. 'Feeling any better, darling?' He gave a sad little nod then stretched his hands up towards her. Gathering him up, she carried him out of the bathroom towards his bedroom.

A stack of clean laundry, dropped off earlier by the wonderful Mrs W sat on top of the dresser and Jess soon had Isaac bundled up in a onesie and a pair of cosy socks. 'Do you want to lie down for a bit?' Another little nod. 'Okay, darling, here you go.' She settled him in bed, coaxed him to take a sip or two from his cup of very weak squash, and sat with him until his sooty little lashes fluttered closed. He was exhausted, and she hoped he might sleep for an hour or two. When she was sure he was fast asleep, she picked up his almost empty cup to take it back to the kitchen for a refill. She stepped from the bedroom to find a grey jersey top sitting in a neat square next to the door. Shrugging into it, she couldn't help but sigh. Soft and loose, it was an old favourite, and she immediately felt better for wearing it.

Padding on her bare feet into the playroom, she found Tristan knelt on the big rug beside Elijah as her son explained the complicated hierarchy of the various superhero action figures laid out between them. He raised his head long enough to give her a ghost of a wink before returning his attention to the relative merits of Thor vs Iron Man. Both she and Steve had thought Elijah too young for the movies, but not all the parents of his classmates had agreed, and awareness of the toys had been all pervasive at his old school. Elijah didn't seem bothered about not having seen them, happy to make up his own adventures with the various characters.

Thankful for a moment to not have to worry about either of her boys, Jess hurried into her room to find that not only had the mugs been removed, but the quilt had been straightened on her bed, the curtains drawn back and the top window opened an inch to let a bit of brisk, fresh air in. In the kitchen, the two mugs had been properly washed and set on the draining board to dry. Such a simple thing, but the sight of them made her stomach flutter. Some men bought you roses; some washed up your dirty mugs. She knew which she preferred. Having washed Isaac's cup and fixed him a fresh drink, she took the time to pour a glass of milk and arrange a couple of chocolate biscuits on a plate for Elijah. He'd been so good – not a single murmur of complaint about being kept home from school and cooped up in the nursery while she looked after Isaac – he deserved a little treat.

Balancing the two cups and the plate, she set down Elijah's treat on one of the little desks in the playroom. 'Snack time, Eli.'

Abandoning Tristan mid-conversation, Elijah scrambled up from the rug and hurried over to take a seat at the desk. 'Thanks, Mummy!' She rested her hand on his head for a moment before heading back to check on Isaac.

He was properly out, thank goodness, and Jess crept around, putting his drink beside the bed then setting the tablet nearby so she would know the moment he stirred. She inched the bedroom door closed, freezing when the latch clicked, but there were no sounds from inside. Turning away, she almost bumped straight into Tristan. 'Oh!' She clapped her hand over her mouth.

'Sorry,' he whispered. 'I didn't want to worry Elijah by talking in front of him. How's he doing?'

She shook her head. 'Not great. I'm really hoping he can sleep it off for a bit, but he's hardly kept anything down. If he doesn't show any sign of improvement when he wakes up, I think I'll have to call the doctor.'

Tristan touched a thumb to her cheek. 'You look exhausted.'

'Gee, thanks.' But she didn't resist when he put his arms around her and tugged her close. It was so nice to give herself up to him, even if it was only for a matter of seconds. 'I needed that,' she said, easing back from his hold.

'I'm here to serve.' His fingers pressed her hips for a moment before falling away. 'Look, why don't you go and grab some rest while Isaac is sleeping? I can take Elijah downstairs with me or bring my laptop up here if you'd prefer. I've got a couple of emails to sort out, but other than that I'm mostly twiddling my thumbs until we can start the set up for the winter festival next week.' He gave her a grin. 'You might be doing me a favour, actually, as I could do with a distraction.'

Her hand went to her head conscious of her greasy hair. 'I should have a shower first.'

'Sleep first, shower later.'

God, had there really been a time when she'd found this bossy side of him unattractive? Right now – if she hadn't been almost dead on her feet – it would be pushing all her buttons. Still, she couldn't quite allow herself to give into it. 'Give me five minutes to have a shower and I'll be right as rain.'

A look of frustration creased Tristan's brow. 'Why is it so hard for you to let someone take care of you for a change? You need sleep, I'm happy to sit with Elijah to allow you to rest. How is this a drama?'

She was sure she had a point, but right at that moment her brain was too addled to find it. 'Okay, if you're sure you don't mind? I'd rather you stayed up here. I'd sleep better knowing there was someone else to listen out for Isaac.'

'Then it's a done deal. Give me two minutes and I'll be back.'

Jess finally surfaced from her nap four hours later. It was pitch dark beyond her half-open curtains and it took her a moment to orientate herself. Slipping from her bed, she padded into the playroom area to find Tristan and Elijah sprawled side by side on the rug watching something on Tristan's laptop. A pair of dirty plates sat on one of the desks and she noticed that Elijah was wearing his favourite Spiderman pyjamas. 'Everything all right?'

Leaving Elijah absorbed in his film, Tristan came to greet her. 'All good. Isaac woke up earlier. He seemed a lot better, but he said he was thirsty, so I gave him a drink and he went right back to sleep.'

Jess rubbed her eyes, trying to get her groggy brain to catch up. 'I didn't hear him.'

'Probably because I snuck into your room as soon as you were asleep and took your phone from the nightstand.' If the expression on his face was supposed to be guilty, it missed by a country mile.

'You had no right!' God, what if she'd been snoring, or drooling, or both?

'Well, I claimed that right anyway, so you'll have to get over it. Next you'll be cross because I gave Elijah his dinner.'

The look he gave her said he thought she was being ridiculous, and she had a feeling he might be right. 'I'm sorry, I'm being ungracious. It's a bit of a shift in gears and my brain hasn't quite woken up. I'm sure he's fine, but I just want to look in on Isaac.'

He stopped her with a gentle hand on her arm. 'I'm just trying to take care of you, Jess. I can't do that without taking care of the boys, and I wouldn't want to.'

'I know.' She raised her hand to cover his fingers. 'I'll get better at this.'

'Me too.' His smile warmed her all over. 'I should've asked before I took your phone, but by the time I thought about it you were already crashed out.'

'It's okay.' And it really was because he hadn't done it because he didn't think she couldn't cope with looking after her children, he was simply saying she didn't have to do it on her own. 'If you're happy to keep Eli company, I'm going to grab that shower once I've checked on Isaac.'

'Of course. We're watching *Wreck-It Ralph*. I can't believe how

145

many great animated films I've missed out on. I've got a lot of catching up to do.'

Isaac was dead to the world still, but he seemed to be sleeping easily and that horrible clamminess to his skin had gone. Feeling like the worst had passed, she paused by the door to turn on the night light in case he woke up, then headed for the bathroom. Showering in peace was a rare luxury so she decided to take Tristan at his word that he was happy to look after Elijah and she took her time. After washing her hair twice, she took the time to massage in a deep conditioning treatment and shave her legs and underarms.

When she finally emerged from the fragrant steam, she felt more like herself than she had in ages. Swathed from neck to knees in a thick cotton robe with a towel wrapped around her wet hair, she returned to the playroom to find it empty. Tristan's laptop sat in the middle of the rug still, so they couldn't have gone far. As she headed towards her bedroom, she heard a murmur of conversation from the little kitchen. She stopped outside the door to listen.

'How about *PAW Patrol* spaghetti shapes?' Tristan was asking.

Elijah giggled. 'No, silly, those are mine' Jess rested her head against the wall, smiling at the easy way her son responded to Tristan.

'Hmm. *Peppa Pig*, then? Is Mummy a fan of Peppa?' Tristan was trying hard to sound serious, but Jess could hear the humour in his tone.

'Those are for Isaac. Mummy doesn't eat sketti. She likes soup.'

'Soup it is then.'

Leaving the pair of them pottering around in the kitchen, Jess tiptoed past to her room to get dressed. Stealing a few extra minutes of me-time, Jess slathered herself with cream from a set of toiletries she'd been given by her former in-laws the previous Christmas. It smelled of cherry blossom and felt like silk sliding over her skin. She dug out a pair of soft yoga pants that matched her grey jersey top then unwound the towel from her hair. Drying it felt like too much effort, so she wove it into a loose plait. The moment she left her room, the smell of chicken soup filled the air, sending her tummy rumbling.

'What's all this, then?' She asked, walking into the kitchen to find the little table in the corner had been set with a single place.

'We're making you dinner.' Elijah skipped over to give her a hug. 'You smell yummy.'

She laughed. 'Why, thank you, and thank you for taking such good care of me and making my dinner. What a lovely surprise.'

Elijah tugged her over to sit at the table, hopping from foot to foot in excitement. 'I set the table.'

'You did a grand job, too. Well done.' Jess waited until he glanced away to flip her spoon the right way around.

Tristan placed a steaming bowl in front of her. 'Here you go.' He returned to the counter to retrieve a plate holding a couple of slices of buttered bread. 'If you want anything else, just let me know.'

Jess couldn't help but smile at his proprietary air. He'd really made himself at home. 'This is perfect, thank you.'

'My pleasure.' He held out a hand to Elijah. 'Time to help me with the washing up.'

As she ate her soup, she watched as Tristan placed the other kitchen chair in front of the sink and helped Elijah to stand on it. With his arms around the boy to stop him from falling, the pair made a big performance of washing up the saucepan and wooden spoon they'd used. She liked how patient Tristan was with her son, how he kept his voice soft and encouraging. Even when he corrected Elijah's scrubbing technique, he did it with lots of warm praise and she could hear how it boosted Elijah's confidence in the way he chatted freely.

'Talk about a dream team,' she said, bringing her empty bowl and plate over to the sink.

'Put it in the water, Mummy, and watch me.' As Tristan held the bowl steady for him, Elijah whirled the scrubbing brush around and around until every inch of it was clean.

'That's amazing, Eli. You're getting to be such a big boy. I'm very proud of you.' She lifted him down off the chair with a hug and a kiss then set him on his feet. 'Now I think it's time you thought about bed.' He pouted but didn't say anything when she held up a warning finger. 'You've got school in the morning, remember? Now say good night to Tristan and thank him for looking after you today.'

'No need to thank me,' Tristan said, hunkering down to give Elijah a quick hug. 'I had a great time. Night night, buddy.'

'Night.' Elijah returned to Jess. 'Night, Mummy.'

She stroked his hair. 'Do you want to sleep in with me, so we don't disturb Isaac? My tablet's beside the bed so why don't you go and snuggle down and find yourself a story and I'll be in soon.'

Happy now he was getting the treat of staying in her room, Elijah skipped out to do as she'd suggested.

Tristan straightened up and turned back to the sink to empty it and rinse away the bubbles. 'No need to do that,' she said. 'You've done more than enough, already.'

'It's been my pleasure. He's a fab kid. If you want me to walk him down to school in the morning so you don't have to take Isaac out in the cold, I'm happy to do it.'

She thought about what he'd said earlier, about wanting to take care of her, and the boys being a part of that. If she was seriously considering pursuing a relationship with him, she needed to know it would work for the boys as much as it did for her. Tristan and Elijah were starting to form a lovely bond and she should do what she could to encourage that. 'That would be a great help.'

Wanting to show her appreciation, she stretched up intent on brushing a kiss to his cheek but he moved at the same time, reaching across her to grab the tea towel from the rack and somehow her lips ended up grazing the corner of his mouth. He froze, their mouths a breath apart. The sensible thing would've been to laugh it off, to move away and make an excuse about having to see to Elijah. His cheek carried a hint of that amber aftershave of his she loved so much and suddenly she wasn't feeling in the least bit sensible. She closed the gap, feathering her lips over the edge of his, coaxing him with tiny kisses to turn and give her more of his mouth. When he did, she sighed into him, offering her parted lips up for him to claim.

The chair stood between them, preventing her from pressing any other part of her body against his so there was no other sensation to distract her from the firm heat of his mouth, the slip and slide of their tongues, tentative at first as they tasted and tested and learned the feel of one another. The pressure of his lips increased, turning their kiss deeper, forcing a little sound of need from her throat as she clutched at the edge of the stainless-steel board, any control she might have started off with completely deserting her.

He kissed her like a man starved; like a man who'd been waiting years for this moment and was determined to make the most of it. All those fears she'd had about whether she was ready to venture deeper into intimacy burned away in the heat of his lips on hers. Passion like she'd never known roared to life inside her. Had she honestly been worried she wouldn't be able to connect to this part of herself again? She'd never felt more alive, more aware of herself as a woman. She wanted . . . hell, she just *wanted*.

She wanted to kiss him all night, to cast aside all her responsibilities and not be Jessica Ridley, not be anything other than a woman in the arms of a man intent on bringing her nothing but pleasure and the sweetest of release. The utter recklessness of it was enough to shock her back into reality and she dragged her mouth from his with a gasp. 'Stop.'

Eyes locked, chests panting for breath they stared at each other across the gap created by the chair between them. 'Jess,' he gasped. 'I'm sorry, I didn't m—'

Pressing trembling fingers to his lips, she shook her head. 'That stop was for me, not for you. You haven't done anything wrong.'

His brow furrowed. 'Then what . . .' He cut himself off this time and she could almost see the gears clicking behind his eyes as he comprehended the reality of their situation. 'Yeah, yeah, of course, okay.'

She smiled at him, sharing his sense of frustration. 'I think perhaps we should call it a night.'

Blowing out a long breath, he tucked his hands in his pockets. 'I think you're probably right.' He strolled across the kitchen, pausing on the threshold to look back at her, a wicked glint in his eyes. 'Jessica Ridley,' he said with a shake of his head. 'Who knew?' And with that he was gone.

Chapter 14

The Saturday morning of the winter festival dawned dry and crisp. *And bloody cold*, Tristan thought to himself as he jogged down the steps of the castle and the shock of the freezing air hit his lungs. Tugging his flat cap down over his ears, he bundled his gloved hands into the pockets of his thick winter coat and marched briskly towards the front gates. Condensation turned the air white with every exhalation, to match the thickly frosted grass all around him. It was hard to tell how clear the day would be with the sky still mostly grey and the sun barely a hint of red on the low horizon, but the forecast was promising sunshine all weekend, and he was putting his faith in the Met Office. As he neared the gate, he could hear the hum of vehicle engines and bits and pieces of conversation. He quickened his pace.

'Morning, Mr Ludworth.' A plump, older man clutching a steaming mug and clad in a bright red bobble hat and a garish green puffa jacket greeted his arrival at the locked gates. 'Lovely day for it.'

'Morning, Mac, I certainly hope so,' he replied, recognising one of the food vendors who'd not only participated in the summer fete with his speciality hog roast, but had also catered for Arthur and Lucie's wedding reception. Tristan unlocked the padlock and

151

tugged loose the thick chain securing the gates before chucking both out of the way beside one of the gateposts. Having worked free the bolt which locked the gate into the ground, he swung back the left-hand side. Without prompting, Mac unfastened the right-hand side and did the same. 'Cheers, Mac. Right, do you remember which way you're going?'

'I do, indeed, and I'm in the same pitch as before, that's right?'

'Absolutely. Arthur and Will are just finishing up their breakfasts and then they'll be down to make sure everyone sets up in the right spot, but if you wouldn't mind acting as the lead for the rest of the early birds.' Tristan wasn't sure how many other vendors were already in the queue, but the headlights on the vehicles disappeared beyond his line of sight.

'Not a problem. I think most of us are returners so we can look after ourselves and help the newbies. I've got a copy of the plan you sent through in the cab of my truck if there's any issues until his Lordship gets down there. How is he, by the way? I'm looking forward to seeing him – and his lovely wife – again.'

'He's doing great,' Tristan said as he walked Mac back to his truck. 'Lucie, too. I've no doubt you'll be able to catch up with everyone during the day as the conversation at dinner last night was how much all of us are looking forward to one of your pork and apple sauce rolls.'

Beaming, Mac clambered into the driver's seat. 'Send 'em all my way. Mate's rates for the family.'

'You've got yourself a deal.' Tristan closed the door and smiled across at the peroxide blonde in the passenger seat of the truck. 'Morning, Mrs Mac.'

'Morning, lovely. All set for the day? It's going to be a good one, I reckon.'

'Just about, and I hope so. You guys are staying over tonight, right?' The festival was running over three consecutive weekends, and most of the vendors who weren't local were either camping overnight or putting up in the village. They had a couple of

B&Bs, but a number of enterprising families had offered overnight accommodation to make a few extra pounds in the run up to Christmas.

'We are indeed, lovely. Forecast is chilly, but it's plenty snug and warm in there.' She nodded back to the special sleeping compartment in the back of the truck. As plump as her husband, Tristan had no doubt it would be both snug and warm once the pair of them were in there.

'Well, we're launching the woodland walk tonight, so if you're not too tired at the end of the day, I hope you'll come and join us.'

Mrs Mac smiled. 'I was telling Mac about it and we've got our walking shoes packed and ready.'

'Fantastic, I'll catch up with you both later.' Tristan stepped back and waved the truck forward.

A sharp whistle rang out as Mac was easing his truck and trailer through the gate, and Tristan glanced behind him to see Arthur jogging down the drive towards them. After a few quick hellos, Arthur was installed in the back of Mac's truck and they were on their way to the showground.

The morning passed in a blur of checking in all the vendors and welcoming the volunteers from the village who were taking admission fees on the gate. Tristan stayed with them for the first hour to make sure they had everything in hand before finally feeling able to head down to the showground. The weather was fulfilling everything the forecasters had promised, the duck-egg blue sky clear apart from the odd streak of high, white cloud. Those early freezing temperatures had eased now the sun was out and everywhere he looked there were smiling faces.

Every stall had people around it and the hot food trucks filled the air with delicious scents. One of the biggest queues was over where the team from the wildlife park had set up. Wandering over, Tristan was delighted to find Jess and the boys in the queue. Though she had the pushchair with her, Isaac was out of it and

153

clinging to Elijah's hand as they waited for their turn to meet 'Santa's' reindeer. Smiling his thanks as people behind them in the queue let him through, Tristan made his way to Jess's side. 'Good morning.' Though he wanted to kiss her, he settled for finding her hand and giving it a discreet squeeze.

'Hello! How are you?' To his delight, Jess planted a quick kiss on his cheek. 'Everything looks wonderful, is it all running to plan?'

'Tris! Tris!'

Laughing, Tristan bent down to scoop up Isaac who was waving his arms for a lift up. 'Hello, matey, nice hat!' He tugged one of the plaited wool lengths hanging down from the ear flaps on Isaac's Nordic-style woolly hat. Settling the boy on his hip, he turned back to Jess. 'I can't believe how smoothly it's all going, it's actually quite terrifying. I saw Iggy earlier and she said she felt the same all the way through the summer fete so perhaps this is normal.'

The people in front of them shuffled forward a dozen steps as the next small group were admitted into the animal pens. 'Have you been queuing long?' He asked Jess as they closed the gap.

She shrugged a shoulder. 'About ten minutes, give or take. I explained to the boys before we started that the reindeer didn't like big crowds so it might be a while. If we all behave then we're going for waffles and hot chocolate afterwards, isn't that right, Eli?'

The little boy grinned up. 'I'm having chocolate sauce AND cream on mine.'

'Wow! That sounds tasty. Do you think if I behave myself, I'll be allowed waffles, too?'

Jess laughed. 'You'll have to be a very good boy.'

Leaning over, Tristan whispered in her ear. 'Hard when I'm this close to you.' He snuck a little kiss on her cheek to prove his point.

Her cheeks, already glowing from the cold, deepened to a rosy blush. 'Definitely no treats for you,' she muttered, but she was smiling as she said it.

As he had something of a captive audience around him, Tristan decided to do a bit of on the spot market research and began chatting to the families in the queue on either side of them. He was gratified to learn the couple in front had travelled over an hour and had driven up in a little convoy with several other family members. 'Did you mind that we don't have a Santa's grotto?' he asked the father of the group in an undertone.

'To be honest, mate, it was a relief. These days are always expensive when you factor in the food and stuff you end up picking up from the stalls. I like this idea, and if the kids enjoy it, we're going to make a trip to the wildlife park in the new year. We hadn't heard of it until we saw about it in the programme, and we're always looking for something to do at weekends.'

'That's great to hear, and one of the things we were hoping would come of their association with us. They do a lot of great conservation work so if we can send a few more visitors their way, then it's win-win.' He hefted a wriggling Isaac higher on his hip. 'What about the woodland walk? Are you planning to stick around for that?'

The man shook his head. 'It's a bit of a long day for our littlest.'

Tristan understood that. 'Well, it's on every night between now and Christmas Eve so if you do decide to come back for it, hang onto your ticket from today and you'll be entitled to the same discount as if you'd bought a joint ticket this morning.'

'Really? That's great news.' The man nudged his wife. 'Did you hear that, Lisa? We can come one night just for the light show in the woods and get a discount if we show our tickets from today.'

'Oh, that's great news.'

They had included it in the programme, and the ticket sellers at the gates had been briefed but perhaps he needed to get Arthur to mention it when he did his little welcome speech they'd planned for around lunchtime. 'Make sure you spread the word!'

Twenty minutes later, they'd made it to the front of the queue, which was just as well as Isaac was getting a bit restless. The moment Tristan approached the keeper standing nearer to a small group of tethered, grazing reindeer, the little boy was trans-fixed. They were bigger than Tristan had expected, and he was surprised to discover as the keeper began his briefing that they were all female, given they all had antlers. The keeper kept her facts short and sweet, including the theory that because the male reindeer shed their antlers in the autumn rut, it could be argued that Rudolph of the famous Christmas song should in fact be renamed Rudolphina.

After the talk, the children were offered the chance to feed the reindeer by tossing a few handfuls of a specially prepared mix onto the grass near the small herd and there was also an opportunity to pet a smaller female who was being held by another keeper. Each child was allowed to approach with an adult and shown how to gently stroke the reindeer's flank. Isaac didn't seem too keen, turning to burrow his face in Tristan's shoulder whenever one of the animals swung its head in their direction. He retreated to the side lines, steering the pram with one hand and keeping hold of Isaac with the other while they waited patiently for Elijah to have his turn.

The next section filled with smaller pens holding rabbits, guinea pigs, miniature goats and a pair of rare breed pigs was much more to Isaac's taste and he clamoured to be let down. Lifting him over the edge of the rabbit pen, Tristan hunkered down beside the fence and watched in delight as the bunnies hopped over to investigate their new visitor. 'Gently,' Tristan said when Isaac stretched out a hand towards a fawn-coloured Lop with huge ears. Taking the boy's wrist in a soft grip, he showed him how to pet the rabbit. 'Like with Pippin, okay?'

''Kay!' The sweet smile Isaac gave him did all sorts of funny things to Tristan's heart, and he had to sit on the grass and catch his breath at the sudden wave of emotion. If he and Jess were really going to do this, then it would be Tristan's job to teach these boys, to help them grow into men of compassion the way his father and uncle had done for him and Arthur. He would never *be* Elijah's or Isaac's father – nor would he ever try to assume a role which Steve already did admirably – but he could be a friend, an advisor and a confidante. One hell of a responsibility, but the rewards might make it the most fulfilling thing he ever did in his life. And maybe, just maybe, somewhere along the line he and Jess might have a child of their own.

A pair of small arms were flung around his neck and Tristan found himself with a very excited five year old in his lap. 'I touched a pig!' Elijah beamed from ear to ear, clearly proud at this amazing achievement.

'Wow! What did it feel like?'

'He was all bristly like a brush, wasn't he Mummy?' The pair of them glanced up to Jess who was standing next to them.

'Yes, he was. I thought he was going to be smooth.'

Tristan laughed. 'Did you touch him, too?'

'Of course. Though it might be the first and last time I do so.' She knelt beside him and leaned over the fence towards Isaac. 'Have you been making friends with the bunnies?' She stroked the rabbit who'd settled between Isaac's legs and was happily nibbling at the grass. 'Oh, he's lovely and soft. Come and give him a stroke, Eli.' Tristan sat quietly, watching the three of them pet the rabbit, heart full to bursting and didn't think he'd ever been happier in his life.

They were just making their way towards the waffle seller when his mobile started ringing.

'Hello?'

'Tristan? It's Will. We've got an issue up at the car park, can you come and give me a hand?'

'Sure, give me five minutes.' He hung up then turned to Jess with an apologetic smile. 'Sorry, duty calls.'

'Don't worry about it, it was lovely we got to spend some time with you, I thought you'd be rushed off your feet all day.' She held out her arms to Isaac. 'Come on, little man, Tristan has to go and do his work.' She settled the toddler on his feet.

'I'll see you later, hopefully?'

She nodded. 'We're heading back in a bit because these two are going to need a decent nap before we go and see the lights later.'

'Wait for me?' It was only as he said it, he realised what he'd said.

Jess glanced down then up at him through her lashes. 'Always,' she murmured.

Euphoria gave his feet wings though Tristan soon came down with a bump when he heard horns beeping. Doubling his pace, he found a frustrated Will at the top of the area they'd set aside for parking. In addition to the orderly queue of cars snaking back towards the gate, there was a second queue cutting at right angles. 'Hey, sorry, what's up?' he gasped, bending at the waist to catch his breath.

'Some idiot didn't want to wait and cut across the field thinking he'd spotted a gap and then couldn't get through. Only by the time he realised all the rest of these jokers had followed suit. A horn beeped and Will immediately turned, cupped his hands around his mouth and yelled. 'Stop that! It's your own fault for trying to push in.'

Fearing Will was about to lose it, Tristan sent him off to placate the drivers who'd obeyed the signs and went to sort out the miscreants. The red-faced driver who'd caused all the trouble in the first place leaned out of his window and began to complain as soon as Tristan approached. 'What a bloody joke this is! Couldn't organise a piss-up in a brewery.'

'Terry!' The woman in the passenger seat snapped. 'I told you to wait, but would you listen to me? No of course you had to decide you knew best, just like you always bloody do!'

Oh, Christ. The last thing he needed was to get dragged into the middle of a domestic. 'You've been very patient, sir. Please, give me a few more minutes and I'll have this sorted.'

'It's a bloody disgrace, it is, and for the amount you're charging to get in an' all! I've a good mind to demand my money back.'

Deciding perhaps Will had the right attitude after all, Tristan pulled his wallet out of his back pocket and withdrew a twenty-pound note. 'Here you go,' he said, thrusting it at the driver. 'Full refund of your entrance fee and a bit towards your petrol besides. I'll escort you back to the gate as soon as I can get these other vehicles shifted and you can be on your way.' He strode off, leaving the man spluttering and his wife giving him another earful.

It took a combination of charm, good humour and firm instructions, but he eventually got the cars turned around and with Will's help they got them integrated into the correct line and everyone moving once more. The only car remaining was Terry, the driver who'd started it all. 'Right, then,' Tristan said, briskly. 'Thank you for your patience, sir. Now if you head towards that yellow arrow over there, you'll pick up the route back to the gate. I'll run up and meet you there and we can get you back out onto the road and on your way. My apologies again for all the inconvenience.

The driver gave him a sheepish look. 'Mary wants to have a look around, so I think we might stay after all.' He held the twenty-pound note out to Tristan. 'Sorry, mate.'

'No harm done.' Tristan accepted the cash with a smile. 'Come on let's get you parked so you can hopefully enjoy the rest of the day.'

Apart from a couple of other minor hiccups – including a hilarious half an hour when one of the miniature goats escaped its pen and was eventually corralled between a burger van and an ice cream truck by a very flustered keeper – the rest of the day ran like clockwork. Tristan managed to find time to stop at Mac's van for a hot pork roll, and was delighted to hear that Mac and all the other food vendors were thrilled with the amount of trade they'd done.

Arthur performed his MC duties with aplomb, while Lucie spent an hour in the craft tent touring each of the stalls and giving each individual vendor some attention. When Tristan crossed paths with his brother, he was hefting two reusable shopping bags stuffed full of trinkets and gifts. 'Lucie felt bad about singling anyone out, so she bought something off every stall in there,' he said with a grin. 'God knows what we're going to do with it all.'

Tristan peered in the top of the nearest bag. 'Looks like you've got some nice stuff. Have a chat with Jess and she might take some of it off your hands for the stockings she's going to make up for the house party guests.'

'Good call. Have you managed to spend any time with her today?' Arthur never had been one for subtlety.

'We took the boys to see the reindeer. You should've seen them, Arthur, they were so excited, it was the sweetest thing ever.'

Arthur grinned. 'You should see the expression on your face right now.'

Tristan could well imagine. 'I know, I know, I am a goner.'

'It's good to see. You've been really restless since Dad died, but it feels like you've got a sense of purpose back. And with Iggy pregnant too, we're making great progress on the next generation already.'

'I hope so. There's still a lot of stuff unresolved between us, but I won't give Jess or those boys up without a fight.' He didn't even try to hide the fierceness of his feelings.

Placing one of the bags down, Arthur gave him a quick slap on the shoulder. 'That's the spirit, and don't forget you've got plenty of reinforcements to call in if you need them. Lucie adores Jess – and the boys, too – we both do. Nothing would make us happier than to be able to welcome them permanently into the family.'

Bless his brother for saying it, even when Tristan knew he'd likely say the same even if they weren't so keen on Jess because he knew they only wanted to see him happy. 'If it was up to me, it'd be a done deal already, but the last thing I want to do is rush Jess into something she might come to regret.'

Arthur nodded. 'You never were one to do things the easy way, were you?'

'At least I haven't scared her off yet.' Tristan couldn't resist the dig at his brother whose own path to true love had been more than a little rocky.

'Whatever, little brother.' Arthur buffed his nails on his shirt then blew on them. 'You wish you had my skills with the ladies.'

Tristan laughed, of course, but deep down inside his most sincere wish was that he and Jess might end up as happy as Arthur and Lucie were together.

Chapter 15

The great hall was the kind of noisy chaos that could only be expected when seven adults, two over-excited children and a rambunctious pack of dogs gathered in the same space. The dogs were milling around by the door, one or other of them giving a bark in the expectation they were being taken out for a walk. As she knelt to buckle Isaac into the harness for his reins, Jess smothered a grin as she watched Arthur and Lancelot's somewhat ineffectual efforts to herd the dogs back towards the fireplace. With Isaac and Elijah both warmly wrapped up, Jess turned her attention to her own coat and hat, then called Lucie over to help her with the backpack carrier she planned to use rather than the buggy. Although the wheels on the buggy were sturdy and had a good tread, she wasn't keen on trying to negotiate her way around the woods with it – even though she'd been assured the paths would be able to accommodate it. Isaac would want to explore and she'd only resort to carrying him when he got too tired. 'I think that's fine, thanks,' she said to Lucie, giving the strap around her middle a quick check.

Another flurry of voices added to the general hubbub as Mrs W, Betsy and Maxwell entered the hall all similarly wrapped up for the cold weather. Arthur had extended the invitation to them when Maxwell served an early supper of stew and homemade bread, and Jess was delighted to see they'd accepted. The boys were particularly fond of the housekeeper and the cook, but she'd come across Maxwell one morning helping Elijah to tie his shoelaces ready for school and had instantly developed a soft spot for him.

With Maxwell there to help, the men had better luck shooing the dogs away from the front door and everyone was soon gathered at the bottom of the steps. It was a cold, clear night and the heavens were already doing their best to put on a light show to compete with the one waiting for them in the woods.

'Where's Tristan?' Elijah asked, glancing around as though realising for the first time he wasn't with them. Though their original arrangement had been to meet at the castle, he'd texted Jess earlier to say he would meet them at the entrance to the walk instead as he wanted to make sure everything was running smoothly.

'He's over at the woods with Will,' Iggy said as she came over and held out a hand to Elijah. 'Come on, let's go and find them!'

Jess followed at Isaac's slower pace with Constance and Lancelot falling in beside them. 'Well, it's a beautiful night for it,' Constance said. 'I must say I'm rather excited to see what they've done.' Only Tristan and Will had seen the full display, the rest of the family having been barred from the woods so as not to spoil the surprise.

Their route from the house took them across some unlit open ground and with Lancelot's help, she got Isaac settled into the carrier on her back, not wanting him to stumble even though most of the adults were carrying torches and she could see well enough. As they approached, the night before them took on an eerie green glow before switching to a deep violet then a bright red, and she stopped to point out the changing colours to Isaac. Little hands patted the thick, woolly hat on her head. 'Pretty!'

'Yes, darling, it's very pretty.' She spoke too soon. Pretty didn't come close to describing the sights awaiting them. A shimmering curtain of lights covered the entrance to the walk, concealing what lay in store for them other than the ghostly glow of colour shining here and there above the tree line. There was only a small queue in front of them. The display had opened a couple of hours previously at dusk, and they'd decided to eat first and let the majority of the crowds pass through before they ventured across. A tall figure silhouetted against the curtain of light waved and began weaving his way towards them. Though he had a flat cap tugged over his hair, Tristan's cheeks and nose were red from the cold.

'How's it going?' Jess reached up to cup his cheek. 'My goodness, you're freezing.'

Tristan leaned into her hand for a brief moment. 'Only my face, the rest of me is fine. Will and I had an Irish coffee from the food van.' He gave her a lopsided grin, and she wondered if the shot of whisky in that coffee had been a single or a double.

'Tris! Tris!' Isaac yelled his usual greeting to his new favourite person, almost deafening her in the process.

'Look at you up there, you're almost as tall as me.' Reaching over her shoulder, Tristan took Isaac's outstretched hand. 'Are you ready to see the lights?' From the way Isaac was bouncing against her back, the answer was most definitely yes.

As they approached the curtain of lights, Jess could feel the anticipation and excitement rising inside. 'Ready?' Tristan asked her, stretching his hand out to pull part of the curtain aside.

She nodded, and then found herself in the midst of a breathtaking fairyland. She wasn't sure what she'd been expecting, but it wasn't anything like the sight before them. Beneath the trees on either side of the path was an amazing array of illuminated toadstools in every shape and size imaginable. On the trunks of some of the bigger trees, spotlights shone on little doors, and every now and then tiny golden lights twinkled in the branches like fireflies or fairies were hiding in the branches. It was so magical, Jess felt tears prickle her eyes for a moment. 'Oh, it's beautiful.' Her gasp of delight wasn't the only one as the rest of the family group crossed from one side of the path to the other pointing out different things they'd spotted to one another.

'Down!' Isaac demanded behind her, and Tristan obliged immediately, lifting him free of the carrier and setting him on his feet.

'Hold on there, mister.' Jess caught his sleeve before he could escape and reached into her coat pocket with her free hand to fish out the strap which she clipped onto the harness of the reins. As soon as she released his arm, Isaac was off, toddling as fast as his little legs would carry him towards a toadstool standing right next to the path. She was about to warn him not to touch, but there was no need as he came to a stop and just stared in fascination at the glowing red and white spotted decoration as though expecting a fairy or a gnome to pop out from behind it. She wasn't sure how long they remained in that first section, and would've happily stayed longer just to enjoy the wonder in her baby's eyes as he explored everywhere but Elijah came running up and tugged her sleeve. 'Mummy, Mummy, come and see!' And she let him drag her along the path.

In the next section, the trees were filled with huge baubles, each tree illuminated in a different colour by hidden lights. Every few seconds the colours changed sending a rainbow ripple around the grove. Beyond the rainbow, the next section of trees appeared to be raining sparks of fire from high in their boughs.

And so it went on, each turn in the path bringing another visual delight. Twenty minutes later, she was standing alone in front of an open grove in the trees filled with a carpet of twinkling stars. Mrs W and Betsy were somewhere behind them with Isaac, having claimed his loyalty with a piece of homemade shortbread the cook produced from her pocket. She could hear Elijah's bright, high voice a little ahead where he'd gone to explore the next bit of the walk with Iggy and Will. Warmth bracketed her side, and the familiar trace of amber filled the air. Her glove was tugged off and Tristan's warm fingers entwined with hers. 'So, what do you think?'

'It's incredible. Beyond anything I could've imagined,' she said, squeezing his hand. 'And it'll be here for our guests to enjoy over Christmas?'

Tristan nodded. 'We're closing everything to the public from the evening of the twenty-third. We want the guests to have exclusive access to the estate, although I was talking to Arthur and we thought we might invite the village up to watch the fireworks on New Year's Eve. We'll open the gates and they can watch from the driveway.'

She grabbed his arm, unable to contain her excitement. 'You've changed your mind about the fireworks? Oh, *thank you*!'

'Arthur, Iggy and I had a chat about it and decided it would be a great way to round out the year and though no one outside the family needs to know about it, it can also be a tribute to Dad's memory. We thought we'd open up the battlements to the guests so they can watch it from up there.'

'Really?' It was more than she could've asked for.

'Really,' he confirmed, grinning down at her. 'There's a staircase that comes out next to a nice wide section of the wall over the front door so they'll be front and centre for the display. We've decided to get a firm in to do it. I know you said you could handle it, but you'll have more than enough on your plate with the masquerade ball. We want to put on something special, especially if we're going to invite the locals. They've done a huge amount to support us all since we lost Dad, and it feels like a nice way to say thank you.'

'And it will be a brilliant way to send our guests off with a memory they'll hopefully treasure for a long time.'

'As long as they tell all their rich mates about it, I'll be happy.'

She tilted her head back to look at him properly. 'You think you'll repeat the house party if it's a success?'

'Absolutely. If we pull it off, I've got my eye on holding four a year – Easter, midsummer, harvest time and Christmas again.

I also want to capitalise on the success of hosting Arthur and Lucie's wedding and add some of those to next year's calendar.'

His enthusiasm was catching. 'You're going to be busy.'

'*We're* going to be busy.' Turning to face her, he took her other hand. 'When I said I wanted a future with you, this is what I was talking about. Not just us living together, but working together, a partnership in every sense.' He squeezed her hands. 'I'm not winging it anymore, Jess. I've got a plan, a vision for how I want my life to go from here on in, and nothing would make me happier than to have you by my side. I know I can achieve the success I want on my own, and whatever you choose to do you'll smash it, but imagine how much better it could be if we combined forces.'

How easy would it be to say yes? To let him sweep her away in the tide of his enthusiasm and chase this dream of his together? It was so tempting, her tongue tingled with the need to shout 'Yes!' And if it was only her own future to consider she wouldn't hesitate. *Head over heart, Jess.* 'It's a risk.'

She watched his face fall for a moment before he sucked in a breath and nodded his head. 'It is. And if it's a step you find you can't take, I'll understand. But whatever you decide, I'm not giving up on you – on us. I said I'd wait for you, Jess, and I meant it. I *mean* it.'

Raising her hand, she cupped his cheek. 'I'm not saying no.'

'Then that's enough for me.' He lowered his head and brushed a kiss across her lips. 'Come on, let me show you the rest of the lights.'

Jess had just shown out the decorating team and stood admiring the triumph of a tree they'd installed in the great hall when she heard a gasp above her. Raising her eyes, she saw Lucie gripping the railing of the balcony at the top of the stairs, her stunned gaze fixed on the glittering white star topping the tree a few inches from the ceiling. 'Oh, Jess, it's stunning!'

She smiled up at Lucie. 'You don't think it's a bit over the top?' She'd debated back and forth with the lead decorator over the merits of a smaller, more subtle tree and had eventually been persuaded that although those would be suitable for the library and the guest drawing room, a space as huge as the great hall deserved a statement tree. They'd chosen a Douglas fir for it's dark green-blue branches and installed it on the left-hand side of the hall. Its position gave maximum impact from the front door, the stairs, and for those entering from the long gallery while also keeping it well away from the huge fireplace. They'd used only white decorations and lights to complement the green and white pattern on the enormous round table which dominated the centre of the hall. A direct replica of the one hanging in Winchester Castle, the table was another of their Arthurian-obsessed ancestor's contributions to the castle's decor. Thick fir garlands studded with twinkling white lights wound around the entire length of the balcony balustrade and down the curving banister of the stairs. A matching garland draped the length of the mantel high over the fireplace.

Lucie jogged down the stairs to join her, dressed in jeans and a soft emerald-green jumper which turned her long red hair into a flame tumbling around her shoulders. 'Oh, I think it's completely over the top.' She grinned at Jess, hooking an arm through hers. 'And absolutely perfect.' She sighed. 'Imagine walking into the hall for the very first time and being confronted with this sight. Our guests are going to be blown away.'

'God, I hope so.'

Lucie hugged her arm. 'Please tell me you're not nervous about this! Honestly, Jess, you've got nothing to worry about. After all the hard work you've put in, you deserve for it to be a success. I was telling Arthur only this morning I wished we were staying here as your guests, because they are going to be pampered and spoiled to within an inch of their lives.'

Jess leaned into her friend's shoulder – that's how she thought of her now, not the lady of the castle, nor the wife of her employer, but a good friend and true confidante. Whenever she'd had doubts over the decorations in one of the guest rooms or was struggling to make a final decision on menus, it had been to Lucie she'd turned for advice. Together they'd debated the pros and cons of a tweed patterned blanket vs a neutral throw – silly little details to some people, perhaps, but Jess wanted everything to be perfect and Lucie had never made her feel like she was wasting her time on trivialities. 'Thank you, Luce, for everything.'

'It's been my pleasure, Jess.' Lucie pecked a kiss on her cheek. 'You look worn out. I hope you're going to get some rest this weekend before the guests arrive on Monday.'

Jess shrugged. 'It's the last weekend for the winter festival so I'm sure there will be lots to do. Besides,' her voice caught in her throat. 'I'd rather keep busy.' Her parents were on their way up to collect the boys and take them back to Somerset for Christmas. It was breaking her heart to think about not being with them when they opened their presents on Christmas morning, but she didn't know what else to do. They deserved to be the centre of attention, and she would be busy looking after their guests. Steve was desperate to see them, and they'd be back with her on the twenty-ninth and then through the new year.

'Oh, Jess, I didn't mean to upset you.' Lucie drew her into a tight hug.

'Ignore me, I'm being silly.' Jess laughed through a sniffle. 'I know the boys will have a wonderful time with Steve and our parents. I just hadn't expected it to be quite this hard.' She straightened her shoulders. 'But this is our life now, and we'll all have to get used to sharing holidays; better to start sooner rather than later.'

Lucie pulled a clean tissue from her pocket and handed it to her. 'And we're going to make such a fuss of them when they come home.' Though she'd protested against it, the Ludworths had decided to postpone their own official Christmas celebrations until the children were back to share it with them.

'You didn't have to do that, you know.'

'We know.' Lucie smiled. 'But Christmas is such a special time when there are little ones to share it with. It was a unanimous decision so don't bother arguing against it anymore.'

'I won't.' Her phone beeped in her pocket. She scanned the text. 'It's Mum. They've stopped at the services for a cup of tea. Dad reckons it'll be no more than an hour once they set off again, I'd better go and make sure everything's ready upstairs.' They were staying overnight and setting off early in the morning to get ahead of the weekend traffic if they could. As the guest rooms were all made up ready for next week, Mum and Dad would sleep in her room and she'd sleep in with the boys. Isaac wouldn't mind the cot for one night, and she liked the idea of having them as close as possible before they headed off.

'I'll speak to Betsy now. If we have lunch at one-thirty that will give them a chance to get their bearings first, and still leave time before we have to head down to the village.' It was the last day of school, and Elijah, long with all the other children, was taking part in the nativity play and carol concert.

'Sounds good to me.' Jess gave her another quick hug and they went their separate ways.

Chapter 16

'You made good time!' Jess called to her parents as she hurried down the steps to meet them. 'How was the drive?'

'Not bad at all,' her dad replied, giving her a huge bear hug. 'You're looking good, flower. All this country air must agree with you.' Stepping back, he craned his neck as he took in the imposing vista of the castle. 'What a place!' He turned to look the other way out of over the gardens. 'What a view!'

'It's pretty amazing, huh?' Jess walked around the other side to hug her mother. Things had been a little stiff between them since the confrontation at Centre Parcs and Jess was hoping they might improve with a bit of face-time. 'Hello, Mum. It's good to see you.'

'Hello, darling.' She returned Jess's hug then smoothed a hand over the jeans she was wearing with a pretty pink jumper and matching gilet. 'I'm not very dressed up, I'm afraid.'

Jess pointed to her own sweatshirt. 'Nor am I. It's very casual here, so don't worry about it. Arthur and Lucie are waiting inside to say hello, and you'll meet the others over lunch.'

Her mum's lips twitched, a habit she had when she was nervous. 'And they're the lord and lady of the castle, is that right? What should I call them?'

Jess slung an arm around her mum's waist and steered her

towards the steps. 'He's not a lord, he's a baronet, and you call them Arthur and Lucie.' She gave her mum a little squeeze. 'They're just people, Mum.'

Whatever nerves her mum might have been feeling were soon swept away by Arthur's natural exuberance and charm. 'Alan, Wendy, how wonderful to meet you both,' he said, striding over to shake her dad's hand and press a quick kiss to her mum's cheek. 'Such a shame you're not staying longer than one night, but we'll do our best to make you feel at home in the short time we have.'

Lucie stepped forward and hugged Jess's parents in turn. 'Welcome to Bluebell Castle. As Arthur said, you must make yourselves at home.' She kept a gentle hand on Wendy's shoulder. 'Come and see what your amazing daughter has done with the decorations. We're quite overwhelmed by this tree.'

While she took Wendy on a little tour around the great hall, Arthur chatted to her dad about the drive up, the route he'd used and the forecast for the morning. 'It'll be icy first thing, but you should have a clear run home.'

Maxwell appeared on cue to relieve her dad of the little overnight case he was carrying and escorted the three of them upstairs, leaving them at the door to the nursery with an instruction to Jess to call if they needed anything.

'Well,' her mum said as she removed her gilet and hung it on the back of one of the chairs in the playroom. 'They've certainly tucked you out of the way up here.'

Jess rolled her eyes in her dad's direction, imploring with him not to let her start. 'We love it up here, it's like our own little flat and we come and go as we please. The boys have settled in very well.'

'I think it's lovely,' her dad said. 'These windows certainly flood the place with sunshine, don't they? Why don't you give us the tour, flower?'

Grateful for his support, Jess showed them around. 'You'll be in here.' She showed them the room she'd come to love with its big high bed and slanted ceiling. 'We have to share the one bath-room, but I'll make sure the boys have a bath tonight so there'll be plenty of time for you to have a shower in the morning.'

'I might have a shower tonight, before bed,' her dad said. 'Give your mum time to do her hair and whatnot before we set off in the morning. If it's as icy as Arthur reckons, we might not want to rush off too quickly. I don't suppose the gritters get out here much.'

'We can play it by ear. There's always a big cooked breakfast buffet at the weekends, and everyone else will be up early as it's the last of the winter festival weekends.'

Her dad rubbed his hands together. 'Sounds good to me.'

'Alan. What did the doctor say to you about your cholesterol?'

'Come off it, Wend, one fry-up isn't going to kill me.' He curled his arm around his wife's waist. 'You can't get rid of me that easily.' Though she tried to duck away from the big kiss he aimed at her cheek, she was laughing.

Jess found herself smiling. She'd forgotten they could be like this together. 'You can have a poached egg, Dad, that'll cut back on the fat.'

His eyes widened. 'Traitor! I might've known you women would gang up on me. Now where's that youngest grandson of mine? I need someone on my side.'

'He's downstairs. Mrs W, the housekeeper has been looking after him while I supervised the last of the decoration instal-lations. Let's go and fetch him and I can give you a quick tour before lunch.'

Lunch passed in a flurry of friendly conversation as the Ludworths went out of their way to make her parents feel welcome. She didn't say anything, but merely raised an eyebrow in Tristan's direction. The look of wide-eyed innocence he gave her only confirmed her suspicions he was behind this full court press of charm. Well, more power to him. If she was going to stay on at the castle, it might help persuade her parents to support that decision now they could see what a nice environment the boys would be living in.

Though she'd tried to be sensible about it and keep her options open, none of the job searches she'd done had turned up anything suitable nearer to her parents or Steve, and going back to London where her best prospects lay still seemed impossible on one salary, never mind the horrendous cost of childcare she'd have to fork out on top of rent, food and all the other essentials. Trying to build a new business with Tristan would be a risk, but if they *could* make it work . . . She closed her eyes for a second. God, if only she had a crystal ball.

There was also the small matter of when and how she was going to tell her parents about Tristan. Her dad would probably take it okay, but she couldn't see her mum responding well to what would be the final nail in the coffin of her dreams that Jess and Steve would get back together. Probably best to play it by ear and see how the rest of the afternoon and evening went first.

They made quite a parade going down the hill towards the village. In addition to Jess and her parents, the entire Ludworth clan, including Betsy, Mrs W, and Maxwell were enjoying the stroll down in the early afternoon sunshine. As they made their way to the village hall, it seemed like most of the residents of Camland had turned out to join them. While Arthur and Lucie spent some time outside saying hello to everyone, the rest of the group made their way in and managed to claim a block of seats a few rows from the front. A flurry of greetings came Jess's way from other parents she'd met at the gates over the past few months. 'You've settled in well, here,' her mum observed as Jess sat down and placed Isaac on the seat beside her.

'Yes, we all have. It's a lovely place, Mum . . .' A waft of amber aftershave stole the rest of her sentence as Tristan scooped Isaac up and settled himself into the empty seat, with the little boy on his knee.

'We miscalculated the number of chairs,' he said with a grin so cheeky she wondered if he'd somehow cooked this up on purpose. Leaning forward she glanced down the row to see it was full, as was the one behind.

'I can take him.' She held out her hands to Isaac, who ignored her gesture and nestled himself into the crook of Tristan's arm.

'He's fine where he is, don't fret.' A soft touch brushed her hand where it rested between their seats, his little finger curling around hers for an instant before moving away.

Don't fret? Was he trying to give the game away? Though he'd kissed her during the woodland walk, they'd been out of the glare of the lights and as far as she was aware no one in the family had seen them. He certainly hadn't made any other public overtures towards her, and she'd not said anything – not even to Lucie, though it had been tempting to ask her advice. And now here he was, holding Isaac like he had every right to, while all but holding hands with her. All it would take was one sharp-eyed observer to put two and two together to set the rumour mill rumbling. Secrets didn't stay very secret in a little place like this. She shifted her chair a little closer to her mum, just in case.

'You'll find it hard to leave, I expect, but then I never understood why you took on this job in the first place, knowing it would only be a temporary position.'

Jess bit the inside of her cheek to stop herself from snapping. Trust her mum to ambush her with this when they were in a public setting. 'I told you why I wanted to come here, and it's the best thing I could've done for the three of us,' she said, trying to keep her voice low enough so as not to be overheard.

'But you'll be wrenching Elijah out of school now he's settled in. I never raised you to be selfish, Jessica, but this past year, it's like you're a different person.'

'Enough, Wendy,' her dad said, placing his hand on his wife's knee. 'We're here to watch our grandson, not make a scene.'

Grateful for his intervention, Jess leaned closer. 'The boys adapted very well to the move here, and they'll adapt again when things change in the new year.' She was prevented from saying any more when Mrs Winters stepped out of the wings onto the centre of the stage and a hush fell over the audience.

'Thank you everyone for coming. Just a quick reminder that you are welcome to take photos of your child in their costume on the set at the end of the performance should you wish, but we do ask you not to do so during the show. And now, it gives me great pleasure to transport you back to a certain little town you might have heard of . . .' As she exited the stage, the curtain opened and the strains of 'O Little Town of Bethlehem' began and Jess forgot about everything else other than watching Elijah and all the other children.

'I think he's finally asleep.' Jess said as she joined her parents in the little sitting room in the nursery. 'I still couldn't get him to take off his costume.' Though he hadn't had a speaking part, Elijah had made the most of being cast as one of the sheep; baaing loudly and generally threatening to upstage the shepherds as he gambolled around on all fours in a white hooded top and black tights and gloves, his face covered in white stage makeup apart from a little black nose they'd drawn in with Iggy's liquid eyeliner. Jess had insisted on scrubbing his face clean but had given up the fight over the rest of his costume, not wanting his last night at home to turn into an argument. Accepting a glass of wine from her dad, she curled her legs up under her and sank into the corner of the sofa opposite him with a sigh. 'Thank you.'

Leaning forward, he clinked his glass against hers. 'Cheers, flower. I was just saying to your mum it's been a lovely day. Almost a shame we have to go home tomorrow and miss the winter festival.'

Though she hadn't been looking for it, this could be the perfect opening. 'Well, you never know, there might be other occasions when you can visit and hopefully stay a bit longer.'

'But your contract runs out in the new year,' her mum pointed out. 'So that hardly seems likely. Speaking of which, what are you going to do next?'

'Well, I've been given the opportunity to stay on here for a bit.' She tried to keep her tone casual, but it was hard over the thundering of her heart. She hated confrontation, always had.

'Doing what, exactly?' Wendy sat up in her chair, brow furrowed in a way Jess knew spelled trouble on the horizon.

'Tristan wants to open an events management company, and he's giving me the chance to come on board as a partner. If the house party goes well, we'll be looking at running several more throughout the year, organise some weddings and might even scout around for other clients in the area who might want our help.'

'There's a lot of ifs and mights in that statement,' her dad pointed out in his soft voice.

'I know.' Jess agreed. 'That's why I haven't committed myself to anything yet.'

'And what about us?' Wendy set her glass down on the coffee table with an angry click. 'Don't we get any say in you moving our grandchildren all the way up here on a permanent basis?'

'It's not like I'm emigrating to another continent!' Though she hadn't wanted to start a row, Jess found it impossible to keep the frustration from her voice. 'How long did it take you to drive up here? Four hours? It doesn't take much less than that to get to London from Somerset, for God's sake. Did I say anything when you decided to move out to the country just after Eli was born, and you know, just maybe I might have needed my mum on hand to help me? No, of course, I didn't because I wanted what was best for you.'

Her mother stared at her, eyes brimming with hurt. 'You never said you needed my help.'

God, it was enough to make her want to scream. 'I'd just had a baby, Mum, of course I needed your help. But you and Isla got it into your head about Somerset, and I was so bloody glad you were selling the Kennington house, I kept my mouth shut and let you get on with it.' Jess hugged her arms around her knees. 'Getting stuck on the A303 for hours on end with a screaming baby in the car was still a better prospect than ever having to walk across that threshold again.' In the years following Marcus's death, she'd never once been able to enter their childhood home without being transported back to that awful night when her world had fallen apart.

Her dad reached out to grip her hand. 'We didn't know you felt that way, flower. You never said anything.'

Jess returned his squeeze. 'Because no one was allowed to say anything, were they? We all had to act like everything was normal.' She choked on a sob, wishing like hell she could keep the lid locked firmly on this can of worms, but unable to help the words from spilling out. 'God, it was like Marcus simply vanished one day, and we had to pretend like nothing bad had happened.'

'How dare you say that!' Her mother's voice was shrill. 'We had pictures of him everywhere, same as we do in the new house. I think about him every day.' It was true. Though her mother had cleared out Marcus's room with an unholy speed, turning it into a guest bedroom with pastel watercolours on walls that used to be smothered in band posters and pin-up girls, the rest of the house had become a shrine to his memory.

'But those pictures were only your version of the truth, Mum. You plastered the walls in all those happy family scenes of when we were kids, but it was like time stopped in 2007 when Marcus first go into trouble and didn't start again until the day Steve and I got married. You erased the last five years of his life, and erased a huge part of me in the process too.'

Her mum was crying now, huge theatrical sobs that shook her whole body, but managed to produce very little in the way of tears. Jess's dad jumped off the sofa and put his arms around her. 'Shh, love, shh. She doesn't mean to upset you, do you Jess?' He sent her an appealing look across the room.

Oh God, he was going to do it again. He was going to let Mum off the hook and allow her to deflect the conversation, just like always. She stared at him for a long moment. 'No. I didn't mean to upset you, Mum. Please don't cry.' The words were empty, as hollow as the feeling inside her.

Wendy sniffled a few times before managing to pull herself together. Funny how quickly she managed to recover from one of her crying fits. 'It's just such a difficult time of year, especially with you not coming home for Christmas,' she said, shredding the tissue between her fingers.

And just like that, Jess was the one in the wrong. It was exhausting trying to get her mother to face anything she didn't want to. Not just exhausting, pointless. 'I am not boarding that guilt train, Mum, so don't even start. You know why I can't come back with you, and at least you're getting to see the boys. I'm doing my best to build a new future for us, and if I decide that means we're staying here in Derbyshire then you are going to have accept it.'

'We'll support you in whatever you choose to do, flower,' her dad said, walking the tightrope between his wife and his daughter. 'Won't we, Wendy?'

The nod she got from her mother was a little begrudging, but Jess accepted it as all the victory she was going to get. 'Okay, then. Let's not fight about it, anymore.'

Needing to get away for a few minutes, Jess grabbed their glasses and headed to the kitchen. As she splashed a bit more wine in her glass, she came to the realisation things were never going to change as long as her father continued to shield her mother from the reality of what had happened to Marcus, and why. Jess had two choices: to keep pushing and risk a permanent fracture, or be the grown-up instead of the child and move on. Even if she got Wendy to talk honestly about what had happened, it wouldn't bring Marcus back. She was holding on to the wrong things and if she didn't let go of those old hurts they would poison the future she was starting to give herself permission to dream of.

Chapter 17

By the time Tristan had waved off the last vendor on Sunday night, he was so cold his numb fingers could barely slide the chain through the gates and secure the padlock. Will had offered to stay with him, but he'd sent him inside an hour earlier to check on Iggy who'd been having one of her off-days and was no doubt feeling miserable. Shoving his hands deep into the pockets of his coat, he forced his aching feet towards the beckoning warmth of the castle. As they had the first time he'd seen them on Friday, the decorations in the great hall took his breath away. The scents of pine, cinnamon and orange filled the air, relieving the aching cold in his bones almost as much as the heat emanating from the fire blazing in the enormous hearth. Kicking off his boots, he tossed his jacket in the general direction of the coat cupboard and padded on stockinged feet across the tiles towards the fire.

Bliss. Closing his eyes, he let the heat soak through him as the dogs milled around his feet, the warmth of their bodies adding to his feeling of well-being. It was over. Six weekends on the trot and the car park had been full to bursting every day. The vendors were already pushing for details of the next event which was a real confidence boost. Now all they had to do was focus on their VIPs arriving tomorrow. He scrubbed a hand through the shaggy hair he'd still not found time to get cut and decided tomorrow morning was soon enough to think about them. He'd grabbed a burger earlier, so he didn't need to worry about dinner. Hot shower, bed, nothing more.

Moving on autopilot, he climbed the stairs and already had his thick jumper pulled off before he'd reached his bedroom door. He pushed it open and stared at the empty expanse of his bed. Though someone had been in and turned down the quilt – probably Mrs W – he felt no urge to move closer. It looked cold and far too empty. Tossing his jumper on the floor, he closed the door and continued down the corridor towards the nursery stairs.

The door to the playroom stood ajar, and though the main room was dark he could see light spilling in from the direction of Jess's little suite of rooms. Not quite sure why he was there, he called out her name.

A few moments later the door to her room swung open and Jess stood framed in the light, clad in a pair of pyjama bottoms covered in rainbows and unicorns and a turquoise blue T-shirt. Her bare feet looked tiny, poking out from beneath the long legs of her pjs and her hair had been pulled into a loose plait which hung over one shoulder. 'Everything all right?'

He nodded, unable to move, just wanting to drink in the sight of her.

'Tristan?' She crossed the room towards him. 'What is it?'

'I'm tired.'

She took his hand. 'You're freezing cold. Have you been outside all day?'

He nodded again, the weight of the day – of the past few weeks bearing down on him.

'Come on then, let's get you warm.'

Instead of leading him to her room, she turned the other direction towards the bathroom, urged him to sit on the closed lid of the toilet and fiddled with the taps on the shower to get it running. When she was satisfied with the temperature of the

181

water, she turned to him. 'Can you manage your clothes, or do I need to give you a hand?'

The idea of her stripping him off was bloody appealing, but not like this when he could barely stand. 'I can manage, thanks. Sorry to crash in on your evening.'

'Nonsense.' Leaning down, she kissed his lips, a fleeting touch that was there and gone almost before he registered it. 'It's about time you let me take care of you for a change. There's a clean towel on the rail. Come through when you're ready.'

For the first few minutes he couldn't do anything other than shudder as the warm water from the shower beat down upon his chilled skin, as sharp as pins and needles. It was only once the worst of the shaking subsided that he realised the water temperature was barely much more than tepid, though it had felt almost unbearably hot to his skin. He must've been close to at least a mild case of hypothermia – unsurprising when the temperature, even in the sun, had barely squeaked over freezing. He remained in the shower for as long as his legs would hold him up, turning up the heat in tiny increments until eventually the bathroom filled with steam. He managed a quick scrub over with a couple of handfuls of the first bottle of shower gel his hands closed around, not caring in the least that he would smell of cherry blossoms.

When he finally stepped out of the stall, he found a pair of his pyjama bottoms and a T-shirt folded neatly on the seat of the toilet. Jess must've gone down to his room to find them, though he'd been oblivious to her coming back in. Drying off seemed like too much effort, so he wrapped the towel around himself and let it blot the worst of the water off while he scrubbed his teeth with the lone pink toothbrush sitting in the holder and hoped Jess would forgive him for it.

Warm and dressed, he followed the light from her room like a wise man following the star and found her curled up on the sofa in her sitting room, a fleecy blanket draped over her knees, e-reader in hand. 'Feeling better?' she asked, pushing back the blanket to rise.

He waved her down, feeling awkward and a little embarrassed for invading her space the way he had. 'I just wanted to say thank you, and I'll leave you in peace now.'

She tilted her head on one side, the long plait of her hair spilling down. 'You came up here for a reason.'

'I needed you,' he admitted.

'Good.' Rising, she took his hand and led him towards her bedroom. 'Now come to bed.'

He wanted to resist, he was in no fit state to give her anything right now, but then he realised that was okay. Every relationship needed balance, and when you were with the right person, taking was as important as giving. He let her lift the quilt and push him onto the bed. 'I sleep on the left,' he mumbled, eyes already closing as the softness of the pillow welcomed his weary head.

'Not anymore, you don't,' she said, tucking the quilt around him. When her little body slid in behind him and curled over his back, he decided that from now on the right side of the bed suited him just fine.

He woke the next morning to the scent of fresh coffee and the disappointing emptiness of the mattress beside him. He'd slept like the dead, for – he checked his watch – ten hours, as it had been barely past eight o'clock when he'd staggered through Jess's door last night. He couldn't remember the last time he'd slept so deeply, and he didn't think it was all down to exhaustion. Though his recollection was hazy, he had the impression of turning over some time in the night and pulling Jess in tight against him, her head pillowing on his chest, one leg thrown over his thigh in a proprietary way that made him smile now as he propped himself up against the headboard and reached for the coffee. It was hot, and strong, and with exactly the right amount of milk he preferred. *She knew how he liked his coffee.* An absurd thing to be happy about, perhaps, but it filled him with as much hope as her sweetness the night before.

He'd drunk almost two-thirds of the mug and was trying to persuade himself to make a move when Jess entered the bedroom, wrapped in the same big towel he'd used the night before, a smaller, matching towel covering her wet hair. 'Awake at last,' she said with a grin as she crossed to the dresser and picked up a wide-toothed comb.

'Come here,' He patted the edge of the bed beside him, and though she hesitated, she eventually came to perch next to him. It would be so easy to tease her into dropping her towel and coax her back into the warmth of the bed, but he recalled their night under the stars and his pledge to himself to take the time to explore every level of intimacy with her before they took that final step. Instead of reaching out to tug at the tempting corner of the towel tucked between her breasts, he took the comb from her hand and slowly unwound the towel around her hair.

Taking the first wet skein, he held it close to the root and pulled the comb through the rest of it until it lay flat and smooth against her back. He took another handful, repeating over and over until every tangle was loosened, every knot unfurled. By the time he finished, her head was bowed, her limbs pliant and soft. 'Thank you.'

'My pleasure.' He leaned forward and kissed the skin of her shoulder, allowing himself a few moments of indulgence to taste the exquisite softness.

'*Tristan.*'

His name on her lips was almost enough to undo all his good intentions, but today was a huge day for them both – Jess, especially – and he was damned if he would derail it. There weren't enough hours in the day for all the things he wanted to do to her, and a lightning fast morning glory was not going to be the way he took her for the first time. 'Put some clothes on, Jess, I'm begging you.'

Laughing, she rose from the mattress. 'At least you're a bit perkier than you were last night.'

'I feel amazing,' he told her. 'Better than I have in forever.'

She cast him a shy glance over her shoulder. 'Me too. I was missing the boys so much; it was good not to be alone.'

He climbed from the bed and crossed to her. 'Would you like to not be alone again tonight?'

Biting her lip, she nodded. 'But would you mind if we kept this between us? Not because I want to hide you from anyone, but I don't have the bandwidth to cope with whatever questions it might raise with your family.'

'That's fine with me. The only thing I want you to concentrate on this week is delivering on all the hard work you've put in. If you want me here, I'm here. If you need space, you can ask for it. Give and take, okay?'

Rising on tiptoe, she pressed a quick hot kiss to his mouth. 'You're something special, Tristan Ludworth.'

Sliding his hand beneath the heavy drape of her wet hair, he pulled her close to steal another kiss. Her lips flowered beneath his, opening, accepting, welcoming the deep stroke of his tongue. When he could finally persuade himself to release her mouth, he pressed his forehead to hers. 'You're everything I ever dreamed of, Jess. Only the reality of you is ten times sweeter than anything I allowed myself to imagine.'

She curled her arms around his waist, pressing her body against his with a groan. 'Damn you, you don't play fair.'

Laughing, he held her tight for a moment before letting her go. 'Not a chance. Not when the stakes are this high, and I'm playing for keeps.'

By 4.30 that afternoon, Tristan was on his way back from a final trip to the railway station with the last of their guests loaded into the family Land Rover. The lady beside him, Ms Abigail Norman, was one of their three solo guests. She'd bumped into Tim and

185

Charlie on the platform while waiting for their connection to the single-carriage train which visited Camland four times a day, and they'd persuaded her to share a gin-in-a-tin from the ample supply they'd provisioned themselves with for the journey. As a result, the short drive up the hill from the station was a giggly one. As he drew up at the front steps of the castle, the laughter in the car faded as his three passengers took in their first proper sight of their home for the next ten days. 'Bloody hell,' breathed Charlie from the back seat.

'It's amazing,' Abigail added.

'Wait until you see inside.' Hopping out, Tristan rounded the four-wheel drive to open Abigail's door and help her out before doing the same for Charlie and Tim in the back. 'Don't worry about your bags, I'll sort them out. Come on in.' He led them up the steps and pushed open one half of the huge wooden doors.

Laughter, conversation and the soft strains of an instrumental backing track playing traditional carols greeted them, together with a blast of hot air and the familiar skitter of claws on tile as a couple of the castle's dogs came to greet the new arrivals. Not wanting to overwhelm their guests until they'd had a chance to grow used to them, Arthur had confined most of their unruly pack to the family room, leaving only Nimrod and Bella, their gentle greyhounds, and little Pippin to mingle amongst the guests.

'Let me take your coats,' Tristan offered, as he shoved the door shut behind him. 'We're having a champagne reception to welcome everyone, and then we'll show you to your rooms.' He spotted Jess weaving through the small crowd around the round table and nodded towards her. 'And here's a familiar face.' Taking Abigail's coat, he smiled at her. 'Jess and I used to work for Tim and Charlie.'

'So, they were telling me on the train.' As they watched first Tim and then Charlie envelope Jess in a big hug, she leaned towards Tristan. 'I must say I was a little nervous about coming here on my own, but if they're anything to go by, I'm going to have a lovely time.'

186

'I certainly hope so. We have a couple of other single ladies staying, although they're already friends. The idea of this break is to do as much or as little as you please. You'll meet a lot of new faces tonight, but don't worry too much about trying to remember who everyone is. Jess and I will be around to make sure you have everything you need, including company anytime you need it.'

'Thank you. I am hoping to get some work done whilst I'm here, but it's good to know there's a friendly face.'

He offered her his arm. 'Come on, let's get you a glass of champagne, and I'll introduce you around.'

In addition to Tim, Charlie and Abigail, there were also the Boltons – the empty nesters trying to avoid their first Christmas alone, and the Carlisles – a retired Canadian couple with the kind of perma-tans which spoke of a very happy retirement spent exploring the world. Tristan steered Abigail towards them and performed the introductions. Bob Carlisle immediately handed her the full glass of champagne he'd taken from a passing tray and set off in search of a fresh one, while his wife, Gloria, and Teresa Bolton complimented Abigail on her pretty sweater, and the three of them were soon planning a trip to the Boxing Day sales, the English women promising to show Gloria all the best stores.

Content Abigail was in good hands, Tristan did a quick circuit to check on their other arrivals. Malcolm Austin, a business executive stood off in one corner phone glued to his ear as it had been since they'd arrived not long after lunch. His wife, Anne-Marie, a timid little thing, hovered nearby looking awkward. Tristan touched his sister-in-law on the back and nodded towards the lonely woman. With a smile of understanding, she excused herself from where she was chatting to Jess, Tim and Charlie and had soon gathered up Anne-Marie and taken her across to meet her mother.

Standing with their backs to the fire, the greyhounds flopped on the floor at their feet, David and Yuki, a couple in their midforties who were both successful artists and hoping for inspiration, gushed to Iggy and Will about the amazing gardens. Marcia and Carole, the two female friends he'd mentally nicknamed the merry widows were laughing up at Lancelot, who could always be relied upon to deliver an outrageous story.

So far so good. He frowned, looked around the room once more, and realised he was one couple short. Spotting Maxwell in his full butler rig, including white gloves, circulating with a bottle of champagne to top up glasses, Tristan called him over. 'Any idea where the Swifts are?' If they'd decided to go straight up to their room, that was their choice of course, but he and Jess had hoped the reception would act as a bit of an ice-breaker and give everyone a chance to get to know each other.

'They're in the long gallery with Sir Arthur. Mr Swift expressed some interest in the family history, I believe.'

'Great, thanks.' Tristan allowed Maxwell to find him a glass of champagne, and after seeing Arthur was making his way back through the gallery towards the hall with the Swifts, he made his way to Jess's side. 'All good?' he murmured as Tim and Charlie wandered off to admire the decorations.

'So far.' She scanned the room. 'They all seem to be having a good time.'

He placed a discreet hand on her lower back. 'Relax, I just checked on everyone.'

Her fingers grazed his thigh. 'Thank you. I'm going to speak to Maxwell and ask him to bring the food out before the champagne flows too freely.'

'Good idea. I need to get the last of the luggage from the car and put it away before it freezes. I'll see you later?'

From the rosy glow on her cheeks, she understood his meaning behind the seemingly innocent question. 'Yes.'

Chapter 18

As Jess stirred awake early the next morning, her first thought was how bloody hot she was, followed immediately by a rush of panic that she might be getting ill. She tried to shove the heavy cover draped over her, only to discover it was the unmoveable weight of Tristan – the human electric blanket – rather than any type of bug responsible for her current high temperature. She still couldn't quite believe they were sleeping together, and sleeping was the operative word because when they crawled under the covers last night, Tristan had curled his arm around her and started watching some silly heist movie on his tablet. The plot had been incomprehensible to her, but she couldn't have cared less, content to lie there beside him and run over the events of the day. She must've dozed off before the ending, because she couldn't recall anything after the robbers had crashed the stolen armoured car off the side of a bridge and that had been quite early on in the movie.

She tried to wriggle out from under Tristan's weight, only to receive a grumbled complaint in her ear as his arm tightened around her waist. The alarm hadn't gone off, so she whisked the covers off her lower half as much as possible and let him sleep. Drowsiness tugged at her eyelids, and she was nodding back off when she realised the room wasn't completely dark, though it had been every morning she'd awoken since not long after the clocks had gone forward. Worried they'd somehow managed to oversleep, she fumbled for her phone on the nightstand and held the illuminated screen in front of her face. 5.20, still ten minutes before the alarm was due to go off.

So why was it so light? With a more determined effort this time, she freed herself from Tristan's embrace and tiptoed to the window. An odd light filtered through a gap in the curtains, and when she twitched them open she couldn't hold back her gasp of delight. Everywhere she looked was covered in a blanket of white. Unable to contain her excitement, she ran back to the bed, flicked on the lamp and bounced onto the bed. 'Tristan! Tristan, wake up!'

'Wha . . .?' Shaking his shaggy hair out of his eyes, he sat up. 'What's the matter? What time is it?'

'Not quite half five.'

'Then unless the castle is on fire, I've still got time to sleep,' he grumbled, lay down and pulled the cover over his head.

'But it's been snowing! Come and look.' She tugged his arm, trying to pull him from the bed.

'We live in the dales, that's what happens in winter.' His complaint was muffled by the quilt still covering his face.

'Aren't you even a little bit excited about it?' She pouted. 'Imagine how the guests are going to feel when they wake up and see we're having a white Christmas. I couldn't have planned it more perfectly if I'd tried.'

'It's not technically Christmas until tomorrow. It might melt during the day.' When she didn't answer, he flipped the quilt down and squinted up at her. 'You're really excited about this, aren't you?'

'A little bit,' she admitted. 'I wonder if it's just up here, or if they've had some down south.' She pictured Elijah's face if he woke later to snow in Somerset. A fist clenched her heart, God, how she wished they were here with her.

'Oh, no you don't.' Tristan scrambled up and pulled her into his arms. 'No feeling sad. We'll have the boys back with us before you know it, and they'll be able to build a whole army of snowmen on the back lawns.'

She nodded against his shoulder. 'I know, it's just . . .'

'Shh, darling.' He rocked her gently, his lips brushing tiny kisses to her temple. 'I know.'

She was gratified when their guests at least shared her enthusiasm for the overnight snowfall. Once the sun had risen, it was clear to see not much more than a couple of inches had fallen, enough to cover the grass and the roof of the stables, but not so much as to present a hazard if they needed to get a vehicle out – especially one of the four-wheel drives.

Breakfast with the family went down well, and Jess was pleased to see Morgana had chosen to join them after deciding to give the welcome reception a miss. She had fallen into conversation with Abigail and the merry widows and, having discovered Abigail was working on an embroidery project, had invited her to use her upstairs sitting room any time she wished as the light was 'far superior to that in the west drawing room.' The general consensus between the guests was everyone was happy to remain at the castle for the next couple of days, content to explore at their leisure. Jess had double-checked everyone had her mobile number programmed into their phones and left them in peace.

They'd opted to place hotel-style 'Do Not Disturb' cards in every bedroom, and when she went up mid-morning to check in with Mrs W and her little team of temporary cleaners, it was to find they'd worked out perfectly and they were just finishing up the last of the rooms. Though she'd not expected anything less from someone as experienced as Mrs W, Jess was delighted to see the bedrooms were spotless, and as she headed down the private staircase they'd allocated for the guests, she could hear the drone of a handheld vacuum down below where one of the cleaning team was finishing off the last few steps.

She headed next for the orangery, where she found Yuki curled up in one of the chairs, the sketchpad on her lap showing the preliminary outlines of an orchid blooming in a pot. 'Can I get you anything?'

Yuki tilted her head back, the black silk waterfall of her hair falling in arrow straight lines from her face. 'I'm fine, thanks.' She gestured around her with the pencil in her hand. 'I might just live in here for the next week.'

Jess smiled. 'It's beautiful, isn't it? And as I said yesterday, you must please yourself while you are here. There's no obligation to do anything other than relax and have a good time.'

'We're relaxed all right.' The humorous remark came from behind them, and Jess turned to see David standing in front of the large plate-glass windows, an easel set up in front of him. 'We were in bed by nine o'clock and I don't think I moved a muscle until half eight this morning. I can't remember the last time I slept that long.'

'That's music to my ears. Right, well, I'll leave you both in peace, but I'll be around if there's anything you need.'

A quick stroll through the library showed her it was empty. Sweeping up a coffee cup left on one of the tables, she poked her head around the door of the west drawing room to find Mr and Mrs Bolton ensconced on the sofa in front of the fire, noses buried in their books. After promising them a fresh pot of tea, she completed her circuit of the guest spaces and made her way back to the great hall. Tim, Charlie and the Carlisles were just coming in, boots encrusted with snow and cheeks rosy from the fresh air. They'd obviously been out with the dogs from the number of wet paw prints on the tiles trailing towards the pile of cushions in front of the fire. Whipping out her phone, she sent a quick WhatsApp to the messaging group she'd set up for the cleaning crew before helping the two couples to hang up their coats, scarves and other paraphernalia.

'I can't get over the air up here,' Charlie said, shaking his head. 'It's like I can feel it clearing out all the muck and emissions from living in the city.'

'So that's why you were coughing every time we walked up the tiniest incline?' Tim raised a sardonic eyebrow at this partner.

'No, that's because I haven't been to the gym in the last six months,' Charlie responded with a grin. 'But that's all going to change. I'm on a health and fitness kick starting from now.'

'And I was going to ask if anyone wanted a cup of tea and a piece of freshly baked ginger cake,' Jess teased. 'So, none for Charlie, but what about the rest of you?'

'Now, hold on a minute,' Charlie protested. 'I've walked off a ton of calories this morning. A slice of cake won't do any harm.'

'Looks like the health and fitness kick is starting tomorrow,' Tim tossed over his shoulder to Jess as he linked arms with Charlie and the pair strolled towards the door leading back the way she'd just come. 'We'll be in the drawing room. Bob, Gloria, are you going to join us?'

'I wouldn't say no to a piece of that cake,' Bob said, curving an arm around his wife. 'What about you, honey?'

'Just the tiniest piece,' she said, placing a hand on Jess's arm. 'The food here is so wonderful, I'll have to watch myself.'

'A sliver,' Jess promised. 'Enough for a taste, nothing more. And some Earl Grey tea to go with it?' she asked, recalling the woman's preferences.

'That'd be delightful.'

To her surprise, everyone opted to attend Midnight Mass and they gathered that night, just after ten-thirty in the great hall for luxury hot chocolate. While she left Tristan manning the table where guests could have huge dollops of fresh cream, marshmallows and dark chocolate shavings added to their drinks, Jess dashed off to lay out the stockings she'd prepared on the end of everyone's beds. She'd gone for a mix of high-end toiletries, and some of the bits and pieces Lucie and Arthur had picked up from the traders at the winter festival such as jars of homemade preserves and hand-carved tree ornaments. She'd add silk scarves for the women and ties for the men, and a few jokey items like miniature versions of childhood games such as Connect 4 and Guess Who?. Her grown up version of a selection box was to include a box of handmade Belgian chocolates, as well as the traditional satsuma and a small bag of nuts. Each item had been covered in cheerful wrappings made from recycled paper and tucked carefully inside the knitted stockings she'd found online, made by a wonderful lady who donated all her profits to a local hospice.

She made it back to the hall as everyone was putting on their coats. She caught Tristan's eye and gave him a quick thumbs-up to let him know she was ready to go. Torches were distributed between the group and they were soon crunching across the snow-topped gravel drive towards the main gate and the old church which lay on the opposite side of the road from the castle grounds.

A steady stream of people from the village were making their way up the hill, torches bobbing and the group from the castle blended in with them as they walked through the old lychgate marking the entrance to the church's sacred ground. Here and there among the gravestones, tiny tealights flickered where people had paused to place a memorial to a relative or friend.

The church itself was ablaze with light. Thick white pillar candles filled every stone window ledge, and two pairs of wrought-iron standing candelabras stood at the front and rear of the small interior. The candles sent strange shadows dancing on the stone walls and lit up the rich jewelled tones of the stained-glass windows. Little sprigs of holly and pine cones had been scattered along the backs of each set of pews interspersed with red-leather bound hymnals. Arthur, Lucie and the rest of the family made their way to the Ludworth pew which sat at the very front of the church at a right-angle to the pulpit. Tristan remained with Jess to help their guests find seats, then slid into the end of the pew next to her.

It was only as a hush began to settle over the congregation, she recalled she hadn't been in a church since her wedding to Steve. She'd been such a different person back then, it was almost like watching a movie as bits and pieces of that day flashed in her mind. As she'd said to Tristan when they'd lain looking up at the stars, she would never regret the choices she'd made back then because that would mean she regretted Elijah and Isaac when they were her greatest joy. But just for a moment she couldn't help but wonder what would have happened if she'd stayed at the party and let Tristan kiss her. Would they have ended up standing side by side at the front of this church, or would that first flush of young love have faded after a few brief months?

Perhaps the fates had known it was too soon for them and intervened, sending them on divergent paths until the time was right. Because it felt right, now. Sitting here in a packed church surrounded by a community she was becoming to feel she belonged in, she truly felt like she was in exactly the right place, at exactly the right time. As the organist struck up the opening bars to 'Once in Royal David's City', a single tear trickled down her cheek. Home. She was home, at last. If only the boys could be there with her, everything would be perfect.

Though Jess managed to hide how much she was missing them throughout most of Christmas Day morning, the Skype call with her boys after lunch was pure torture. They were so full of excitement and stories about what they'd been doing with their dad she couldn't help but smile, even though her heart was breaking at being apart from them.

When she finally crawled into bed that night, she was too tired to fight back the tears and buried her head in her pillow. A creak from the attic stairs a few minutes later alerted her to Tristan's imminent arrival. Sitting up, she did her best to mop her face and put on a bright smile.

With a bottle of champagne under one arm and a pair of

crystal flutes dangling from the fingers of the other, he gave her a rakish smile as he kicked the bedroom door shut behind him. 'I think you deserve this, after all your hard work today.' His face fell almost immediately. 'Hey, what's wrong?'

'Nothing, I'm being silly,' she managed through a fresh sting of tears. 'I just miss the boys.'

After setting the champagne and glasses down on the nightstand, he climbed onto the bed and drew her into his arms. 'Shh. You're not being silly, and of course you miss them. Have a little cry if you need to.'

Safe and snug in his embrace, she wept herself out, grateful for his understanding. When she finally felt better, she wriggled away from him to go to the bathroom and wash her face. By the time she returned, he'd opened the champagne. Accepting a glass, she clinked it against his and took a sip. 'Oh, that's good.'

'I've got something else that might make you feel even better,' he said with an exaggerated wink.

She couldn't help but laugh. 'Come on then, show me what you've got.'

Reaching into his pocket, he drew out his phone, opened a video clip and handed it to her. 'I recorded this the other day.'

Elijah's laughter filled the air. 'Watch me, Tristan! Watch how fast I can go.' Little legs pumping he cycled around the stable yard, eyes shining with joy. The image changed and they were inside the stable block. She watched as Lancelot led out a pony from a stall and hitched him to a railing. With gentle encouragement, he introduced first Elijah and then Isaac to the animal. The wonder on their faces put a lump in her throat.

'When did you film this?' she murmured, unable to tear her eyes from the screen.

'Last week when you went shopping with Lucie. I meant to show you that evening, but I got distracted. They were so happy that day, I thought it might help cheer you up.'

'Thank you.' As the clip ended, her guilt eased. Yes, her boys were happy to be spending time with Steve and their grandparents, but they were happy here at Bluebell Castle, too. She raised her glass to Tristan's. 'Merry Christmas.'

Instead of clinking glasses, he leaned forward and kissed her. 'Merry Christmas, darling.'

*

'Mummy, Mummy, Mummy!' Elijah barely gave his father time to unbuckle his seat belt before he was flying across the gravel towards her.

Crouching down, she hoisted him into her arms and held him tight, showering his little face in kisses until he squirmed in protest. 'Welcome home, darling! Did you have a lovely time?'

'I did! I got lots of presents. I was worried that Santa wouldn't be able to find us, but Daddy said he wrote to him and told him where we'd be, and when I woke up in the morning, all my presents were there under Granny's tree.'

'That's good to know, and well done Daddy for making sure Santa got the right house.' She grinned up at Steve as he came over to them, carrying Isaac. 'Everything all right?'

He nodded. 'The journey was fine, thanks, and the boys have been good as gold all week.' He raised an eyebrow at the castle next to them. 'Nice place you've got here.'

She laughed. 'We've only got a tiny bit at the top, but it suits us just fine. You can come up and have a look if you like?'

Steve shook his head. 'Maybe another time?' She'd messaged him to say she was thinking about extending her time at the castle, without elaborating on all the reasons why, and he'd been fully supportive, saying he could see the boys were thriving up here. He set Isaac down on the ground. 'Eli? Why don't you take your brother inside while I have a quick word with Mummy?'

'Okay, Daddy.' They exchanged hugs and kisses and Steve promised he would Skype them the next day.

197

Jess watched with an eagle-eye as Elijah helped his little brother up the big stone steps one at a time to where Lucie was waiting at the top to greet them. 'Are you sure you won't come in?' she asked, turning back to Steve once Lucie had waved to say she had them okay.

'I'd rather just unpack and run, if it's all the same to you.' He scuffed a foot in the gravel. 'It's a couple of hours from here to Wrexham, I'd like to try and get there in the daylight.' She'd been surprised when Steve had told her he would be bringing the boys back, until he'd explained the reason behind it. He and Holly, his geologist friend had certainly progressed beyond coffee.

'Meeting the parents, eh?' She said, giving his shoulder a playful push.

He laughed. 'It's nothing serious. Holly told them I was spending time with the boys, and they thought I might be feeling a bit blue afterwards and might like a few days away.'

'Don't believe a word of it! You're going to be inspected, so you'd best behave yourself.'

A polite cough came from behind them, and she turned to see Tristan on the steps.

'I thought you might need a hand bringing the boys stuff in,' he said, not moving closer.

'Good idea.' She waved him over. 'This is Steve, be kind to him as he's off to meet his new girlfriend's parents.'

'Hi. Tristan Ludworth, it's good to meet you.' Tristan shook Steve's hand. 'Well they can't be any scarier than Wendy, so I'm sure you'll be fine.'

Steve laughed. 'Good point, and it's nice to meet you, too. I've heard a lot about you.'

When Tristan raised an eyebrow at her, Jess shook her head. 'Not from me!'

Steve laughed again. 'From the boys. They've told me about everyone here. It's good to know they've got so many people looking out for them.'

'They're a credit to you. The whole family adores them, you

should see the pile of presents underneath the tree ready for later.'

'I hope you'll find room for everything, because I've got a boot full of stuff already.' Steve raised his eyes to the castle. 'Not that you're short of space.'

'Very true.' Tristan rubbed his hands, reminding Jess of how chilly it was outside. 'Look, let's not stand around here, come inside and have a coffee.'

'I won't, but thanks, I appreciate the offer.'

Tristan shrugged like it was nothing. 'As long as your boys are under this roof, I want you to feel welcome here.'

Jess felt her heart swell as she watched them interact. Here was the crossover between her past and her future, and it could've been awkward as hell. Instead, she felt only blessed to know these two very decent men, and her boys were blessed too for no matter whether they were with her or their father, they'd have a wonderful role model to guide them.

It was later that evening, when Jess slipped out from the chaos of the family room for a quick check on their guests. Elijah and Isaac were in their element, any upset they were feeling at being separated from their dad skilfully deflected by the fuss Tristan and the rest of the Ludworths had made of them. A stack of presents sat next to the small tree they'd put up in the corner. Nothing too grandiose, rather lots of small things including practical gifts like new wellies and coats as both were already threatening to outgrow what they had. The main gift had been a contribution from them all, and she'd left the boys sprawled on the carpet between Arthur and Tristan, a couple of big kids themselves, as they slotted together the tracks of an amazing train set. There would be enough track to cover half of the playroom floor as well as a fantastic array of old-fashioned locomotives, heavy goods diesels with stacks of shiny trucks to tow behind them and even the latest version of a high-speed passenger train.

Closing the door behind her, she pressed her back to it and

listened for a moment to the piping laughter of her sons. They were so happy here, and it made the decision she'd been moving towards that much easier to make. Yes, there would be risks to starting a new business with Tristan, but that feeling which had started in the church – no, before that, when they'd first sat together beneath the starlight – cemented itself in her heart. This was home now, not just for her, but for Eli and Isaac, as well. She couldn't wait to put the boys to bed so she could be alone with Tristan and tell him.

'Here she is!' Tim's warm voice greeted her the moment she entered the library to find him and Charlie sprawled in a pair of wing-backed leather chairs, china cups full of coffee and a pair of brandy balloons on the table between them.

'I was just coming to check on you but looks like you're already well taken care of.'

'That marvellous butler came through not ten minutes ago,' Charlie replied. 'We were just plotting to steal him away. Speaking of which,' he held out a hand to her as he rose from his chair. 'Come and sit for a minute, we wanted to talk to you.'

'Everything's okay?' she asked, taking the vacated seat while Charlie perched opposite on the arm of Tim's chair.

'Everything's fine, couldn't be better. We've both been so impressed with what you've done here, haven't we?' Charlie glanced down at his partner, who nodded in agreement.

'That's what we want to talk to you about, Jess. You're wasted up here, and I am mad as hell we didn't fight harder to keep you at the firm. We should've done more to help you manage your personal situation.' Tim said.

'And that's why we want you to come back,' Charlie burst out. 'Whatever you need, we'll work out a package to help you. Rent allowance, childcare provisions, flexible working so you'd only need to be in the office one or two days a week. Whatever it will take to bring you back, we're ready to do it.'

If she hadn't already been sitting down, she might have fallen over. Part of her was exhilarated to know all her hard work here at the castle had left them with such a good impression, the other part . . . the other part wanted to throw itself on the ground and cry at the unfairness of it all. Just when she thought she knew what she was doing, these two came along and pulled the rug out from under her. Heart had been able to overcome head when she'd not had a solid career option on the table, but this was more than that. She wouldn't be starting over, she'd be going back to a place where people knew her, to a job she excelled at, and if what they were saying was true, she might even be able to afford somewhere in her old neighbourhood so Elijah would be able to go to school with the friends he'd made in pre-school. Isaac could go back to his old nursery, too. Her finances would be stable, as well. Although she'd been paid a regular salary for her work here at the castle, if she and Tristan were to start their own business, there'd be no certainty of income for at least the first few months.

But if she went to London, she wouldn't have him. And the boys wouldn't have him, or all the other wonderful members of this eclectic, loving family they'd found themselves in the middle of.

'What's the matter?' Charlie asked, deep lines furrowing his brow. 'We thought you'd be over the moon.'

Jess forced a smile, trying to cover the heartbreak and turmoil inside her. 'I am, I mean, thank you. I'm just a little taken aback, as it was the last thing I was expecting. Can I have some time to think about it?'

'Of course.' Tim leaned over to pat her hand. 'Take all the time you need.'

Rising on unsteady legs, Jess sent them both a more grateful smile. They really were two of the most wonderful, generous people she knew. 'Thank you again. I'll let you know as soon as I can.'

She made it out of the library and around the corner before sliding down the wall to hug her knees in a tight ball. *What the hell was she going to do?*

Chapter 19

New Year's Eve dawned crisp and bright. Scowling at the beam of bright sunshine breaking through where he'd forgotten to close his curtains properly the previous evening, Tristan climbed out of bed to drag them shut, then crawled between his sheets once more. How had everything gone to shit in the space of forty-eight hours? He'd been so sure, so bloody certain Jess was going to stay – especially after the way she'd been with him on those few stolen nights when the boys had been away.

Only Tim and Charlie had opened their very generous hearts – and wallets – and offered her the one thing he didn't have to give her right now – financial security. Oh, he knew they'd be fine. Arthur wouldn't let them starve, for God's sake, and he was sure in his heart that between him and Jess they had the perfect combination to make a success of a new business. But he didn't want to have to go cap in hand to Arthur, and he was damn sure Jess would baulk at the idea. He didn't even have a proper home to offer her, as he'd not had time to sort out the renovations on the gatehouse, so, he'd be expecting her to squat up in the attic for the foreseeable future.

If he was her, he knew which option he would choose, so he couldn't be mad at her about it. At Tim and Charlie, sure, that pair of interfering bastards were off his Christmas card list forever. But he knew Jess well enough to know she'd make the right decision in the best interest of her boys. It didn't have to spell the end for the two of them; he'd sworn he would wait for her, and he'd meant it. He could split his time between here and London, assuming that's what she wanted, and work hard to establish the business so once the boys were older and he could prove to her that he could give her that security she needed, they could build a future together.

It hurt. It hurt so much he felt like he'd been punched in the gut, but they weren't kids, and whatever he'd told himself before about wanting to be her Prince Charming was a fantasy more suited to a child than a man. Life didn't care about aching hearts and empty beds, it just kept rolling inexorably forward and it was up to him to adapt. He was the free agent, the one who could afford to be flexible. Give and take, that's what love was. Well if he had to spend the next few years giving, so what? Jess was worth it.

He didn't have much time to sulk over the next few hours as he worked with Arthur, Lancelot, Will and Maxwell to dismantle the enormous round table. Unlike the original, the replica had been designed and put together in sections, and although it took several hours of hard work, sweat and enough swearing from Will to fund as many luxury weekend breaks as Iggy could possibly want, they finally had the last piece stacked in one of the store rooms. Mrs W and her little crew moved in straight afterwards, scrubbing and polishing the tiles until they gleamed. The dogs and all their paraphernalia had been relocated to the family room, leaving the vast expanse of the great hall free for the dancing to come.

Dusty and tired, he headed up to his room for a shower and a catnap. It would be a late night, and he had a couple of hours to kill before the final preparations got underway, and the castle had fallen silent as most of the other residents had decided on the same thing. As he entered his room he stopped short at the sight of something sitting on the end of his bed. Moving closer, he found he couldn't stop a smile from tugging at his lips as he worked out what it was. A harlequin mask, crisscrossed in diamonds of dark blue and black with glitter-gold edgings stared up at him, a midnight blue silk handkerchief folded neatly beside it. A note rested on top of the handkerchief and when he unfolded it, it simply said 'From your Columbine xxx'

Feeling a lot cheerier, he set the little gift to one side and headed for the shower. No, things were far from perfect between him and Jess, but they had love and they had hope, which was a hell of a lot more than most had.

Dressed in his tuxedo, mask in place and the new handkerchief spilling from his pocket, Tristan worked his way around the room to where his brother stood in a mask the same style as his, only pure black apart from a red glitter heart encircling one of the eye slits.

'Nice mask,' Tristan grinned as he offered Arthur one of the two champagne flutes he was holding. 'Who are you supposed to be?'

'The King of bloody Hearts,' Arthur grumbled, taking the glass and swigging a mouthful. 'I blame that girlfriend of yours for coming up with the stupid idea in the first place. Why can't we have a normal party?'

'Because that wouldn't be as much fun.' Tristan gestured with his glass across the room at the array of glitter, feathers and beads adorning all the faces. 'And, besides, Jess is not my girlfriend.' Not officially, anyway, until she chose to make it public.

'Well, that's not what Lucie reckons.' Nudging his arm, Arthur pointed across the room. 'And if she's not your girlfriend, why did she make you matching masks, eh?' Clinking his glass against Tristan's he added. 'I hope you know what you're getting yourself into because that looks to me like a family waiting for you to fill the missing gap.'

Tristan barely noticed his brother walking away, his gaze transfixed across the room. Beside the shining Christmas tree, stood Jess, bracketed by two little figures dressed in black shirts and trousers, their masks miniature versions of his own. The one fixed over Jess's eyes was a more elaborate version, with blue and gold feathers rising from the centre of the eyepiece to form a delicate crown. Her gorgeous curves were draped in midnight blue velvet, just as they had been all those years ago when she'd stolen his breath and his heart. This version was a more grown-up take on the original, the waist tighter, the bodice cut lower in a stunning v which revealed enough of her creamy skin to make his mouth water.

His feet moved of their own volition, the crowd already on the dance floor fading away until all he could see was the three figures waiting for him. 'You look incredible,' he murmured as he bent forward to press his cheek to hers, careful not to dislodge their masks. 'Simply stunning, and I love you.'

Her soft gasp made him realise it was the first time he'd said, and for a moment he couldn't believe that was right. Surely, he'd told her that before? When they'd been curled up together in her bed. He'd certainly thought it, even if he hadn't. She gave her a slightly lopsided smile. 'I love you, too.' It was barely a whisper of sound, but it was enough. It was everything. But this wasn't just about the two of them, as much as he longed to sweep her in his arms and twirl her around the dance floor until they were both dizzy.

Crouching down, he met two grinning little faces. 'Wow, don't you two look smart? Are you ready to party?'

'I want to dance!' Elijah said, tugging at Jess's hand. 'Can we dance, Mummy?'

'Of course we can, Eli, though we'll have to take care with Isaac as we don't want him getting squashed.'

'Here, I've got him.' Tristan scooped the toddler up, accepting a sloppy kiss on the cheek from Isaac with a laugh. Offering his free hand to Jess, he led her and Elijah out onto the dance floor.

Their moves were neither stylish, nor elegant, but that didn't matter. Tristan twirled Isaac around in happy circles, while Jess held up the long flowing skirt of her dress and stepped from side to side in a rhythm that had nothing to do with the music blasting from the speakers and everything to do with the bouncing boy holding her hand. It was silly, and exuberant, and Tristan didn't know when he'd had so much fun.

They were joined on the floor by other members of the family, Lancelot foxtrotting up and down with a laughing Constance pressed cheek-to-cheek. Arthur and Lucie, who was in a stunning black lace gown and a mask covered in those red glitter hearts, swayed beside him and Jess as they chatted about anything and everything that came to mind. Iggy rocked up, looking a million dollars in a red velvet smoking jacket and black satin trousers, a black and red mask over her eyes. Will had eschewed a tuxedo for his beloved leather jacket, teamed with a white dress shirt and black bow tie. He'd opted for a Phantom of the Opera style white mask, which only served to make the ugly scar twisting down his cheek stand out.

'Here you are at last,' Arthur cried out as they joined them. 'I've been dying to share the good news with everyone, but I didn't want to do it without you.'

'What's going on?' Tristan's gaze swivelled between his siblings.

'Iggy's decided to stay here at Bluebell Castle, haven't you, Iggle-Piggle?' Arthur tugged at the elegant French plait she'd drawn her curls into.

'If you call me that once more, I'll change my bloody mind,' she snapped, before breaking out in a huge grin. 'I couldn't face the thought of going back to town, so Will's agreed we can stay.' She threw her arms around her lover and hugged him tight.'

'Bluebell Castle is where we want to raise our kid,' Will said. 'All we need to do is sort out some proper living accommodation for us.'

Arthur waved that away. 'Easy as. We'll knock a few rooms together, make you a suite like ours.'

'There's always the nursery,' Jess said, her soft voice cutting through the celebrations and sending Tristan's heart plummeting like a stone.

'What are you talking about? I thought you were staying on here?' Iggy shot Tristan a sharp glance.

He curled his free arm around Jess's waist. 'Jess is going back to the city for a while. Tim and Charlie have made her a job offer that is too good to turn down.'

'It is a good offer,' she agreed, not making him feel any better. 'But not the best offer I've had recently.' She stepped closer into Tristan's side, placing her hand over his heart. 'They can have the nursery, because we're going to be moving into the gatehouse with you.'

Stunned, he swung around to face her. 'But, I can't give you anything like the financial security you need, and the gatehouse is a wreck!'

'Well,' she said, those ruby red lips beneath her mask stretched wide in a saucy grin. 'You'd better pull yourself together and get on with the renovations, hadn't you?' Glancing down at Elijah, she cupped his cheek and hugged him to her side. 'We had a talk about it this afternoon, and we decided, didn't we?'

Elijah gave an emphatic nod. 'We want to stay here.' His eyes lifted to meet Tristan's, and the love and trust shining in them was enough to almost send him staggering. 'With you.'

'Oh, Christ.' His eyes were growing wet behind his mask and he didn't have enough arms to do everything he wanted to do. He hugged Isaac to his hip with one hand, and reached out to cup Elijah's cheek with the other. 'Having you all here will make me the happiest man in the world.'

A sniffle came from behind them, and he glanced over to see Lucie laughing as she blotted her cheeks with Arthur's hand-kerchief. Lancelot swooped in and before Tristan knew what he was doing, he'd taken Isaac from his arms and he and Constance twirled him around until his high giggles filled the air.

'Come on, Eli, let's boogie!' Iggy took the boy by the hand, blowing a kiss at Tristan with the other as she and Will led him away to dance.

The rest of the family melted away, leaving him and Jess alone in the centre of the dance floor. 'Here we are again,' he murmured, reaching for her hands to drape them over his shoulders.

'Here we are again,' she agreed, nestling against his chest with a happy sigh. 'And I do believe you owe me a kiss.'

His hands found her waist, his fingers relishing the dip and curve of her lush body which was his to savour, his to cherish and adore. 'I do believe you're right.' Lowering his head, he claimed her lips with his and there was nothing and nobody on earth right then other than the woman in his arms. Wait, he'd promised her, and wait, she'd asked him to do, but no more. Tonight was the start of the rest of their lives, and he couldn't bloody wait to see what the future had in store for him and his perfect little family.

Epilogue

Arthur stood on the battlements of Bluebell Castle and stared out over the grounds of his home; his castle. Around him the excited chatter of his family and their guests filled the chilly air. More noise rose from the driveway below as the villagers gathered ready for the firework display.

This time last year it had still felt like his father's home, and that Arthur was little more than a pretender to the title – a boy dressing up in his dad's shoes. Now, knowing not only was the future of the castle secure, but that he, Iggy and Tristan were moving forward with their lives, he finally felt worthy of calling himself Baronet Ludworth.

A warm arm curled through his, and the familiar weight of his wife's head rested against his shoulder. Of the many things he had to be grateful for, Lucie was the best and the brightest. *God, how his father would've adored her.*

'You're very quiet,' Lucie said, snuggling close. 'Is everything, all right?'

'I was just thinking about Dad, about how much I miss him, and about how much he would've loved you. I only wish you could've met him.'

Rising on tiptoe, she pressed a sweet kiss to his lips. 'I do, too, but then again, if he was still around, none of this would've happened.' She gestured with her free hand to the others gathered around them.

Arthur took in the sight of his family, and knew she was right. To his left, a laughing Tristan hoisted Elijah onto his shoulders for a better view. At his brother's side, Jess chatted to Morgana, the pair of them wrapped in glittering evening shawls to ward off the bite of the wind. Beyond them, Lancelot held little Isaac in the crook of one arm, the other wrapped around Constance's waist. To Arthur's right, Iggy stood wrapped safe and warm in Will's arms as he whispered something in her ear which made her giggle. Though he longed for his father's presence, nothing would make him give up one single piece of the joy and heartache they'd all shared over the past twelve months.

As the first bright splashes of red and gold lit up the skies above his head, Arthur sent up the same wish he'd uttered exactly twelve months ago. 'Blaze bright, Dad, always.' Surrounded by the love and warmth of his family, he pledged in his heart to do the same.

Acknowledgements

As I sit and write these acknowledgements, it's hard to believe it has been three years since I signed the contract for the series which became Butterfly Cove. Since then, we've explored picturesque Lavender Bay and the wild, untamed beauty of Bluebell Castle together. It's been so much fun to share with you these stories born from my own love of reading romantic fiction.

I've had a number of readers ask if I will revisit any of the locations for a follow-up book, and while I can never say never, there are no current plans to return. To make a story interesting there needs to be conflict, and it doesn't seem fair to the happy every after covenant I pledge with each story to throw a wrench into the lives of any of my couples who have worked so hard to find each other. I prefer for each hero and heroine to live on in the imaginations of my readers.

I have a number of people I need to thank:

First and foremost my husband, who is simply my world. x

I don't have enough superlatives to describe my editor, Charlotte Mursell, who has been with me every step of the way. Thank you for championing me from the moment you found me in the submissions pile. x

Everyone at my publisher, HQ Digital, for making my books shine. x

The usual suspects – Philippa, Jules, Bella, Darcie and Rachel who are the best support system anyone could ask for. x

And thanks to you, dearest reader, for making this the very best job in the world. These stories are yours as much as they are mine. x

Turn the page for an exclusive extract from
Spring at Lavender Bay, the first book in Sarah
Bennett's enchanting Lavender Bay series . . .

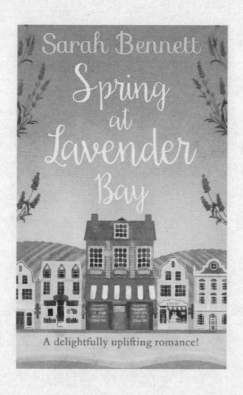

Chapter 1

'Sort this for me, Beth.' A green project folder thumped down on the side of Beth Reynold's desk, sending her mouse arrow skittering across the screen and scattering the calculation in her head. Startled, she glanced up to see a wide expanse of pink-shirted back already retreating from her corner desk pod. Darren Green was her team leader, and the laziest person to grace the twelfth floor of Buckland Sheridan in the three years she'd been working there. She eyed the folder with a growing sense of trepidation. Whatever he'd dumped on her—she glanced at the clock—at quarter to four on a Friday afternoon was unlikely to be good news. Well, it would just have to wait. Sick and tired of Darren expecting her to drop everything, she ground her teeth and forced herself to ignore the file and focus on the spreadsheet in front of her.

Fifteen minutes later, with the workbook updated, saved and an extract emailed to the client, Beth straightened up from her screen. Her right ankle ached from where she'd hooked her foot behind one of the chair legs and there was a distinct grumble from the base of her spine. Shuffling her bottom back from where she'd perched on the edge of the cushioned seat, she gave herself a mental telling off. There was no point in the company spending money on a half-decent orthopaedic chair when she managed to contort herself into the worst possible sitting positions.

Her eyes strayed to the left where the file lurked like a malevolent toad. If she turned just so, she could accidentally catch it with her elbow and knock it into the wastepaper basket sitting beside her desk. Brushing off the tempting idea, she grabbed her mug and stood up. Her eyes met Ravi's over the ugly blue partition dividing their desks and she waggled her cup at him. 'Fancy a brew?'

He glanced at his watch, then laughed, showing a set of gorgeous white teeth. 'Why am I even checking the time; it's not like I'm going to refuse a coffee, is it?'

Everything about Ravi was gorgeous, she mused on the way to the kitchenette which served their half of the huge open-plan office. From his thick black hair and matching dark eyes, to the hint of muscle beneath his close-fitting white shirt—the only thing more gorgeous than Ravi was his boyfriend, Callum.

Though she'd never admit it to anyone other than Eliza and Libby, she had a huge crush on her co-worker. Not that she would, or could, ever do anything about it, but that wasn't the point. Ravi being unobtainable and entirely uninterested in her as anything other than a friend and co-worker made him perfectly safe. And it gave her a good excuse for not being interested in anyone else. An excuse to avoid dipping her badly-scorched toes back into the dating pool. Once had been more than enough.

Until she recovered from the unrequited attraction, there wasn't room in her heart for anyone else. She could marvel at the length of the black lashes framing his eyes and go home alone, entirely content to do so. He was the best non-boyfriend she'd had since Mr Lassiter, her Year Ten history teacher. He also provided a foil on those rare occasions she spoke to her mother these days. Lying to her didn't sit well with Beth, but it was better than the alternative—being nagged to 'get back on the horse', to 'put herself out there', to 'settle down'.

Eliza and Libby knew all about both the hopeless crush and her using a fake relationship with Ravi as a shield against her mother's interference. And if they didn't entirely support the white lie, they at least understood the reasons behind it. Just like they'd known everything about her since the first day they'd started at primary school together. They knew what her mum was like, and they understood why Beth preferred the harmless pretence of an unrequited crush. She'd never been one for boyfriends growing up, and the more her mum had pushed her, the more she'd dug her heels in.

Beth had been eight years old when her dad had walked out with not so much as a backward glance. Her mum had spent the rest of Beth's formative years obsessed with finding a replacement for him—only one who could provide the financial security she craved. Before he'd left, there'd been too many times her mum had gone to pay a bill only to find the meagre contents of their account missing. If Allan Reynolds hadn't frittered it away in the bookies, he'd blown it on his next get-rich-quick scheme. Given the uncertainty of those early years, she had some sympathy for her mum's position. If only she'd been less mercenary about it. A flush of embarrassed heat caught Beth off guard as she remembered the not-so whispered comments about Linda Reynolds' shameless campaign to catch the eye—and the wallet—of newly-widowed Reg Walters, her now husband.

Determined not to emulate Linda, Beth had clung fiercely to the idea of true love. She had even thought she'd found it for a while, only to have her heart broken in the most clinical fashion the previous summer. Trying to talk to her mother about it had been an exercise in futility. Linda had no time for broken hearts. Move on, there's plenty more fish in the sea. She'd even gone so far as to encourage Beth to flirt with her useless lump of a boss for God's sake. Beth shuddered at the very idea. In the end, she'd resorted to making up a romance with Ravi just to keep Linda off her back.

Beth clattered the teaspoon hard against Ravi's coffee cup, scattering her wandering thoughts. Balancing the tea and coffee mugs in hand, she returned to her coveted corner of the office. People had offered her bribes for her spot, but she'd always refused, even if sitting under the air-conditioning tract meant she spent half the summer in a thick cardigan. Her cubicle with a view over the grimy rooftops of London was worth its weight in gold. When her work threatened to overwhelm her, she needed only to swivel on her chair and glance out at the world beyond to remind herself how much she'd achieved. The ant-sized people on the pavement scurried around, travelling through the arteries and veins of the city, pumping lifeblood into the heart of the capital.

Moving to London had been another sop to Linda. Based on her mother's opinion, a stranger would believe Lavender Bay, the place where Beth had been born and raised, was akin to hell on earth. A shabby little seaside town where nothing happened. She'd moved there after marrying Beth's father and being stuck on the edge of the country had chafed her raw, leaving her feeling like the world was passing her by. When her new husband, Reg, had whisked her off to an apartment in Florida, weeks before Beth's fourteenth birthday, all of Linda's dreams had come true. She'd never stopped to consider her daughter's dreams in the process.

Though she'd never been foolish enough to offer a contradictory opinion, Beth had always loved Lavender Bay. The fresh scent of the sea blowing in through her bedroom window; the sweeter, stickier smells of candy floss and popcorn during high season. Running free on the beach, or exploring the woods and rolling fields which provided a backdrop to their little town. And, of course, there was Eleanor The older woman had taken Beth under her wing and given her a Saturday morning job at the quirky seaside emporium she owned. The emporium had always been a place of wonder to Beth, with new secrets to be discovered on the crowded shelves. Hiding out in there had also given her a haven from Linda's never-ending parade of boyfriends. Beth suspected she'd been offered the few hours work more to provide Eleanor with some companionship than any real requirement for help.

When it had looked like Beth would have to quit school because of Linda and Reg's relocation plans, Eleanor had intervened and offered to take her in. Linda had bitten her hand off, not wanting the third-wheel of an awkward teenage daughter to interrupt her plans. It hadn't mattered a jot that a single woman nearing seventy might not be the ideal person to raise a shy fourteen-year-old. Thankfully, Eleanor had been young at heart and delighted to have Beth live with her. She'd treated her as the daughter she'd never had, and Beth had soaked up the love she offered like a sponge.

Under Eleanor's steady, gentle discipline Beth had finally started to come into her own, Desperate not to disappoint her mum in the way everyone else had seemed to do, Beth worked hard to get first the GCSEs and then A levels she'd needed in order to go to university. With no real career prospects in Lavender Bay, she'd headed for the capital, much to Linda's delight. Her mother's influence had been too pervasive and those early lessons in needing a man to complete her had stuck fast. When Charlie had approached her one night in a club, Beth had been primed and ready to fall in love.

For the first couple of years working at the prestigious project management company of Buckland Sheridan, she'd convinced herself that these were her own dreams she was following, and that her hard work and diligence would pay off. Lately she'd come to the realisation she was being used whilst others reaped the rewards. Demotivated and demoralised, she was well and truly stuck in a cubicle-shaped rut.

Raising the mug of tea to her lips, Beth watched as the street lights flickered on below, highlighting the lucky workers spilling out of the surrounding office blocks. Some rushing towards the tube station at the end of the road, others moving with equal enthusiasm in the opposite direction towards the pubs and restaurants, rubbing their hands together at the thought of twofers and happy hour. Good luck to them. Those heady nights in crowded bars with Charlie and his friends had never really suited her.

Checking the calendar, Beth bit back a sigh. She was overdue a weekend visit to the bay, not that Eleanor would ever scold or complain about how much time it had been since she'd last seen her. She'd tuck Beth onto the sofa with a cup of tea and listen avidly to all the goings on in her life. Not that there'd been much of anything to report other than work lately. Unless she counted the disastrous Christmas visit to see her mum and Reg in Florida, and Beth had spent the entire month of January trying to forget it.

Even surrounded by Charlie's upper-class pals she'd never felt more like a fish out of water than she had during that week of perma-tanned brunches and barbecues. She would much rather have gone back to Lavender Bay and Eleanor's loving warmth, but Linda had organised a huge party to celebrate her 10th wedding anniversary to Reg, and insisted she needed Beth by her side. Having people believe she had the perfect family had always mattered more to Linda than making it a reality.

With a silent promise to call Eleanor for a long chat on Sunday, Beth drained her tea and turned back to her work. The dreaded contents of the file Darren had dumped on her had to be better than thinking about than the surprise date her mum had set her up with on New Year's Eve. She glanced across the partition between their desks. Ravi might be gay, but at least he had all his own teeth and didn't dye his hair an alarming shade Beth had only been able to describe to a hysterical Eliza and Libby as 'marmalade'.

Ravi caught her eye and smiled. 'Hey, Beth?' He pointed to the phone tucked against his ear. 'Callum wants to know if you're busy on Sunday. We're having a few friends around for a bite to eat. Nothing fancy.' They exchanged a grin. Nothing fancy in Callum's terms would be four courses followed by a selection of desserts.

'Sounds great. Can I let you guys know tomorrow?' It wasn't like she had anything else planned, but going on Darren's past record whatever was hiding in the file he'd dumped on her would likely mean she'd be working most of the weekend.

Ravi nodded and conveyed her reply into the handset. He rolled his eyes at something Callum said in reply and Beth propped her hands on her hips. 'If he's telling you about this great guy he knows who'd be just perfect for me then I'm not coming. Not even for a double helping of dessert.' The only person more disastrous at matchmaking than her mother was Callum.

Her friend laughed. 'You're busted!' he said into the phone then tilted it away from his mouth to say to Beth in a teasing, sing-song voice, 'He's a very fine man with good prospects. All his own teeth!' She closed her eyes, regretting confessing all about the New Year's date to Ravi on their first day back after the Christmas break. He'd never let her live it down.

She shook her head. 'Aren't they all? I'll message you tomorrow.' Which was as good as accepting the invitation. There was always a good mix at their parties and the atmosphere relaxed. Leaving Ravi to finish off his conversation, she turned her attention to the dreaded file.

Three hours and several coins added to the swear jar on her desk later, she decided she had enough information together to be able to complete the required draft report and presentation at home. Darren had left the office on the dot of five, laughing with his usual pack of cronies as they made their way towards the lifts. He'd not even bothered to check in with her on his way out, assuming she would do whatever was necessary to ensure their department was ready for the client meeting on Tuesday. The project had been passed to him by one of the directors a fortnight previously, but either through incompetence or arrogance he'd chosen to do absolutely nothing with it.

Stuffing the file, a stack of printouts, and her phone into the backpack she used in lieu of a handbag, Beth swapped her heels for the comfy trainers under her desk and disconnected her laptop from the desk terminal. Coat on and scarf tucked around the lower half of her face, she waved goodnight to Sandie, the cleaner, and trudged out of the office.

The worst of the commuting crowd had thinned so at least she had a seat on the train as it hurtled through the dank Victorian tunnels of the Underground. The heating had been turned up full blast against the February chill but, like most of the hardened travellers around her, Beth ignored the sweat pooling at the base of her spine and kept her eyes glued on the screen of her phone. Music filled her ears from the buds she'd tucked in the moment she'd stepped on board, drowning out the scritch-scritch of a dozen other people doing exactly the same thing.

She never felt further from home than when crammed in with a load of strangers who made ignoring each other into an artform. In Lavender Bay everyone waved, nodded or smiled at each other, and passing someone you knew without stopping for a ten-minute chat was unthinkable. After three years in London, there were people she recognised on her regular commute, but they'd never acknowledged each other. Nothing would point a person out as not belonging faster than being so gauche as to strike up a conversation on public transport.

The anonymity had appealed at first, a sign of the sophistication of London where people were too busy doing important stuff to waste their precious time with inane conversations. Not knowing the daily minutiae of her friends and neighbours, the who'd said what to whom, was something she'd never expected to miss quite so much. Having everyone in her business had seemed unbearable throughout her teenage years, especially with a mother like Linda. But on nights like this, knowing even the people who shared the sprawling semi in the leafy suburbs where she rented a room for an eyewatering amount wouldn't be interested in anything other than whether she'd helped herself to their milk, loneliness rode her hard.

Cancelling the impending pity party, Beth swayed with the motion of the train as she made her way towards the doors when they approached her station. A quick text to Eliza and Libby would chase the blues away. The odds of either of them having Friday night plans were as slim as her own so a Skype chat could probably be arranged. Smiling at the thought, she stepped out of the shelter of the station and into the freezing January evening air.

Clad in a pair of her cosiest pyjamas, Beth settled cross-legged in the centre of her bed as she waited for her laptop to connect to the app. The piles of papers she'd been working from for the past hour had been replaced by the reheated takeaway she'd picked up on her way home, and a large bottle of ice-cold Sauvignon Blanc. With perfect timing, Eliza's sweetly-beaming face popped up in one corner of her screen just as Beth shovelled a forkful of chow mien into her mouth. 'Mmmpf.' Not the most elegant of greetings, but it served to spread that smile into an outright laugh.

'Hello, Beth, darling!' Eliza glanced back over her shoulder as though checking no one was behind her then leant in towards the camera to whisper. 'I'm so glad you texted. Martin's obsessed with this latest bloody game of his, so you've saved me from an evening of pretending to be interested in battle spells and troll hammers.' She rolled her eyes then took a swig from an impressively large glass of rosé to emphasise her point.

Fighting her natural instinct to say something derogatory about her best friend's husband, Beth contented herself with a mouthful of her own wine. It wasn't that she disliked Martin, per se. It was almost impossible to dislike someone so utterly inoffensive, she just wished her friend didn't seem so unhappy. The two of them had made a sweet couple at school, but Beth had always assumed the attraction would wear off once Eliza gained a bit more confidence and expanded her horizons beyond the delicate wash of purple fields encircling their home town.

When Martin had chosen the same university as them both though, her friend had declared herself delighted so Beth had swallowed her misgivings and watched as they progressed to an engagement and then marriage. They'd moved north for Martin's job, and fallen into a kind of domestic routine more suited to a middle-aged couple. Eliza never said a word against him, other than the odd jokey comment about his obsession with computer games, but there was no hiding the flatness in her eyes. Beth suspected she was unhappy, but after her own spectacular crash-and-burn romance, she was in no position to pass judgment on anyone else's relationship.

Opting yet again for discretion over valour, Beth raised her glass to toast her friend. 'Bad luck for you, but great for me. I miss you guys so much and after the day I've had I need my girls for a moan.'

A sympathetic frown shadowed Eliza's green eyes. 'What's that horrible boss of yours done this time?' She held up a hand almost immediately. 'No, wait, don't tell me yet, let's wait for Libs. She'll be along any minute, I'm sure.'

Beth checked her watch before forking up another mouthful of noodles. It was just after half past nine. The fish and chip shop Libby helped her father to run on the seafront at Lavender Bay closed at 9 p.m. out of season. With any luck she'd be finished with the clean up right about now . . .

The app chirped to signal an incoming connection and a pale and harassed-looking Libby peered out from a box on the screen. 'Hello, hello! Sorry I'm late. Mac Murdoch decided to try and charm his wife with a saveloy and extra chips to make up for staying two pints over in The Siren.'

Beth's snort of laughter was echoed by Eliza as she pictured the expression on Betty Murdoch's face when her husband rolled in waving the greasy peace offering. Considering she looked like a bulldog chewing a wasp on the best of days, she didn't fancy Mac's chances.

Eliza waggled her eyebrows. 'She won't be sharing his sausage anytime soon.'

'Oh, God! Eliza!' Libby clapped her hands over her eyes, shaking her head at the same time. 'That's an image I never wanted in my poor innocent brain!' The three of them burst into howls of laughter.

Gasping for breath, Beth waved a hand at her screen. 'Stop, stop! You'll make me spill my bloody wine.' Which was a horrifying enough thought to quell them all into silence as they paused to take a reverent drink from their glasses.

Libby lifted a hank of her hair, dyed some shade of blue that Beth had no name for, and gave it a rueful sniff. 'So, I get why I'm all alone apart from the smell of fried fish, but what's up with you two that we're hanging out on this fine Friday night?'

'Work,' Beth muttered, digging into her takeaway.

'Age of Myths and bloody Legends.' Eliza said.

'Ah.' Libby nodded in quiet sympathy. She knew enough about them both that nothing else was needed. People who didn't know them well found their continuing friendship odd. Those bonds formed in the classroom through proximity and necessity often stretched to breaking point once they moved beyond the daily routine. Beth and Eliza had left their home town of Lavender Bay, whilst Libby stayed at home to help her father after the untimely death of her mum to cancer when Libby had been just fourteen.

They made a good trio—studious Beth, keeping her head down and out of trouble; warm, steady Eliza who preferred a book or working on a craft project to almost anything else; and snarky Libby with her black-painted nails and penchant for depressing music. She'd taken immense pride in being Lavender Bay's only goth, but both Beth and Eliza had seen beyond the shield of baggy jumpers and too-much eyeliner to the generous heart beneath it. Though it might be difficult to tell from the hard face she turned to the world, Libby was the most sensitive of them all.

A sound off-screen made Libby turn around. She glanced back quickly at the screen. 'Hold on, Dad wants something.' Beth took the opportunity to finish off her takeaway while they waited for her.

Pushing the heavy purple-shaded fringe out of her red-rimmed eyes, Libby stared into the camera in a way that it made it feel like she was looking directly at Beth. 'Oh, Beth love. I've got some bad news, I'm afraid.'

A sense of dread sent a shiver up her spine and Beth took another quick mouthful of wine. 'What's up, not your dad?

Her friend shook her head. 'No. He's fine. Miserable as ever, grumpy old git.' There was no hiding the affection in her voice. Mick Stone was a gruff, some would say sullen, bear of a man, but he loved his girl with a fierce, protective heart. 'It's about Eleanor. She had a funny turn this evening as she was closing up the emporium, and by the time the ambulance arrived she'd gone. Massive heart attack according to what Dad's just been told. I'm so sorry, Beth.' Streaks of black eyeliner tracked down Libby's cheeks as the tears started to flow.

The glass slipped from Beth's limp fingers, spilling the last third of her wine across her knees and onto the quilt. 'But . . . I only spoke to her last week and she sounded fine. Said she was a bit tired, but had been onto the school about getting a new Saturday girl in to help her. It can't be . . .'

'Oh, Beth.' If Eliza said any more, Beth didn't hear it as she closed her eyes against the physical pain of realisation. Eleanor Bishop had been a fixture in her life for so long, Beth had believed her invincible. From the first wonder-filled visits she'd made as a little girl to the sprawling shop Eleanor ran on the promenade, to the firm and abiding friendship when she'd taken Beth on as her Saturday girl. The bright-eyed spinster had come to mean the world to her. All those years of acting as a sounding board when Beth was having problems at home, dispensing advice without judgement, encouraging her to spread her wings and fly, letting Beth know she always had a place to return to it. A home.

If she'd only known, if she'd only had some kind of warning, she would have made sure Eleanor understood how much she meant to her, how grateful she was for her love and friendship. Now though, it was too late. She'd never hear Eleanor's raucous,

226

inelegant laugh ringing around the emporium as she made a joke to one of her customers, or passed comment on the latest shenanigans of the band of busybodies who made up the Lavender Bay Improvement Society.

The unpleasant dampness of her pyjama trouser leg finally registered, and she righted the glass with trembling fingers. Through the haze of tears obscuring her vision, she saw the worried, tear-stained faces of her friends staring back at her from the computer screen. 'I'm all right,' she whispered, knowing they would hear the lie in her voice if she spoke any louder. 'Poor Eleanor.'

Libby scrubbed the cuff of her shirt beneath one of her eyes. 'I don't think she suffered, at least. Dad reckoned she was gone before she would have known anything about it. At least there's that.' Her voice trailed off and then she shook her head angrily. 'What a load of bollocks. Why do we say such stupid things at times like this?' Noisy sobs followed her outburst and Beth ached at the distance between them.

Eliza pressed her fingers to the screen, as though she could somehow reach through and offer comfort. 'Don't cry, darling, I can't bear it.' She addressed her next words to Beth. 'What are you going to do about the arrangements? I'm sure Mum and Dad will be happy to host the wake. Eleanor doesn't have any other family, does she?'

Eliza was right. Eleanor had been an only child, never married and apart from some distant cousins she'd mentioned whose parents had emigrated to Australia somewhere under the old Ten Pound Poms scheme, there was no one. Which meant one thing—it would be up to Beth to make sure her beloved friend had a decent send off. She sucked in a breath as she shoved her sorrow down as deep as she could manage. There would be time to deal with that later. 'I'll sort it out. I don't think it can be Monday as I'll have to straighten up a few things at work, but I'll be down on the first train on Tuesday morning. Can you let

227

your dad know, Libs? See if he'll have a word with Mr Bradshaw for me.' There was only one funeral director in town so they were bound to be dealing with the arrangements.

Libby sniffled then nodded as she too straightened her shoulders. 'I'll give Doc Williams a call as well and then we'll track down whoever's got the keys for the emporium. Make sure it's properly locked up until you get here. You won't be doing this alone, Beth. We'll sort it out together.'

'Yes, we will,' Eliza added. 'I've got some leave accrued at work and Martin can look after himself for a few days. I'll call Mum and ask her to get my room ready. If there's not a spare available at the pub, you can bunk in with me for a couple of days.' The Siren had guest rooms as well as accommodation for the family, and although the bay would be quiet this time of year, they were one of the few places to offer rooms year-round so they got some passing trade from visiting businessmen and families of local people who didn't have room to accommodate their own guests. Eliza paused, then added softly. 'If you'd rather stay at the emporium, I'll sleep over with you.'

The thought of being in the flat above the shop without Eleanor's bright presence was something Beth couldn't bear to contemplate. She shook her head. 'No, I think with you would be best.'

'Of course, darling. Whatever you need.' Eliza's face crumpled. 'Oh, Beth, I'm so sorry.'

Beth nodded, but couldn't speak to acknowledge the love and sympathy in those words. If she gave in, she'd never get through the next couple of days. She stared down at the papers she'd set aside until the lump in her throat subsided. Darren would never give her the time off unless she got that bloody report finished. 'Look, I'd better go. I've got an urgent project to sort out for Monday.'

'Message me if you need anything, promise me?' Eliza raised her fingers to her lips and blew a kiss.

Beth nodded. 'Promise.'

'Me too. Love you both, and I'm sorry to be the bearer of such awful news.' Libby gave them both a little wave. 'I know it's terrible, but I'm so looking forward to seeing you both even under such awful circumstances. It's been too long.'

They signed off with a quick round of goodbyes, and the screen went dark in front of Beth. The greasy smell from her plate churned her stomach and she gathered it up, together with her glass and the bottle of wine. Trudging down to the kitchen, she thought about what Libby had said. She was right, it had been too long since the three of them had been together. They'd been drifting apart, not consciously, but life had pulled them in different directions. No more though, not if Beth could help it.

Now that Eleanor was gone, they were all she had left in the world. Crawling beneath the covers, Beth curled around the spare pillow and let her tears flow once more. The one person in the world she needed to talk to more than Eliza and Libby would never pick up the phone again. What was she going to do?

Dear Reader,

Thank you so much for taking the time to read this book – we hope you enjoyed it! If you did, we'd be so appreciative if you left a review.

Here at HQ Digital we are dedicated to publishing fiction that will keep you turning the pages into the early hours. We publish a variety of genres, from heartwarming romance, to thrilling crime and sweeping historical fiction.

To find out more about our books, enter competitions and discover exclusive content, please join our community of readers by following us at:

🐦 *@HQDigitalUK*

f *facebook.com/HQDigitalUK*

Are you a budding writer?
We're also looking for authors to join the HQ Digital family!
Please submit your manuscript to:

HQDigital@harpercollins.co.uk.

Hope to hear from you soon!

DIGITAL HQ

If you enjoyed *Starlight Over Bluebell Castle*, then why not try another delightfully uplifting festive romance from HQ Digital?

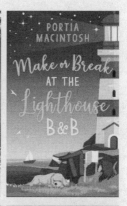